SONG

of the

CRIMSON
FLOWER

ALSO BY JULIE C. DAO

Forest of a Thousand Lanterns
Kingdom of the Blazing Phoenix

SONG

of the

CRIMSON FLOWER

JULIE C. DAO

PHILOMEL BOOKS

PHILOMEL BOOKS
An imprint of Penguin Random House LLC, New York

First published in the United States of America by Philomel,
an imprint of Penguin Random House LLC, 2019.

Visit us online at penguinrandomhouse.com

Library of Congress Cataloging-in-Publication Data

Names: Dao, Julie C., author.
Title: Song of the crimson flower / Julie C. Dao.
Description: New York : Philomel Books, 2019.
Summary: Bao, a poor physician's apprentice, and Lan, the wealthy nobleman's
daughter he loves, work together to break a curse and save the kingdom of Feng Lu.
Identifiers: LCCN 2019018026| ISBN 9781524738358 (hardback) |
ISBN 9781524738365 (e-book) | Subjects: | CYAC: Fantasy. |
Blessing and cursing—Fiction. | Social classes—Fiction.
Classification: LCC PZ7.1.D314 Son 2019 | DDC [Fic]—dc23
LC record available at https://lccn.loc.gov/2019018026
Printed in the United States of America
1 3 5 7 9 10 8 6 4 2

Edited by Jill Santopolo.
Design by Jennifer Chung.
Text set in Fairfield LT Std.

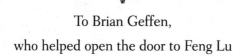

To Brian Geffen,

who helped open the door to Feng Lu

❦ CAST OF CHARACTERS ❦

- **Lan**—*pronounced lahn*
- **Chau**, her maid—*pronounced chow*
- **Minister Vu**, her father—*pronounced voo*
- **Lady Vu**, her mother
- **Bà Trang**, a seamstress—*pronounced ba jahng*
- **Bà Danh**, an acquaintance—*pronounced ba den*
- **Hieu**, Lan's nephew—*pronounced hew*
- **Bà nội** (Vietnamese for paternal grandmother), now deceased—*pronounced ba noy*
- **Phong**, Lan's eldest brother—*pronounced fum*
- **Chung**, the youngest of Lan's older brothers—*pronounced choom*
- **Tam**—*pronounced tum*
- **Master Huynh**, his father and a physician—*pronounced win*
- **Madam Huynh**, his mother
- **Bao**—*pronounced to rhyme with how*
- **Ông Hung**, a fisherman in the river market—*pronounced ohm hoom*
- **Chú Minh**, a younger fisherman in the river market—*pronounced choo min*
- **Khoa**, who dies of the bloodpox—*pronounced khwa*
- **Cô Ha**, Khoa's sister—*pronounced co ha*
- **Lady Yen**, a noblewoman—*pronounced eeeng*
- **Lord and Lady Phan**, her parents—*pronounced fahng*
- **Lord Nguyen**, her betrothed—*pronounced weeng*

- Empress Jade
- Lord Koichi—*pronounced ko-ee-chee*
- Wren
- Commander Wei—*pronounced way*
- Huy, a young man who lives in the village—*pronounced hwee*
- Cam, an old woman who lives in the village—*pronounced kahm*
- Tao, Cam's husband—*pronounced to rhyme with how*
- Mistress Vy, leader of the Gray City—*pronounced veee*
- Sinh, Vy's husband—*pronounced sing*
- Huong, the river witch—*pronounced hoohng*
- Quang, captain of the Gray City—*pronounced wahng*
- Ly, a worker in the Gray City infirmary—*pronounced lee*
- Master Chu, a patient in the Gray City infirmary—*pronounced chew*
- Kim, Master Chu's daughter—*pronounced keem*
- Thuy, a patient in the Gray City infirmary—*pronounced twee*
- General Yee, Commander Wei's second-in-command—*pronounced yee*
- Lo, the Imperial war surgeon—*pronounced low*

NOTE TO READERS: The above pronunciations are not 100 percent accurate as it can be difficult to translate Vietnamese names, which are often tonal, into phonetic English for the Western tongue. They are merely my closest approximation.

SONG

of the

CRIMSON
FLOWER

1

The music came in on the breeze.

Lan rushed to the window, the sleeves of her pale-yellow robe fluttering like butterfly wings. "He's here! Quick, put out the light!"

Her maid blew out the candles, plunging the bedroom into darkness, and Lan saw outside with a sudden sharp clarity: the great oaks sheltering the Vu family home, bending close together as though sharing a secret; the sunset-pink blossoms in the garden that smelled of summertime; and the grassy hill sloping down to the river two levels beneath her window. The warm breeze ran playful fingers through her long hair as she leaned out.

"Be careful, miss!" Chau begged. "What will I tell your parents if you fall?"

Lan brushed away the maid's hands. "I've never fallen yet, have I? Hush, now."

A boat glided over the water and stopped near the riverbank. In the moonlight, Lan could only see a sliver of the young man's face, turned up toward her, and the shine of his bamboo flute. *Tam*, she thought, her mind caressing his beloved name. Her heart soared as he began to play, every sweet note ringing out as clearly as though he were in her room with her.

The music seemed a living, breathing thing. It whispered to her and danced in the air before her. The notes clung to her skin and the back of her throat. Lan pressed her hands against her flushed cheeks, thrilling at the beauty of it. Tam had come every night for two weeks and had played this song each time—*her* song, the melody he had written for her. He had tucked the lyrics into the hollow of their favorite tree, and she had learned them by heart:

> *Little yellow flower,*
> *You crossed the grass and the wind kissed every blade*
> *Your feet had blessed.*
> *I see springtime in the garden of your eyes.*

The flute sang for her, and her alone. It was his voice, telling her in music what he had always been too shy to say in words: that he loved her, that he couldn't wait to spend his life with her, that both their families' dearest hope was also his own. When he finished, he gazed up and lifted his hand to her, and Lan noticed the soft blue scarf tied around his wrist. She had given it to him along with a ruby dragonfly brooch, the heart-jewel a woman presented to her true love.

Chau, well versed in the routine by now, handed Lan several bundles of *hoa mai*. Lan kissed the sweet-smelling yellow flowers before tossing them to Tam. Most of them scattered on the surface of the water, but it was no matter. She knew he would gather each and every one, for she had watched him do it for fourteen nights. As she watched, he stooped to pluck a blossom from the river and kissed the petals her lips had touched.

The maid sighed. "How lucky you are to have such a beautiful romance, miss."

"I am," Lan said softly, stretching her hand to the boatman. She felt like a princess in the ancient ballads her father loved, with stars in her unbound hair. But the girls in those tales were always falling in love with men far beneath them. Tam was of a family equal to Lan's, and the prospect of their marriage was as close to their approving parents' hearts as it was to their own. "He's perfect, isn't he?"

If only he would find his courage. If only he would get past the shyness that forced him to express his feelings only in moonlit visits. In the two weeks since he started playing her music on the river, he had not come by once during the day. *He's busy learning how to become a great court minister like his uncle,* she told herself sternly. *It's silly to complain when he is building a good life for us.* Tam was devoted to her, and when the time was right, he would finally allow the fortune-teller to choose an auspicious date for their wedding. In the meantime, she would try to learn patience and understanding, two of her mother's strongest qualities.

As though Lan's thoughts had called her, Lady Vu's footsteps sounded in the corridor. "Why is it so dark in here?" she asked, entering her daughter's room. Two servants flanked her, their lanterns illuminating the crisp turquoise silk of her long, gold-collared *ao dai*. The overdress fluttered against her cream trousers. "What on earth are you looking at?"

Lan jumped back from the window. "Nothing, Mama. Just stargazing." She didn't have to fib; her parents approved of her betrothal to Tam, after all, and there was nothing improper about these visits. But she was nearly eighteen, and Ba and Mama allowed her so few secrets from them; she wanted these nights of moonlight and music to belong to her and Tam alone. "I was thinking about Tam and how hard he works."

"Of course you were, my love," Lady Vu said, her face softening. "I am certain your wedding will take place soon. You needn't worry."

"I'm not worried," Lan answered, but it sounded forced even to her ears.

Her mother signaled for the servants to relight the candles, and the room in which Lan had grown up came back into view: the bright oak walls, the yellow-and-white embroidered rug, and the cheerful gold silk pillows on the bed. Lady Vu patted a lacquered sandalwood chair. "Sit. I will brush your hair," she said, and the servants left the room to allow mother and daughter their nightly chat. She ran the teeth of the ivory comb tenderly through Lan's hair. "You'll be a happy wife and mother, like me. You have nothing to fear from your Tam."

"I know he cares for me, Mama." Lan fixed her eyes on the night sky, imagining Tam gathering flowers on the river outside and watching the square of light from her room. "I'm just eager for a wedding date to be chosen. If there's a task to be done, better to do it right away."

Lady Vu laughed. "How like your dear father you are in that."

"And like you in my face," Lan returned, lifting an ornate bronze hand mirror. Her face and her mother's looked back at her, both rosy and round with wide noses and wider eyes, dark and shining as the river. Even their dimpled smiles were the same.

Her mother stroked her hair. "Master and Madam Huynh have always spoiled Tam. He's their only son, which is why they indulge him in everything. Ba and I know better than to give your brothers such freedom. *We* are their parents, and we know best." She set the comb down and met Lan's eyes in the mirror. "Tam may be shy, but his nerves will soon pass."

"Do you think that's why he keeps putting off the fortune-teller?" Lan asked, turning to look at her. "Because he's nervous about marrying me?"

"I don't think it has anything to do with you, my treasure." Lady Vu laid a hand on her daughter's shoulder. "Some men are still children at twenty, and Tam may be feeling anxious about the responsibilities he will take on as a husband and head of a household."

"Was Ba anxious?"

The older woman smiled. "No. But he has always been a decisive person."

"He left flowers for you every day after you were betrothed," Lan said, remembering Ba's story. It was both funny and sweet to imagine her proper, formal father as a youth in love.

"Your father and I were well matched from the start. Sharing my life with him has been a joy, and I want that happiness for you," Lady Vu said, squeezing Lan's shoulder. "Ba will speak to the Huynhs and see if they can't push Tam a bit. It's long past time to choose a wedding date."

Three dates had been proposed by the fortune-teller and all refused by Tam. The first had landed in the middle of the rain season, which he insisted was not a propitious time to marry. The next had fallen too close to the Festival of the New Year, which might have symbolized a fresh beginning, but Tam had insisted it would be disrespectful to the gods to celebrate a marriage instead of spending time in reflection and prayer. And the third date—for which both the Huynhs and Vus had pushed—had been in the winter, and Tam did not wish his bride to be cold and uncomfortable in the journey to her new home. No matter that the Huynhs lived only on the other side of the river, no more than a half hour's journey by palanquin.

Lan had been disappointed each time, but had excused these concerns as proof of Tam's thoughtful, conscientious nature. "He's superstitious, and also cautious," she told her mother now. "Our marriage will be the most important event of his life, and he wants it to be perfect."

"Of course he does. Ba will speak to Tam's parents, and by year's end, you will be a bride." Lady Vu dimpled. "Just think of the finery you'll wear and how beautiful you'll look. The first of your cousins to marry, even though you're the youngest. How jealous they will be."

Lan beamed, picturing herself in her festive red wedding clothes and gold headdress. "Will you lend me your jade necklace, Mama?"

"Better than that. I will give it to you as a gift," her mother said indulgently. "And we will have Bà Trang add *ten* times the gold embroidery to your wedding clothes. They'll be so much prettier than the hideous silks Bà Danh's great-niece wore at her wedding." They giggled at the great-niece's expense and sat up late together, gossiping and planning for the future.

When Lady Vu finally retired for the night, Lan gazed out at the star-dappled river, now empty of her passionate boatman. As a child, she had sat by this window with her grandmother, making up wild stories about all the adventures she would have as a bold, brave young woman. Bà nội had loved tales of daring quests and far-off lands and had transferred her passion to Lan, encouraging her to dream and imagine herself as strong and courageous as anyone in the old legends. But Bà nội had died last summer, leaving an empty place in Lan's heart where her grandmother's love and her thirst for adventure had once been.

It made Lan feel lonesome and a little sad, wondering when she had changed so much. But she supposed that letting go of her flights of fancy and her desire to see the world came with growing up. *And getting married will be an adventure, too,* she told herself.

The pieces of her life were falling perfectly into place. Soon, she would make Ba and Mama proud, and she would have everything: a lovely, elegant wing of the Huynhs' home, servants to tend to her every wish as a cherished daughter-in-law, and Tam, the handsome young man who wove his love for her into the melody of a flute beneath the moon.

2

Long before sunrise and the first rays of peach and gold touched the sky, the river market came to life. Boats swept over the water, packed with nets of wriggling fish, buckets of jackfruit and spiny durian, and baskets of sweet, fragrant pastries wrapped in banana leaves. Neighbors shouted greetings to one another, having seen the same faces and heard the same voices year after year. Men and women who had once played as children on the riverbank now rowed their goods to shore, setting up stalls of wood and bamboo along the sand as their small sons and daughters tottered after them. They wore loose cotton clothing, cheap but comfortable in the stifling heat, as they hammered, tied rope, lined up wares on tables, and carried crates.

Bao would have given anything to be one of them.

He knew it was a hard life. The people of the river market were always at the mercy of nature—one year might bring a drought, and then the next, the monsoon rains might last for months, flooding boats and damaging goods. But they all *belonged*, from the oldest man to the newest baby. They all had a place; they all had someone to love and miss them if they were gone.

He couldn't say the same for himself.

"Bao! You're here early," said Ông Hung, a cheerful, red-faced man in his sixties. In the eight years Bao had known him, the man had only ever worn one outfit: a gray hemp tunic over brown trousers. He stood under a lopsided cloth tent, behind a table lined with gleaming catfish. His many daughters sat cross-legged on the ground around him, their hands and legs stained with fish blood as they cleaned the day's catch. The youngest, a girl of fifteen, turned bright red when she saw Bao, causing her sisters to titter.

Bao pretended not to notice, to spare the poor girl further embarrassment. He was too tall to stand up straight beneath Ông Hung's tent, so he stood outside and stooped his head to speak to him. "You look better today, Uncle." He used the term out of respect, but still it gave him a thrill, like addressing a real family member.

"You know why?" called Chú Minh, an adjacent vendor. He was a short, slim man in his forties, with kind, twinkling eyes above a thin mustache. "After he collapsed the other morning, he finally took your advice and rested yesterday."

"Mind your own business," Ông Hung told him good-naturedly. "As the saying goes, an idle man courts the gods' ill will. Lazing about means less money to feed my family."

Bao studied the older man's color. He still looked a bit too peaked for Bao's taste, but at least his eyes were bright and his movements quick. "Your family wouldn't want you to work yourself to death," Bao said. "One day of rest is worth it if it means you can work for years longer."

Chú Minh grinned, and Ông Hung put his hands on his hips, saying,

"Listen to the boy! Wah, so you've decided to become the king's court philosopher instead of a physician now."

"I'm not a physician yet, just an apprentice," Bao said, chuckling. "I tie bandages and hold patients' hands and carry Master Huynh's medicine bag for him."

"You're too modest, son," Chú Minh scolded him. "That fancy Master Huynh may be a retired court physician, but you're the one who takes care of us lowly folks. Who else would set our broken bones or treat our coughs? Or tell this old sack of rice to take a day off?" He clapped an affectionate hand on Ông Hung's shoulder, and the older man grumbled about lack of respect.

"I feel at home here," Bao said honestly, looking at the bustling market around them. He wouldn't trade these haphazard tents, these rickety stalls, and the sharp, pungent smell of fish and dust for anything. It was his escape from the servants' quarters of the Huynh family house, where he slept and studied in a tiny, stuffy room that always smelled of greasy cooking. He had only a thin straw pallet for a bed, a tiny scrap of a table, and a single chair with uneven legs, and still Madam Huynh complained to her husband about the price of keeping a charity orphan like Bao, no matter how gifted he was at medicine. "Everyone in this river market is the closest thing to a family that I have."

Ông Hung fixed Bao with a piercing gaze. "You're a good boy, with a good head on your shoulders. What are you, nineteen? If you get tired of treating rich people's imaginary ailments, come work for me. Learn the business with my sons and marry whichever of my daughters you want." The girls erupted into giggles, and the youngest hid her face in the flank of a catfish.

Bao cleared his throat. "That is much too generous of you, Uncle."

"I'm serious. I'd be honored to have you for a son-in-law." The fisherman's eyes narrowed. "Unless another man has chosen you for his daughter?"

Chú Minh's grin widened. "I think you've hit upon the truth. The boy is blushing."

Bao's face burned as though the midday sun shone upon it, though dawn had only just crept over the limestone mountains. The girl he loved was still his own, and he would not share her yet—not when he might never summon the courage to speak to her. "Even if I ever wished to make a marriage proposal, I have no parents to speak to the parents of my intended."

"Do you think that matters to me at all?" Ông Hung exclaimed.

Beneath the older man's teasing demeanor, Bao saw kindness. Ông Hung was honest and good, and a life with his family would mean hard but decent work and plenty of food. Bao imagined living on the man's boats as children ran around him and scolding aunties told him to eat more, he was getting too skinny. Ông Hung's youngest daughter would be there, too, smiling shyly from behind her dark curtain of hair. They would all love Bao and care for him, and for an orphan who had drifted alone for almost ten years, the hunger for that life was physically painful. But Bao's heart belonged to another. He didn't know whether *her* father would welcome him so readily, but he wanted no other wife but her.

"Thank you, Uncle," he said sincerely. "Well, I should be on my way. I've got a lot of people to check on before my work with Master Huynh begins. I'm going to see Khoa first."

Both men sobered at once. "If anyone can do anything to help poor Khoa, it would be you, my boy. You and the gods . . . and maybe the river witch," Chú Minh said, ignoring Ông Hung's snort of derision. "People may sneer, but there's no denying she's helped many a sick or ailing person. Her methods may be untraditional—"

"Untraditional!" Ông Hung laughed. "The king would throw her into prison for her unnatural practices if she were important enough for him to know."

"She's the closest thing we've got to a magic-wielder," Chú Minh argued.

The older man shook his head. "You can keep your mountain magic and enchantresses. I am a citizen of the Kingdom of the Sacred Grasslands, and we are rooted in the earth and good, reliable medicine we can see. I'll take Bao here over that witch any day."

They looked at Bao, who hesitated. Growing up, he had often heard Madam Huynh telling her son, Tam, the tale of the river witch to frighten him into good behavior. The story went that the woman had been born in the southern Grasslands, among magic-wielders with benevolent powers like the gift of healing or foresight. But the witch had chosen dark magic, *blood magic*, to manipulate and control others, and her people had thrown her out because of her evil ways. She had gone north to make her home in the darkest part of the river, and anyone wandering her forsaken banks might have the hair cursed right off their head or a second nose magically sprout from their chin, just for her sheer pleasure at hearing them scream.

Unlike Tam, Bao had never been scared by the story. Perhaps it was because he lived with the Huynhs' servants, who often joked about the witch and talked of how a former cook had successfully sought her out to erase all of her memories about her unfaithful husband. Or perhaps Bao liked hearing about someone who had come from the southern Grasslands, just like him, the only nugget of information he had about his past. Perhaps they had crossed paths once.

Now Bao shrugged, not wanting to take sides. "I always try to do what I can."

Chú Minh glanced at the small package in his hand. "I don't have a strong opinion either way about your employer, but I'll say this much for him," he remarked. "Even if Master Huynh doesn't deign to serve us peasants, it's decent of him to give you medicine for us."

Bao forced a smile and said nothing.

"Well, go on, then," Ông Hung said. "Let's hope Khoa isn't too far gone to be helped."

"No one is too far gone to be helped," Bao told him, but the men's grave expressions made him wonder whether he should have had Master Huynh accompany him today. He had asked the physician for advice on Khoa's case just the other day.

Khoa was a hale, hearty man who traveled south frequently to harvest milk fruit for his sister to sell in the river market. He rarely stayed more than a day or two at home, but had felt so ill this week that he couldn't make the usual trip. Master Huynh had listened to Bao's description of the symptoms that had developed slowly over the past few months—paleness, lethargy, and chills—and put it down to a case of travel exhaustion. But the physician had not been there to see the transparent quality of Khoa's skin or the dazed look in his eyes.

As Bao bid the men goodbye, he saw a small woman hurrying toward him. It was Khoa's sister, Cô Ha, who was a feminine copy of the man, as though living together for forty years had turned them into each other. But her usually cheerful face was stricken with panic today.

"Bao, please come with me now!" she cried.

"What happened?" Bao asked, alarmed.

Sudden shouts rang out up and down the market. Chickens ran and children shouted as a short, husky man came into view, staggering drunkenly through the market and upending crates of fish and vegetables. It was Khoa, clutching a basket of milk fruit, his ashen face covered with bright scarlet blood. He crumpled to his knees as people backed away, screaming, the basket crashing to the ground. One of the milk fruits rolled to Bao's feet, drenched in the man's blood.

"He's got the bloodpox!" someone screamed.

"Cover your noses and mouths! He'll get you sick if you breathe in his air!"

Men grabbed their sons and ran. A woman fainted, and several vendors jumped over her body in their haste to flee, while an elderly lady ushered her grandchildren away.

Bao stopped one of them, a tall boy of thirteen or so, and pressed a coin into his palm. "Run for Master Huynh. Tell him to come here right away," he said, and the boy took off at once. Bao pushed gently past the weeping Cô Ha toward Khoa, but Ông Hung grabbed his arm.

"Are you crazy? If it's bloodpox, you'll die soon. This is not worth your life!"

"Someone has to help him," Bao said firmly, but he tore off a good chunk of his tunic and wrapped it securely over his nose and mouth. He rushed over to Khoa, who lay flat on his back. Blood flowed freely from every opening in the man's face, including—to Bao's horror—both of his ears and the tear ducts of his eyes. The man gagged, as though blood was coming up his throat, and Bao quickly turned him onto his side so that it wouldn't choke him. He tore some more cloth from his tunic—one of only two good ones he owned—and tried to stem the bleeding from Khoa's eyes and nose, but it was soon clear that he might as well try to stop the river from flowing. He had never witnessed internal bleeding to such a violent degree.

As he murmured soothing words and wiped the man's face, Bao's mind raced like frantic fingers turning the pages of a book. For years, he had cared for the river market people and had seen many different illnesses, but whatever Khoa had was worlds away from anything he had ever experienced. *Bloodpox*, he thought, his heart thundering. *A rare disease that began in the south twenty years ago, before I was even born. The patient experiences uncontrolled bleeding from all orifices.* There had been isolated cases here and there, enough for Bao to have learned about it from Master Huynh, but never one so close to home. He prayed that the physician would come soon, for this was far beyond his training.

"Breathe in and out slowly," Bao said, trying to calm Khoa down, but it was clear that the blood was blocking his airways. "Master Huynh will be here soon."

Two years ago, a former colleague of Master Huynh's had come to visit. They had talked about the many fascinating cases they had come across while serving as court physicians to the king of the Sacred Grasslands. Bloodpox had come up in conversation, Bao remembered, for it had been the first time he had ever heard of it. The disease was thought to have come from overseas, since many foreign merchants and sailors docked their ships in the Gulf of Talon, the southernmost coast of Feng Lu. But whether there was actual proof of that, or the belief stemmed from prejudice against outsiders, Bao didn't know.

What are the chances that it came all the way up here? he thought, gazing down at Khoa.

"He goes south so often," Cô Ha wept. "He must have caught it from someone while he was bringing the last load of milk fruit home. Oh, what will I do if he dies? I'll be all alone."

"Don't think like that," Bao urged her, though the futility of trying to stop Khoa's bleeding was obvious. A powerful smell of rot and damp earth lingered beneath the sharp iron scent of the blood. This man needed medicine beyond anything Master Huynh had in his stores. Bao rubbed Khoa's back and continued murmuring reassurances, not knowing if they were true, but hearing his voice seemed to calm the poor man. Khoa lay motionlessly, his chest rising and falling with his labored breathing as the blood drained from his eyes, ears, and nose. "Stay back," Bao warned Cô Ha, but the woman seemed to be beyond fear.

She knelt beside her brother, clutching at him helplessly. "He's felt poorly for months, but never so bad as this. I didn't know how sick he was," she sobbed. "Just the other day, he complained about wanting his pipe—he always said it made him feel well—and I mocked him for being dependent on it. We haven't any extra money, or else he would be smoking."

"You couldn't have known," Bao reassured her. "What does he smoke?"

"I don't know. Anything he can get his hands on."

But before Bao could question her further, Khoa went limp like a boneless fish. His chest stopped rising and falling, and his eyes stared sightlessly as Cô Ha threw herself upon him, crying as though her heart would break. Bao backed away, aching at the sight of her devastation.

He heard the sound of running feet and looked up, his eyes wet, to see Master Huynh and the boy who had summoned him. The physician's fleshy face was damp with sweat as he gently extricated Cô Ha from her brother. He set his medicine bag on the ground, utterly useless now, and wrapped a clean cloth around his nose and mouth before bending to examine the dead man.

"I couldn't do anything for him," Bao said softly, and Master Huynh's gaze met his.

"This isn't your fault, son," the physician said, closing the dead man's eyes with a gentle hand. "Not much can be done when bloodpox takes hold."

"So it *is* bloodpox?"

"Nothing else causes bleeding to this degree. The ears are the telltale sign," Master Huynh explained. "There was only one way this could have ended for the poor man."

"Then there is no cure?" Bao asked.

The physician shook his head grimly. "My colleague tells me there is a treatment they've studied in the south, but the poppy plant from which it is derived is illegal now."

"The same plant they used to make black spice?" Bao asked, and Master Huynh nodded. But before Bao could ask more questions, Cô Ha let out a piercing wail and rocked back and forth on her heels, and Bao put his arms around her. "I'm so sorry," he whispered, wanting to weep with the poor woman. He knew what it was to be all alone in the world.

Master Huynh was still examining Khoa. "My colleague tells me there is some argument over whether bloodpox is contagious or not," he said. "Just the same, both you and this woman ought to have a healing tonic to strengthen your body's defenses. I'll make it myself."

In the heat of the moment, Bao hadn't spared much thought for his own health. He had taken what little precaution he could and covered his nose and mouth. But if the bloodpox was as terrible as people feared, and Bao got sick and died, who would grieve for him? He had no sister like Khoa, no wife and son like Master Huynh. The people with whom he chatted at market would feel sad, and then forget him. The physician would find another apprentice to replace him. Bao made no impact in the world; he had not a single person.

That isn't entirely true, he reminded himself.

There *was* one person, but she did not know of his love. And if Bao did fall sick by some unlucky turn of fate, perhaps he ought to tell her how he felt about her at last. He had no hope of winning her. Her heart and her hand had been claimed by someone else, but at least by speaking his truth, he might leave a piece of himself behind on this earth. Perhaps the girl he loved would not forget him, even when she did marry another.

I'll tell her, Bao resolved. *It's time.*

3

A few days later, Lan went downstairs to find a cool room in which to do her needlework when the sound of raucous cheering distracted her. The Vu family home stood two levels high, with three interconnected buildings around a central gated courtyard. It was in this courtyard that she found her father and uncles sitting in the shade of the mango trees, drinking rice wine and playing a game that involved stone figurines and much shouting. She watched them bend intently over the board, and then one of her uncles threw up his hands in triumph and provoked a general uproar. Lan shook her head, bemused.

"Ah, Lan," said Minister Vu, looking up at his only daughter. "Are we being too noisy?"

"It sounded like someone was fighting out here." She opened her mother's silk sunshade and held it over her head, squinting in the hot sun. "You're not losing again, are you, Ba?"

The men laughed and Minister Vu pretended to look hurt. "What do you mean, *again*?" He was in his early sixties and still looked every bit as stately and dignified as he had in his younger days, when he had served as a royal official. Even at home, he insisted on formal clothing similar to what he had worn at court: a navy silk overdress with gold piping at the collar and loose matching trousers. But the laugh lines around his eyes and mouth betrayed his sense of humor. "What are you doing outside when your mother wants you to protect your skin?"

"I won't stay long. Where *is* Mama?"

"She went to temple with your aunties, to pray for Bà Danh's grandson."

Lan nodded, knowing how sick the child had been. "Is he getting any better?"

"I believe so, but Master Huynh can tell you himself. He should be here any minute."

Second Uncle raised an eyebrow. "Since when is a busy physician able to take time off?"

"He's not here on a social call. He wants to get my opinion on something," Minister Vu said. "And Bao can always fill in for him, if need be. A most capable young man, that apprentice of Huynh's. Only nineteen and as hardworking and honest as you could wish."

Third Uncle sniffed. "He *should* be hardworking; he's a no-name orphan without family or connections. It was good of the physician to take him in when he already has a son."

Lan's heart picked up, as it always did at any mention of Tam. "Will Madam Huynh and Tam accompany Master Huynh, Ba? Should I have the servants prepare tea?"

Minister Vu smiled. "That's a good idea. She won't be coming, but Tam might, and I'm sure Master Huynh would enjoy some refreshment."

"Why are these Huynhs taking so long to choose a wedding date?"

Second Uncle asked. "Lan and Tam have been intended for each other since birth. What are they waiting for?"

"Perhaps they've changed their minds," Third Uncle said darkly. "Did they ever truly mean to make a proposal, brother? Or were they just trying to win your favor?"

"Huynh is just as high in His Majesty's esteem as I am and has no need to win my favor," Minister Vu said. "It's Tam who is being picky about the fortune-teller's chosen dates."

Third Uncle snorted. "What does a boy of twenty care about the right date? Most of them like to hurry things along when they have an intended bride."

Lan averted her eyes, her cheeks hot at their implication. Tam played her music every night, and if that wasn't a sign of devotion, she didn't know what was. But her uncle had a point: if Tam wanted so much to marry her, why put off choosing a date? She loved being treated like a princess, but she wanted something *real*.

She excused herself to order the tea, and as soon as she had done so, she heard her father's voice raised in greeting and Master Huynh's gravelly response. *Today has to be the day*, she thought, straining her ears for Tam's voice. *He has come to tell me when we will be wed.* She longed to go back out, but decided to let him come to her. Setting her sunshade in the corridor, she went into the sitting room, an elegant chamber filled with ornate woodwork and painted scrolls Lady Vu had inherited from her parents. Lan sat on a rosewood chair and listened as Tam's footsteps approached. She smoothed the skirt of her dusty pink silk overdress and tried to slow her breathing. She wished she'd had time to check her appearance first.

A young man appeared in the doorway, so tall that he had to duck his head as he came in. "Good afternoon," he said, bowing, and it was all

Lan could do to return the greeting politely, for it was not a passionate, shining-eyed Tam after all. It was only Bao, Master Huynh's apprentice, dressed in a plain gray tunic and dark pants with his work-roughened hands folded before him.

Lan struggled to hide her disappointment. "What a surprise," she said. She couldn't recall the last time Bao had spoken to her of his own volition. "Won't you sit down? I've ordered tea."

"Thank you." Bao nearly overturned a chair in his haste to take it, and as he sat, his long limbs knocked the table askew. He attempted to pull it back into position, but did so a bit too hard, and Lan's needlework slid off the polished surface, tumbling in an untidy heap. "I'm so sorry," he said, banging his head soundly on the table while retrieving her needlework.

"That's quite all right," Lan said, amused. "I hope you've been well?"

"Yes, thank you." His fingers tapped an embarrassed rhythm on the table as he stared at the wall behind her head. "And . . . and you, Miss Vu?"

"I am well, thank you." The silence dragged on and Lan searched for something to say, but she knew they hadn't anything in common, except for having played together a few times as children. Her mother had always had aches and pains of an uncertain nature, and when Master Huynh came to attend to her, he would often bring Bao and Tam. Tam, who was light on his feet and quick with a smile, would easily join in on the fun with Lan and her brothers. But Bao, she remembered, had always been shy and retiring and had to be encouraged to join in.

Now, as he shifted uncomfortably in his seat, looking like an overgrown colt with his gangly arms and legs, Lan was surprised to find how much he had grown up. She still saw him from time to time, but had never bothered to look closely, not with bright, careless, handsome Tam around. It was a shame Bao was so quiet and uninteresting, she thought, for he had a face she rather liked and supposed many girls would find attractive, with a long nose, a thoughtful, thin-lipped mouth, and deep-set eyes that always looked a bit sad.

Lan opened her mouth to say something about the weather, out of desperation, when the tea tray came in. Gladly, she poured Bao a cup, hoping he wouldn't break the fragile porcelain. Their fingers touched when he took it, and he jerked backward, wincing as the hot tea splashed onto his leg. She hid a smile, wondering what on earth her father saw in Bao to praise him so.

"It's a hot day. It must have been an uncomfortable carriage ride for the three of you. You, Master Huynh, and Tam," she added, when Bao gave her a puzzled look.

"Unfortunately, Tam couldn't come today," he answered, and Lan felt the now-familiar swoop of disappointment in her belly. "He left this morning to go to his uncle and won't return until tonight. But he asked me to send you his apologies and regards."

His apologies and regards. Lan's fingers clenched on her teacup, her chest tight with anxiety. Perhaps Bao would not be the one to break her mother's porcelain after all. *All of these excuses. All of this putting off the wedding and coming to me only under cover of night.*

"He also sends you this." Bao gave her a folded message, which she tucked away to read later—or throw to the mercy of the river, whichever she felt like doing at the time.

Lan took a deep breath. "Tell me," she said, grasping for something, *anything* to distract her from this sinking feeling, "how has work been for you?"

At once, Bao's whole demeanor changed. He sat up straight, his eyes bright and alert, and began to talk very fast about what he was studying and someone named Khoa who had died the other day. Lan tried her best to listen and to keep her eyes on his face, but her mind had already drifted back to the mystery of Tam. Bao must have sensed her disinterest, for he fell silent.

"I'm sorry to hear about Khoa," she said quickly. "Did he have any family?"

"Yes. A sister, who is now alone in the world." Bao set his teacup on the table and put his hands gently around it, like cradling a baby bird. "It's just like you to think about that."

"What do you mean?" she asked, startled.

"You're kind. You worry about other people." His eyes met hers at last, so earnest that Lan felt a stab of guilt for not listening more carefully about Khoa. "I remember years ago, when Tam and your brothers tried to leave me out of their games, you would insist that I play, too."

She chuckled. "I was always frustrated with you for hanging back. I'm surprised you still remember that."

"Of course. I always will." He looked down at his cup, the tips of his ears bright pink.

"Do you remember," Lan said suddenly, "how my grandmother goaded us to climb that tree in the courtyard? Tam and my brothers were already in the highest branches, but you and I hesitated. Bà nội asked if we were going to let them tease us like that—"

"Or show them that we were just as brave. She promised not to tell your mother if we did." Bao's smile lit up his whole face like sunshine, but it disappeared as quickly as it had come. Lan found herself wanting to see it again.

"I don't think we've spoken in years, you and I," she said slowly. "You're often here with Master Huynh, tending to my mother, but you've never so much as looked at me. Why did you come in here today? It couldn't have been just to deliver Tam's note."

Bao blinked down at the table, seemingly at a loss for words, but he was spared by the appearance of Minister Vu and Master Huynh. The men joined them at the table without breaking stride in their conversation and Lan poured them tea, thinking proudly how well dressed and distinguished her father looked compared to portly, weak-chinned Master Huynh.

"I do wonder how these explosives will change our military tactics," the physician was saying. "It doesn't seem fair to have a weapon that will blow a man up before he's had a chance to fight back, does it? But perhaps I'm a bit old-fashioned in my views. Everyone else seems to wholeheartedly support Lord Nguyen and his ferocious new weapon."

"When it comes to war, my friend, survival is more important than fairness," Minister Vu returned. He accepted his teacup from Lan. "You may leave us if you wish, my dear. I want to catch up on the news with Master Huynh and Bao."

"I'd like to stay, Ba," Lan said eagerly. It was rare that she had an opportunity to listen in on her father's discussions. Her mother hated anything to do with *men's talk* and had forbidden Lan to soil her gentle mind with war and politics . . . however much Lan longed to do so.

"Do as you like," her father said indulgently.

"You mentioned Lord Nguyen," Lan said, recognizing the name of the nobleman who had been one of her father's closest friends at court. "Isn't he getting married soon?"

Minister Vu nodded. "The lady's family is of high rank and close to Empress Jade. They're hoping that this union between a lady of the Great Forest and a nobleman of the Sacred Grasslands will further strengthen relations between our two kingdoms."

"Lord Nguyen's explosives finally work?" Bao asked.

"Yes. After years of developing and testing, he has made yet another modern military advancement," Minister Vu said proudly. "My old friend is a credit to the Sacred Grasslands. In fact, he's held in such high regard that the Gray City has made several overtures of friendship, all of which he has rejected. He's too faithful to our king."

Bao listened with rapt attention. "The Gray City wants him as an ally? Because they want his explosives to help fend off the coming war?"

"There's a war coming?" Lan repeated, alarmed. She blushed when they all looked at her. All she knew of the Gray City was what she'd heard from snippets of her brothers' conversation: that it was a walled stronghold at the southernmost edge of the Sacred Grasslands, that it was on the coast, and that they had family who didn't live far from it. "Will our relatives there be safe?"

Minister Vu patted her hand. "Quite safe. Our king and Empress Jade take issue with the Gray City alone, not with ordinary, respectable citizens."

Lan nodded, wishing she knew more about the conflict. She had fought tooth and nail to sit in on some of her brothers' history and geography lessons, and her grandmother had supported her desire to learn. But as soon as Bà nội had died last year, Lady Vu had put a stop to it. "Please forgive my ignorance," she said, embarrassed, "but what has the Gray City done to offend?"

Master Huynh hid a smirk, but Bao leaned forward and spoke, to Lan's surprise. "The Gray City is in the Unclaimed Lands, the territory between us and Dagovad," he said. "We share ownership of it, but now the Gray City wants to become its own kingdom."

"And our king doesn't like this?" Lan guessed.

"Not one bit," her father said. "The Gray City has been flouting His Majesty's authority for years. They're famous for making a drug called black spice, derived from the poppy flower. Our king and other rulers of

Feng Lu declared it illegal years ago and even burned the poppy fields outside the city, but somehow the Gray City has continued to produce and sell it."

"They're not afraid of anything," Bao said, and Lan glanced at him, wondering if she was imagining the admiration in his voice. He turned to Master Huynh. "Sir, when Khoa died of the bloodpox, you said there was a possible treatment, one that is made from that same poppy plant."

"Not that exact plant, but a derivative," the physician said. "Rumor has it that before the poppy fields burned, the Gray City salvaged parts of the plant and cross-bred it with another flower, creating a new plant from which a powerful medicine might be extracted. It would be a fascinating area of study if it didn't break the laws of four kingdoms of Feng Lu."

"Illegal or not, could it have saved Khoa's life?" Bao asked.

Master Huynh shrugged. "I don't know enough to tell you. I've never seen such violent symptoms as the ones he had. Excessive bleeding from the nose, mouth, and ears."

Lan leaned forward, horrified and intrigued, but Minister Vu gave her a swift glance and said, "This isn't a fit conversation for young ladies' ears, Huynh, and I fear what my wife would say if she knew Lan was listening. Perhaps it's time my daughter went upstairs."

Lan bit her lip, longing to argue that women saw more blood in their lifetimes than men ever would, but she knew it would be disrespectful to contradict her father. "All right, then," she said reluctantly. "I'll go and let you get back to your discussion."

"My apologies for such an unpleasant topic, my dear," Master Huynh said mildly. "We'll let you get back to your sewing. And by the way, Tam hopes to call on you soon."

"Does he?" she asked, trying not to sound too eager, but she knew she wasn't fooling anyone from the significant look her father exchanged with Master Huynh.

"He's been busy studying with his uncle and playing the flute and doing whatever it is that fills his hours, but you can expect a visit not long from now," the physician promised.

"Thank you, sir," Lan said gratefully, and got up to go with a much lighter heart.

Bao jumped to his feet as she passed him. The sudden movement startled them both, and she grabbed his shoulder for balance as he mumbled a clumsy apology. Beneath his tunic, his arm was solid and strong. She had never stood so close to him, not since they were little, and she realized now just how tall he was. She barely came up to his shoulder. "It was nice to see you again, Miss Vu," he said, his fingers resuming their nervous tapping.

"Good day to you." Lan let go of him hastily and hurried out of the room. Upstairs, she unfolded the message from Tam with hungry fingers, now feeling much more disposed to read it.

My dear Lan, he wrote, *I write to let you and your parents know to expect a visit from my mother tomorrow. I regret that I will not be able to come with her due to business . . .*

Lan's stomach lurched despite Master Huynh's reassurances. She skimmed the rest of the note, but there was no mention of when Tam *would* come. She crumpled the message, hurt by its impersonal tone, as though addressing an acquaintance who did not matter much. But she told herself, desperately, that Tam might have written in such a guarded manner because he feared Bao would be nosy and read it before delivering it to her. Yes, that had to be it.

She reminded herself, yet again, that Tam had come every night for weeks to play the song he had written for her. He loved her, and his true love letter was in his beautiful music.

Still, she couldn't help the tears that spilled down her cheeks. She would have happily traded an entire year's worth of moonlit music to have Tam with her in person, where he belonged, and not in a boat far beneath her window.

4

In the two days since having tea at Minister Vu's house, Bao had gone over every look and every word from Lan at least a hundred times in his head. He cursed the absurd flutter that took over his brain and body every time they were in a room together. His arms felt too long, his conversation too clumsy, and his manners too unrefined, and every clever, witty thing he meant to say would fly right out of his head. For years, it had been easier to pretend she didn't exist, when he was aware of every breath she took. To avert his eyes, when all he wanted to do was look at her. To speak to everyone else, when she was the one he wanted to talk to.

And she had noticed.

"You've never so much as looked at me," she had told him at tea.

She had seen him, and perhaps she had thought he was ignoring her because he was stuck-up, or he didn't care, or he disliked her. But even if she knew the truth, it wouldn't matter: she was meant for another. *You're a mess, Bao*, he told himself.

"Why are you scowling?" Madam Huynh demanded. "I realize that bringing me to the Vu home is no pleasure of yours, but you needn't show it."

Bao jolted back to the present: his hands on the reins of the horse pulling the covered carriage, his eyes on the road, and his body sitting—most unfortunately—next to the physician's wife. "I'm happy to take you to see Lady Vu. I have to go there myself, for Master Huynh charged me with delivering medicine." He felt the hatred in her gaze like a splatter of hot oil.

"Impertinent and ungrateful," she muttered. "The only reason you're still working for my husband is because of *my* generosity. *I* let you live in my house and eat my food. I could have had him throw you on the streets years ago, but I didn't."

He shut out the woman's nagging voice. It was easy, since he had been doing it for eight years, ever since he had come to live with the Huynhs. All he had to do was call up a pretty melody, perhaps one of the ones Tam played on the flute, and pretend to be alone. Madam Huynh's words had hurt more when he was little, but at almost twenty, he had learned to spare himself the pain by becoming a wall. *Wall*, after all, was her favorite insult for him, with his long lanky frame and wide shoulders, and he liked the idea of twisting it into a shield against her.

Bao knew he had earned his place through hard work and relentless study. Master Huynh was a kind teacher, but he couldn't always be around to deflect his wife's abuse. She wasn't a noblewoman like Lady Vu, but she had been born to one of the wealthiest families in the Sacred Grasslands, one that had been esteemed by the Emperors of Feng Lu when the continent was still an empire. Marrying her had elevated Master Huynh, a low-born scholar, to court physician, and though he had long since retired from the king's service, his wife still ruled his household.

I'm the only decision he ever made without her approval, Bao thought.

That was why she hated him—that, and the fact that rich people like her and her precious son, Tam, believed that a person's birth determined their worth. Tam had always resented the orphan his father had brought home like a stray dog. Better blood flowed in him and his mother; a penniless orphan like Bao was no more important than the dirt beneath their feet.

But Bao reminded himself that not everyone thought that way. Minister Vu was not just rich, but also highborn, and he had always been kind to Bao. And as for his pretty daughter . . . Bao had never seen Lan treat anyone with less than courtesy or civility, from her father's guests to the lowliest servants, and she had spoken to Bao like a human being at tea. Like an equal. The thought of her warmed him in the face of Madam Huynh's coldness.

He pulled the carriage to a stop in front of the wooden gate carved with the Vu emblem: a circle of *hoa mai* around a meadowlark, a symbol of the family's pride in their Grasslands roots. Bao wondered what it was like to belong to a clan like that.

"Well, go on and help me down," Madam Huynh snapped.

Bao obeyed, trying not to grimace as her cloying perfume overpowered his nostrils. As a servant escorted them through the courtyard, Bao checked to make sure he had the packet for Lady Vu. It was only a simple herbal tea, but Bao knew that Master Huynh had to give her something. She was terrified of illness and was constantly convinced she had caught some horrible disease or another. If she had been near Khoa that day in the market, Bao thought wryly, she would be on her "deathbed" right now—not walking around like Bao, after a dose of snake's-blood tonic.

They found Lady Vu in the sitting room, looking fresh and elegant in her pink-and-gold *ao dai* with mother-of-pearl clasps at the double collar. Though many people considered Madam Huynh to be a beauty, Bao liked Lady Vu's face much more—perhaps because she shared her wide, dancing eyes and rounded, dimpled cheeks with her daughter, Lan.

The two women exchanged warm greetings. "Please forgive my daughter's tardiness," Lady Vu said, glancing toward the doorway. "Today marks one year since my husband's mother died, and Lan wished to spend a bit more time in prayer. She was very close to her grandmother."

"That loving girl of yours must take all the time she needs, then," Madam Huynh said in a sweet, breathy voice reserved for people she regarded as equals. "What a treasure she is."

"As is your Tam," Lady Vu said politely, to which the physician's wife smiled, though lines of tightness formed around her eyes. Lady Vu raised her eyebrows at Bao, and he quickly handed over the packet of tea. "Please thank Master Huynh for me. You may leave us now."

The women continued conversing without a second glance at him. Bao left, torn between disappointment at not seeing Lan and relief that she hadn't witnessed her mother dismissing him like a servant. On the day he had come for tea, he had been so ready to tell Lan that he loved her, but his resolve had wavered. After all, he was as strong as a horse, and it was clear that he had not contracted Khoa's bloodpox. *I should still tell her*, he thought. *A healer's health is never certain.*

And there were other things he had to say, too . . . truths she deserved to know.

Bao lingered in the corridor, searching for an inconspicuous place to wait, when he heard her soft voice coming from a nearby room—the family shrine.

"Hieu is growing fast," she was saying. "He's the biggest of all my nephews, and he has your sweet tooth. He loves *chè ba mau* because of the colors of the bean paste. How I wish you were here to see him, Bà nội." Her voice cracked, and Bao felt a pang at the love and longing in it. He crept past the door, hoping to make it out to the courtyard without her seeing.

"Bao?"

He froze as Lan appeared in the doorway, blinking away tears. He reached into his pocket for a handkerchief, but his fingers shook so much that he ended up dropping it on the floor. He knelt to retrieve it, cursing his awkwardness, and held it up to her. "It's still clean on this side."

Lan accepted it and dabbed at her cheeks. Her composure had returned, and so had her expression of polite disappointment whenever she looked at him. Bao bowed his head, knowing she had hoped, as always, that he was someone else. "Madam Huynh is with my mother?"

"Yes, I drove her here. I was bringing your mother medicine."

"I suppose the two of you came alone," she said. It wasn't a question, but Bao nodded anyway, and she sighed. "I presume Tam is still with his uncle? At the rate he's been studying, he'll be every bit as good a court minister as my father was."

Bao looked at her downcast face, scrambling for something to say that would comfort her. "The villagers are worried about bloodpox spreading." The moment he said it, he felt like kicking himself, knowing that Minister Vu didn't want Lan hearing about such things. But Lan was looking at him, puzzled, and it was too late to take it back. "Master Huynh says that there is a lot of interest in that new medicine the Gray City is making. It might treat bloodpox. People want support from important officials like Tam's uncle to persuade His Majesty to legalize the poppies again, or at least allow research to be done." *Stop babbling,* he told himself, flustered.

But Lan looked more interested than annoyed. "Has the new medicine been successful yet?"

"Master Huynh's colleague says it has. But more work needs to be done." Bao noticed her eyes darting to his fingers, which were tapping a relentless, anxious rhythm against his legs, and made an effort to be still. "Tam must be busy learning everything he can." He didn't know why he was making excuses for Tam, but the dejection on Lan's face was too much for him to bear. She deserved better—she deserved to know.

Lan smiled, her eyes sad. "Thank you for trying to make me feel better, but Tam has been like this long before the bloodpox scare. Will you take any refreshment before you go?"

Bao hesitated. He knew she was only being polite, but he couldn't shake the hope that she wanted his company, too. Perhaps if he stayed, he would finally muster enough courage to tell her what she needed to hear. But he dreaded going back to sit with Madam Huynh and Lady Vu.

"I don't want to go in there, either," Lan said, laughing when he stared at her in surprise. She understood him so well. "Would you like to sit in the courtyard? I won't keep you long. I don't want to join my mother yet, but . . . I also don't want to be alone today."

He nodded and followed her outside, his throat dry and heart hammering at the good fortune of having time alone with her. The afternoon sky was gray with the looming threat of rain, and the air hung heavy with moisture and the sweet smell of the fruit trees. They each took a chair and sat down, looking across the expanse of limestone tiles to where a few maids were doing the day's washing. For a fleeting moment, Bao let himself imagine that this was his house, those were his servants, and Lan was his wife. She would put her small, soft hand in his, and he would tuck a tendril of hair behind her ear and listen to her talk about her day.

But the illusion vanished when he saw the faraway look in her eyes. She was thinking of someone else, someone who would never care for her the way Bao did. This was the moment of truth. He drummed his fingers on his leg, struggling to find the right words. It was now or never.

"I . . . I have something to tell you," he said haltingly. "Something to give you, in fact."

Lan closed her eyes. "Please don't say it's another note from Tam."

"It's not."

"Well, what is it, then?" Her eyes were so deep and soft that he feared looking into them for long. "If it's bad news, tell me at once."

It was too late to go back now. Bao exhaled as he pulled out two objects from his pocket: a crumpled blue silk scarf and a brooch set with dark rubies in the shape of a dragonfly.

Lan stared at them blankly. "I gave those as gifts to Tam. Why do you have them?"

"I've had them for almost a year."

"No, that can't be right. I saw Tam recently with my scarf tied around his wrist."

"While playing the flute to you, on the river."

"Of course. That's what I'm trying to tell you," she said impatiently, and then her eyes slid from the objects to Bao's face. "Please tell me he told you that. *Please* tell me that's how you know." Her voice got smaller with each word until it was a whisper.

"I found your scarf and brooch in a pile of clothing last winter," Bao told her, miserable. Every word he spoke was a double-edged knife, hurting her, and hurting him, too, because of it. But there was no help for it; this was one wound from which he had to drain the poison for Lan's sake. "Every year, Madam Huynh has the servants discard the family's old possessions. I knew that these were gifts from you to Tam, so I asked him if the maids had discarded them by mistake. He told me he had thrown them out himself."

Lan's lips were pressed so tightly they had turned white. "Go on."

"He wasn't himself that night. He'd had an argument with his parents," Bao said quickly. Again, he was unsure why he was making excuses for someone who didn't deserve them. "They had been pressuring him about your wedding, and his studies, and how much money he was spending, and he . . . exploded. He said he was tired of them telling him what to do. He wanted to live his own life. To study what he liked, choose his own profession, and marry a woman he loved. Madam Huynh fainted, and Master Huynh . . . I've never seen him so angry."

Bao wished he could erase the memory of that night and forget the awful things Tam had shouted at his parents. That evening had been the closest Bao had ever come to hitting him, and the gods knew he'd been tempted many times before. But it had devastated him to hear Tam talk that way to the mother and father he ought to honor—to tell them, to their faces, that he wished they were dead. Bao would have given *anything* to be loved the way the Huynhs loved Tam. And to see Tam throwing that away, so careless, so arrogant . . .

Lan rose shakily to her feet. "He said he wants to marry a woman he loves. Which means he doesn't love me," she said, lips trembling. "You tell me this happened a year ago, but I have received many notes since, all written in his hand. I have been given presents. I have heard music on the river at night. And my scarf and my brooch weren't discarded after all."

"No," Bao said, his heart aching. He got to his feet, too, and gazed down at her, wishing he could take her pain away. She looked so small and sad, and when she covered her eyes with her hands, it was all he could do to keep from wrapping his arms around her. He could imagine it so vividly, the way she would fit softly against him, her head tucked beneath his chin.

Lan's hands fell away. She looked up at him, tears beading on her lashes like dew. They were standing so close together that he could have bent his head and kissed the drops away. "It was you, wasn't it?" she whispered. "You wrote the messages to look like they came from him. You left gifts for me. And you . . . you were the boatman."

"Master Huynh asked me to do it," Bao said, fumbling for words. "I didn't want to join in the lie, but I couldn't refuse him. I needed the money he gave me."

"So they paid you to keep up the pretense. To avoid offending my father. To save face by hiding the fact that their only son had gone against their wishes." Lan's voice was calm in the extreme, and for some reason that made his stomach clench even harder. "I did wonder how Tam had suddenly become so gifted at poetry. You're quite talented, you know."

Bao looked down at his hands, still holding her gifts. "They paid me to write messages and stall for time," he said, wanting desperately for her to understand. "But everything else, the poems, the gifts, the music . . . everything else came from me. Tam never *saw* you the way I did. He never valued your kindness, your generosity. Your love and respect for your family. I see you. I see *you*, Lan." Her name slipped carelessly from his mouth, but she didn't seem to notice.

She was shaking her head, her fists clenched at her sides.

"You deserve to be loved," he told her, nearly dropping the brooch in his agitation. "I have loved you for half my life, though I'm not worthy of you. The thought of you kept me waking up each day and working hard, rather than giving in. I felt less alone because of you."

Lan kept her head bowed and did not make a single sound.

Bao put the scarf and brooch on his chair, wanting so much to hold her that it was physically painful. "I wanted you to know what you have meant to me," he said. "That's why I did it. That's why I helped them lie."

She murmured something.

"What did you say?" he asked anxiously, leaning forward.

At last, Lan stared up at him with wet, red-rimmed eyes. And then she slapped him across the face with all of her strength. "I said, get out of my sight!" she screamed.

5

I have never heard Bao talk so much before.

That was the nonsensical thought that ran through Lan's mind as Bao told her, his face red with shame, that Tam had never loved her back. She listened, feeling disoriented, as though *this* were the dream and the nights of music had been the reality. But as her eyes returned to the gifts she had given to Tam along with her heart, she began to understand, with a cold sickening feeling in the pit of her stomach, that she had been wrong. So, so wrong.

Tam had not written her the love song.

Tam had not played her such beautiful music.

Tam had not bothered to come and see her.

He would rather defy his parents than marry her, and he had even thrown her brooch away. She remembered, with painful clarity, the day she had bought it for him at market. The woman who had been selling unusual pieces of jewelry had explained to Lan that they were heart-jewels, a custom from her mountain village: a girl would give one to her true love as a token of endless devotion, and once bestowed, it should never be given back for fear of bad luck. She had beamed when Lan selected the dragonfly, saying, "Be sure you choose the right man."

And Lan had failed to do that.

She stood in a nauseated daze, only half listening to Bao. Everything had been a lie. The Huynhs had tricked her and she had cultivated their false seed of hope in her mind. She was pining for someone who did not want her. She thought of all the times her relatives had teased her and expressed doubt that her wedding would ever happen. Perhaps everyone else had known . . . everyone except her. Oh, what a fool she had been.

A raging headache pounded in her temples. For the first time in her adult life, Lan wanted to kick and scream and hit something. Why, oh, why was Bao still talking? And those long fingers of his, forever tapping against his legs, seemed to drive his nervous energy right into her skull.

"Get out of my sight," she whispered.

"What did you say?"

She looked up at him, at his mouth crooked with worry and his deep-set eyes full of pity. She was sure the servants were watching—a scandal like this would fuel their gossip for months. She didn't care. All she knew was that the young man looking at her was not the one she wanted. He was only a messenger, but his message had shattered her heart.

Lan hauled back and slapped him across the face. "I said, get out of my sight!"

Bao pressed a hand over his reddening cheek. He looked so stunned that she might have regretted it if she hadn't felt like breaking a chair with her bare hands just then.

"You dare make a proposition to me at a time like this?" she shouted.

"Not a proposition," he protested, still holding his face. "I wanted to tell you the truth, because you deserved to hear it. And I wanted you to know why I went along with it."

"I don't care why!" Lan yelled, hearing gasps from the maids across the courtyard. She knew that later, when they described this scene to all of their friends, she would be painted as the villain and Bao as the wronged suitor and that made her even angrier. She felt herself unraveling before him like a spool of discarded thread. "You've made a fool out of me."

"Please, I never wanted to . . ."

Spots danced in her vision and she could barely hear him for the roaring sound in her ears. Somewhere beneath her roiling fury, she knew Tam was the true object of her fury. But it was poor, sweet Bao who had the bad luck to be here, towering over her with wide, wounded eyes like a hurt fawn's. "Do you truly think this is a good time to confess your love?" she raged. "You, an *orphan* of no family! And I, the daughter of a royal minister! How dare you!"

Bao's hand fell away from his face. "I thought that didn't matter to you," he said, his voice low and shocked. "You were always so kind to me."

"I am kind to everyone," she spat, in a low, acidic tone she hadn't known she was capable of, "because my mother taught me well. You mean nothing to me, Bao. You never have. You're a peasant." She choked on the rest of her words, but she had said quite enough.

He staggered backward, his eyes full of tears, and it was so unsettling that Lan forgot her anger. She had never seen a man cry before, not even her father when Bà nội had passed away. Feeling faint, she groped for the edges of her fury. It was her only shield, and she knew that when it vanished, there would be nothing left but terrible, burning guilt at her cruel behavior.

"Lan!" Lady Vu hurried over and threw her arms around her daughter, glaring at Bao. "We heard everything. I think you ought to leave and never show your face here again."

"In fact," Madam Huynh told him, her voice guttural with glee as she went to stand beside Lady Vu, "I think you should never show your face again in this town. You won't work for my husband another minute once I've told him of your disgraceful conduct toward Miss Vu."

Lan collapsed against her mother. "Oh, Mama, help me," she said as the ground tilted beneath her. She caught sight of Bao, whose eyes had never left her. The cheek she had slapped was red, but the rest of his face was white as a funeral sheet, and the look he wore—so much like what Lan imagined her own expression to be, thinking of Tam—was more than she could bear. She buried her face into her mother's shoulder and let the tears come, gushing out like rain.

"You fancied yourself one of my husband's sons, didn't you?" Madam Huynh taunted Bao. "You thought yourself on an equal footing with Tam, to even dare to desire his betrothed."

The anger came back, sharp and hot as an iron in the fire. "Tam is not my betrothed," Lan shrieked at the woman. "And I want *you* to leave as well, Madam Huynh."

"Lan!" her mother cried, horrified by her uncharacteristic rudeness.

But then Bao turned and ran out of the courtyard, leaving Lan's scarf and brooch behind, and the world disintegrated into shimmering dots. As her vision went black, Lan gave in to her devastation, her body crumpling in her mother's arms.

Lan lay in bed in a stupor of humiliation.

Her mother had ordered everyone to leave her in peace, and in the dark and quiet, she pulled the pillows over her head, shutting out the world. But, try as she might, she couldn't shut out her thoughts. They came like pebbles, disturbing the surface of her mind with the truth she had never been able to admit: that she had imagined a Tam who did not exist.

The real Tam, on the rare occasions when he *had* bothered to visit, had never spoken of love or talked about their future. She had fallen for his charm, his wit, and his careless smile, and she had seen his parents' flattery and her parents' hope, and had filled in all the rest herself. She had wasted years fantasizing about a future that would never happen. How her cousins must have laughed to see her swanning around, smugly choosing wedding clothes and hoarding the love notes that the Huynhs had paid Bao to write her.

Bao.

Lan dug the heels of her hands into her eyes. Her shame was a knife in her stomach, and several times she sat up, heaving over her chamber pot but bringing up nothing. She had been so cruel to Bao. It wasn't his fault the Huynhs had used him to hide their son's shameful behavior. He had needed the money, and he had only wanted to make Lan happy. He *had* made her happy.

I see you, he had said. *You deserve to be loved.*

And she had flung his love and his lack of family in his face, as though he could help any of it. She had always been so self-satisfied, so certain she would never grow up to be as horrible as Madam Huynh . . . and in the span of five minutes, had proven that she was no better.

Years ago, she had heard her father telling her mother that he thought Madam Huynh was beating Bao. She remembered how Ba had slipped coins and sweets into the little boy's pockets at every opportunity, and how Bà nội, too, had gone out of her way to be kind to the child. Lan had felt superior to Madam Huynh then, because her father and grandmother had taught her that a man's greatness lay not in in his birth, but in who he chose to become.

And then she had called Bao a peasant to his face.

She despised herself.

All through the night, she tossed and turned and listened in the silence, though she knew she would not hear the boatman's music again. When the sun rose at last, she swallowed her self-loathing and forced herself to get out of bed. Her grandmother would *never* have let her sulk like this. She would have said, "You have done wrong yesterday, but you have a chance to do right today," and figured out a way for Lan to make amends.

And so Lan made an effort to put herself together and go down to join her family. Meals were a chaotic event in the Vu household, with three generations under one roof. Minister and Lady Vu presided at one end of the table, with their four sons, their sons' wives, and assorted grandchildren filling up the rest. Today, Lan welcomed the commotion, hoping it would shield her from attention. She went through the customary round of respectful greetings to her parents and older brothers, then took a seat beside her mother. Lady Vu touched her hand and Minister Vu gave her a loving smile, and Lan felt she could better weather the day with them beside her.

She dug her chopsticks into a bowl of sticky rice speckled with egg and listened to her brothers talk, hoping it would distract her from thoughts of Tam and Bao. Unfortunately, they appeared to be talking about bloodpox, which explained the elegant grimace on Lady Vu's face.

"The disease doesn't seem to be contagious," Phong, her eldest brother, was saying. "Master Huynh and Khoa's sister were both there when he died, but neither of them fell ill."

Nor did Bao. A stab of guilt lanced through Lan's gut, and she put her chopsticks down.

"But how do you explain this other case, then?" asked Chung, the youngest of Lan's brothers. "A man died of bloodpox, surrounded by his family and faithful manservant. Only the servant fell ill and died a month later, and everyone else survived."

"Contagious or not, people are frightened," Minister Vu said. "A few men from the river market came yesterday, begging me to use my influence with the king. They're visiting all of the officials in our region, retired or not, to try to have the Gray City's new medicine legalized. They think it could help stop bloodpox from spreading, if His Majesty approves the research."

Chung shook his head. "It won't happen, Ba. There's a reason the poppy fields were burned and black spice was outlawed eight years ago. It is a dangerous and highly addictive drug, and I doubt anything else the Gray City makes would be safer."

"But isn't it worth a try, if people are dying such violent deaths?" Phong argued.

"I don't trust the Gray City one bit," Chung said. "Nor do I believe in that woman who is leading them. Do you know why her family has grown so rich and powerful over the years? Because they're good at courting the favor of whoever happens to be in power at the time."

Lan looked up, surprised into speaking. "The Gray City's leader is a woman?"

Lady Vu frowned at her, but Chung answered seriously. "Mistress Vy's family grew the Gray City from nothing," he told Lan. "They gifted black spice to the barbarian kings who ruled over them for a century, and then to Empress Xifeng. And look what happened to them all!"

"An epidemic killed off the barbarians, not black spice," Phong pointed out. "And as for Empress Xifeng, she was defeated in the Great War by her stepdaughter."

Chung threw up his hands. "My point exactly. Anything having to do with Mistress Vy or the Gray City is bad luck. I think it's because they still revere the Serpent God," he said, and Lan leaned forward eagerly, distracted at last. Their parents had never before allowed talk of the fallen deity who had aided and abetted wicked Empress Xifeng during her reign of terror.

But before Chung could say more, Minister Vu cleared his throat. "I think we ought to talk of pleasanter things now," he said, with a swift glance at his scowling wife.

As her brothers obediently began to discuss the weather, Lan sat poking listlessly at her food. All of this talk of the Gray City, of places and people and happenings far from home, stirred something in her that had lain dormant for a year. Since Bà nội's death, she had shut away any lingering desire to see the world. She had closed off that side of her, focusing all of her effort on becoming a bride and making her parents proud. But that was all over now.

A deep, sinking grief settled into Lan's core, where her love for Tam had once been . . . and yet there was a thread of an idea, too: what if this was a chance to go somewhere new at last? To fulfill the child-hood hope her grandmother had encouraged? She could leave home, Tam, the Huynhs, and her terrible shame behind her, at least for a little while.

Impatiently, she waited for her brothers and their families to finish eating and leave the table. "Ba, Mama," she said, when she and her parents were alone at last. "May I go and stay with my aunt in the south for a while? I need some time away."

Minister and Lady Vu exchanged glances. "It isn't safe for you to travel south just now, my child," her father said gently. "My guess is that our king and Empress Jade are days away from declaring war upon the Gray

City. They've rejected every royal order to stop producing black spice, and the roads are teeming with smugglers going north to sell the drug."

"But you said our relatives would be safe," Lan told him, agitated. "My aunt there—"

"She and her family are far enough away from the Gray City that I do not fear for them. But it will be risky for a young woman to travel that road. I'm sorry." Minister Vu gave her a kindly smile, but Lan knew he would not budge on this matter. "I cannot part with my daughter—unless perhaps you manage to persuade the Commander of the Great Forest to escort you."

Lan knew he was trying to make her laugh, so she forced a smile for him. The deflated hope clung to her chest like trapped air—she had wanted so badly to escape for a time.

"And we still don't understand enough about that horrid disease. Even if the roads were safe, I wouldn't want you to risk your health," Lady Vu pointed out. She placed a gentle hand on Lan's shoulder. "Poor little daughter, you've been through a difficult time."

"I blame myself," Minister Vu said. "I should have been harder on the Huynhs. I should have gone to greater lengths to find out the reason behind this delay."

"Please don't be hard on yourself, Ba. You only wanted the best for me." Lan sighed. "In any case, I plan to find Bao and apologize today. I was unkind, and I need to make amends."

Once again, her parents exchanged glances. "I'm afraid that's impossible, my love," Lady Vu said carefully. "Bao is gone for good. He took his belongings and his boat and left yesterday."

Lan's stomach dropped. "Gone for good? Can this be true?" she cried. He had vanished without giving her a chance to make things right . . . but considering how awful she had been to him, she couldn't blame him. A stitch formed in her chest, cold and tight, at the thought of him out there somewhere, despising her, while she held on to this terrible guilt forever.

"Don't fret," Minister Vu reassured her. "I am sure that time will soften your words."

But Lan knew that her father didn't understand. He hadn't been there. He hadn't heard her speak the most painful words she could find, eager to make Bao hurt as much as she did. He hadn't heard her use the poisonous sentiments Madam Huynh had flung at Bao his entire life.

And when Lan went back up to her lonely, dark room, all she could think was: *Bao will never know how I regret it, and he will never forgive me.*

6

Bao flung himself into the rowboat and pushed off from shore, grateful that the Huynhs lived close enough to the river that he could make a quick getaway. He thought with regret of Ông Hung and Chú Minh and everyone else in the river market he would never see again, but he couldn't stay a second longer. He couldn't let anyone see his tears and demand to know what was wrong, because speaking of what had just happened might destroy him.

He had fled the Vu house an hour ago, taking the carriage and stranding Madam Huynh. She deserved it, and anyway, it wasn't like he would have a job to lose anymore. He was sure she would go home and fill her husband's ears with her glee and hatred, and Bao would rather leave before seeing the shame and disappointment in Master Huynh's eyes. And so he had gathered his few possessions and made for the river, sailing away as fast as his oars could take him.

The bamboo flute slipped out of his bundle as Bao rowed, despite all of his efforts to hide it from view. He couldn't bring himself to destroy it, not when it had been such a comfort once. But he also didn't want to look at it. He would never play it again without thinking about today.

He turned the oars furiously, desperate to put distance between him and the girl he loved. The girl he had *once* loved. But Lan's voice kept echoing in his mind.

"You, an *orphan* of no family! And I, the daughter of a royal minister!"

The way she had spat the words had brought back terrible memories of cowering in corners, eating scraps from the floor, and crying himself to sleep whenever the physician was away, for that was when Madam Huynh had been cruelest. Bao had never spoken of Lan and Madam Huynh in the same breath; one he had adored, and the other he had reviled. But now he saw that underneath it all, they were the same.

"You mean nothing to me, Bao. You never have. You're a peasant."

He roared with frustration, but still it could not block out Lan's voice.

All these years, he had built her up to be perfect. He had worshipped everything about her: the shine of her midnight hair, the graceful way she walked, her laugh, her smile. He had adored the way she loved and respected her parents, and marveled over how her entire family cherished her, from her older brothers to her youngest nieces and nephews.

What he hadn't known was that it had all been a façade. She and Tam were the same—they were selfish and prejudiced and had never seen Bao as worthy of anything. The princess Bao had imagined in his mind—with her head tipped to the moon, as though his music made her feel closer to the heavens—had been a trick his own hungry soul had played upon him.

"Hello, there!" a man called.

Bao's throat went dry when he recognized Chú Minh rowing in the opposite direction. Every fiber of his being longed to ignore him, but Bao didn't dare show such disrespect, not to someone who had been so kind to him. He stopped, palms stinging from gripping the rough oars.

The fisherman pulled up alongside Bao. "Why are you rowing like a demon is after you?"

"Just taking some air," Bao said shortly.

Chú Minh studied him. "Is everything all right? I don't mean to pry, but if I can help—"

"There's nothing. Thank you, sir." Bao prayed that the man would take the hint and move on, but he stayed where he was. His gaze fell on the flute and the bundle in Bao's boat.

"You're leaving, then," Chú Minh said softly.

Bao could almost taste the bitterness of his own smile. "Eight years ago, I thought I had found a family who wanted me at last," he said. "I thought I might find someone to love me here. But now I know that the gods have always meant for me to be alone."

"What happened? Did that Huynh woman do something to you?" Chú Minh demanded.

"No. But someone I cared for turned out to be just like her."

The fisherman's face softened. "So there's a girl at the heart of it. I knew you had one when Ông Hung kept teasing you. You don't have to tell me who she is, but—"

"I will never speak her name again."

Chú Minh blinked at the despair in his voice. "Please don't do anything silly, Bao."

"Would breaking this flute in half and disappearing off the ends of the earth be silly?"

"You cannot break that flute," Chú Minh said calmly, "because you told me once who gave it to you. Do not be so quick to assume that you're unworthy of love. Think of everyone at market who cares for you. Think of who gave you that flute and taught you how to play."

Bao bowed his head, tears burning his face at the memory of Baba and Ma. He had been six, alone and rummaging for food in their garden. The elderly couple had taken pity on him and taken him in despite their own poverty. Ma was a singer, and Baba often said that the birds wept for joy when they heard her voice. He had accompanied her on his hand-whittled instruments, and together, they had given their love of music to Bao. The flute's smooth, reedy tone had called to Bao in particular, and it had been the happiest day of his life when Baba had given one to him.

"You told me they died, one after the other," Chú Minh said gently, "and you were flung back to the mercy of the world, with only that flute. Don't throw their gift away so lightly."

"I do nothing lightly," Bao said, exhausted. "I'm sorry to leave you now, but I must go."

"At least tell me where you are going."

Bao closed his eyes, but opened them just as quickly, frustrated, for behind his lids he saw Lan's face. Would he never be free from her memory? If only there was a way for him to clear his mind of her. If only there was a way to forget her, as though they had never met. And then the words slipped out. "I'm going to see the river witch," he told Chú Minh. "I'm going to ask her to make me forget everything, and then I'm going to start a new life far away."

The older man's face was carefully impassive. "Are you sure you want to do that?"

But Bao had already picked up his oars. "I apologize for my rudeness today. I am not myself," he said, and began to paddle. Some of the despair slipped from his shoulders as he moved. He had a purpose now, a destination. If the river witch was just a silly tale after all, there would be no harm done. But if she was *real*, this might be a way to leave Lan behind for good.

"Just remember," Chú Minh called after him, "you will always have help in the market. Come to us if ever you are in trouble."

"Thank you," Bao called back, and he meant it wholeheartedly, though he had no intention of returning. He watched Chú Minh get smaller and smaller until he disappeared. As much as Bao would miss him and the friends he had made in the market, they were part of that old life he no longer wanted. He wished them the best and rowed with his thoughts on the future.

The sun slipped behind the limestone mountains, painting the sky salmon pink and ocean blue. Bao passed boat after boat on the water and house after house on the shore without noticing any of them. He kept seeing Lan's silhouette in the window, her hair cascading over one shoulder as she leaned out toward him. He felt the ghost of her hand on his shoulder, touching him that day at tea. He heard her angry voice, shouting at him because he was not the man she wanted.

He wished that he had never agreed to the Huynhs' ruse. He wished he had let Lan's flowers sink beneath the river. He wished he could take back every minute of undeserved happiness he had ever given her. He couldn't change any of that now, but he *could* try to forget it.

Bao rowed on through the night.

Strange, unsettling dreams plagued him. Bao alternately rowed and slept, and when his head drooped onto his chest, he would see Lan running to him with arms wide open. Sometimes, he pushed her away from him and reveled in the sight of her grief, but other times, he let her embrace him, her soft body pressing against him as she lifted her mouth to his. He would wake with his throat dry and his heart pounding, only to sink into other dreams of swaying golden fields, moonlit rivers, and clouds of smoke around the walls of a great unknown city.

In one of these visions, he fell to his knees as flames devoured a field of crimson flowers. And then a woman came, tall with iron-gray hair and eyes like fire, calling Bao's name as she searched the tall grass. He heard the love and loss in her voice and felt the overpowering urge to run to her, but for some reason, his legs wouldn't obey him. At the last minute, she turned and looked directly at him, smiling like a cat that had found its prey.

Bao woke abruptly in broad daylight.

It was the next afternoon, judging by the sun's position in the sky. If he had to hazard a guess, he had been rowing and sleeping on and off for twelve hours. In his hurry to flee, he had neglected to pack any food, a mistake about which his stomach was loudly reminding him.

He looked around, disquieted by the silence. There was not a single soul or boat on the river and no birds sang in the trees. He had never seen the river so empty, but then again, he had never ventured this far south. The vegetation was so thick that he couldn't see any signs of habitation, and some of the large trees had branches drooping into the river like outstretched arms. Bao paused to move one so that his boat could pass, sweat trickling down his forehead in the damp, cloying heat that smelled of rot and dead plants.

"I'm going to see the river witch," he had told Chú Minh.

Bao's laugh sounded hollow in the silence. Surely the fisherman thought he had lost his mind and reason. The river witch was only a tale told to frighten small children into submission, and the servants' silly rumors—of maids who came back with powerful love potions or aging

gardeners who returned decades younger and in the peak of health—
were only that: stories meant to entice and entertain. He must have
sounded so childish to Chú Minh.

And yet, as night began to fall, Bao could easily imagine this part of
the river to be home to a witch. Here the trees bent their ropy necks
over the water, blocking out the sun, and the limestone mountains
hovered like malicious giants casting shadows over the land. The riverbanks seemed to close in on either side, and the branches in the water
were sentinels, lifting their thick, mold-strewn leaves in warning.

Bao shivered despite the pungent heat, forgetting his hunger. He
considered turning the boat back and trying an alternate route; he was
certain that while dreaming his disturbing dreams, he had missed other
possible paths. But his resolve hardened before he could dig his oar
into the riverbank and flip himself around. Going back in the direction
from which he had come felt like losing a battle. It felt like returning
to Lan, like admitting his worthlessness. This was meant to be a new
beginning, and what was a new beginning without adventure?

"I won't go back," he said aloud, and pushed on with renewed zeal.

Master Huynh had trained him well. Bao was certain he would be
able to find work as a healer in a village somewhere. He would live comfortably, and live alone. And day by day, time would heal his painful
memories until he had forgotten the people he had left behind.

He didn't know why a thought that should have been freeing only
made his heart heavier.

He came across a plant groaning with dragon fruit and gratefully cut
down several with his knife. He sliced into the deep pink fruit and ate
the sweet, mild flesh, only just realizing how thirsty he was. He saved
a quantity for later and continued down the winding river, and long
after the sun had gone down, he still had yet to see a single person or

dwelling or hear any sound but the splashing of his oars in the stagnant water.

To add to his uneasiness, there was a stale, sickly sweet smell to the air, as though the river was filled with dead fish. Bao wished for one fleeting moment that he *had* turned back; if he had, he could be eating a hot supper right now with Chú Minh and his family.

And then, suddenly, the vegetation cleared, and in the darkness, Bao saw shapes rising from the riverbanks on either side. They were abandoned huts, fashioned crudely from bamboo and enormous palm leaves. He saw no one, no washing hung out to dry, and no smoke indicating cooking, until a movement in the bushes made him cry out and hold his oar out like a weapon. But it was just a family of mangy rodents, scavenging for food in a pile of rotted timber.

"Get a hold of yourself," Bao told himself out loud, and immediately wished he hadn't. The heavy, watchful silence sharpened around him, as though listening. The hairs on his arms rose as he passed a shabby hut draped in shadows.

Bao had long learned to trust his intuition, as an orphan surviving alone before the Huynhs, and right now it was telling him that he needed to row as fast as he could away from this place. But as he readjusted his oars, his boat hit a large rock with a sickening crunch. He had been so focused on the huts that he hadn't seen the obstacle in the dark. As he muttered a curse and leaned over to check the damage, the back of his neck began to prickle. There was a presence, very near, and within seconds the tip of a spear pointed at his chest.

Someone asked, "What do you want? Speak or I stab you through the heart."

7

A short woman stared down the handle of the brutal-looking weapon. If not for her white hair, Bao might have mistaken her for a child, with her thin arms and legs sticking out from a worn, shapeless tunic. But her face wasn't that of an old woman, either—she might have been forty.

"I told you to speak, boy!" Her gravelly voice sounded as though it wasn't often used.

Bao held both palms out. "I mean you no harm. I'm only passing by."

"No one who comes here is ever just *passing* by."

"I am a lonely traveler. There was only one path, and my boat followed it . . ."

The woman jabbed the spear forward, and he felt the tip graze his tunic. "You are either a liar or very simple," she said in a low, hateful voice. "This river is massive. It is a maze made of waterways, with more twists and turns than you can imagine. You expect me to believe that the current took you here by chance? To the infamous river witch?"

"The river witch?" Bao reared back in shock. He didn't know what he had expected the witch to look like, but it was not this. Perhaps she was lying. His eyes took in every inch of her, from the snowy tangles of her hair to the dirt and scratches on her bare feet. And despite how small and harmless she appeared, his intuition warned him to be cautious. There was a quality to the way she stood and spoke that brought to mind a hungry, haggard tiger, ready to pounce.

"It is impossible to find me unless you are looking for me," she said.

"I wasn't looking for—"

"Liar!" she roared, stunning him into shamed silence. But then she leaned close to study him, the ripe, overpowering smell of her unwashed body filling his nostrils. "Now, I want you to tell me the truth. Where did you come from?"

"The river market about a day's journey north. I ran away from home."

"No," she said softly, and Bao winced as the tip of the spear pressed harder into his skin. One flick of her wrist, and she would draw blood. "That is not your true home. You're of the southern Grasslands, like me. I can tell by the look of you, and by your accent."

He blinked at her in surprise. "It's true. I was born there. But I'm an orphan, and I remember nothing about my birth family."

"Is that so?" The woman lowered the spear, her narrowed eyes taking him in. "People never seek the river witch without a reason. An elderly man hungering for borrowed time. A young man craving riches. A woman in need of a spell that will guarantee her a baby son."

"I don't want any of those things. I just want to go south so I can start a new life," Bao said. "Now, I must be on my way. I apologize for disturbing you."

She ignored him. "You're not in possession of a broken heart, are you?"

"Of course not," he said, a little too loudly.

The woman cackled. "You're an even worse liar than I thought. I can see her in your eyes, plain as day. A girl with a little yellow flower in her long, shining hair."

Little yellow flower. Bao's eyes widened at the phrase from the song he had written for Lan, but it was impossible that the woman could know anything of that. It had been a lucky guess—likely there were many heartbroken young men whose lovers favored the sunny petals of *hoa mai*. "I'll take my leave now," he said shortly, using his oars to detach his boat from the rock. He heard a loud crunch and groaned, seeing a large crack in the wood through which water was already seeping. "Do you have any tree resin I might borrow to patch this up?"

But the woman did not answer. She was staring in openmouthed silence at his right shoulder, from which his tunic had slipped. "What did you say your name was, boy?"

He yanked the cloth back over his skin. "I didn't."

After a long moment, she spoke again with an odd expression on her face. Her rough voice had changed to be almost polite. "I do have some resin. Pull your boat over here."

Bao had no choice but to obey. As he jumped out and dragged his damaged vessel onto the bank, he felt her shrewd eyes on him all the while. She gestured for him to follow, and he did so reluctantly, tucking his possessions under one arm, though he couldn't imagine anyone wanting to steal anything from this desolate place.

The woman's hut had an empty chicken coop beside a sad, scraggly garden. She held the door open for Bao, but when he didn't move, she rolled her eyes. "Stay there, then, brave heart, and I'll bring it out." In a minute, she returned with a basket of dark tree resin and a dirty brush, which he accepted. Up close, she looked even more frail and fragile, and Bao felt a wave of pity for her. He could see on her weathered face the hardship of poverty and loneliness. She was only scared and confused, and the locals had all turned her into some kind of evil witch.

"Is there anything I can do to help you in return?" he asked gently.

She gazed at him with eyes so keen, he thought she might be probing his innermost thoughts. "Why did you lie to me?"

"Because I wasn't *really* meaning to look for the river witch . . ."

The woman made an impatient gesture. "Not about that. Why did you say you were from the river market up north when I know you're from the Gray City?"

"I'm not from the Gray City," Bao protested, but she lunged forward until her face was inches from his. For a small, harmless-looking person, she was faster than he had imagined.

"Full of lies, just like your mother. So, after almost twenty years, she has decided to come and find her little sister at last." She laughed, a bitter, poisonous sound. "No doubt she has found another use for me. She only ever cared about what I and my magic could do for her."

"I don't know what you're talking about!"

"Spare me." The woman's sharp, sarcastic voice cut through his words. "We both know your mother wants me back in the Gray City, and she sent you to do her dirty work because she knew I would kill her on sight. Well, if she's hoping that seeing you will soften me and make me forget everything she's done, then she's wasting her time."

The dark fury in her eyes sent a chill down Bao's spine. Clearly, she was confused and delusional, but she believed in everything she said. And judging from the way she glowered at him, she would not let him go without a fight. He darted a glance at his boat, wondering if he could stall for time. He needed only a few minutes to plug up the crack and get away.

"I see nothing of your mother in you. Only Sinh," she said, shutting her eyes with such a look of grief that Bao paused. "She had everything: our parents' love and the people's respect, and still she took him from me. She didn't love him; she has never *truly* loved anyone in all her life. She only wanted him because he was mine. Well, perhaps, it is time *I* took something from *her*. Perhaps it is time your mother was punished for her deeds."

"I'm going to fix my boat now," Bao said, sidestepping her, and his bundle slipped from under his arm as he did so. The bamboo flute fell to the ground, and he hurried to pick it up and carefully wipe off the dirt with his tunic.

The woman watched him, her mouth twisted. "Your father played the flute, too, long ago. He loved it as much as you seem to love yours. Is it your most prized possession, Bao?"

He froze. "I never told you my name."

"You didn't have to. I was there the day you were born. How do you think I recognized the birthmark on your shoulder? It looks like the number three, doesn't it?" She laughed at his shock. "That's not a lucky number. And *you* are not a lucky boy."

Bao's mind spun, racing for answers. But there was no rational explanation for how she had known his name, and no way she could have so clearly seen the shape of the birthmark in the darkness. "Who are you?" he whispered, feeling cold all over.

"I have had many names in my long, sad life," she said, advancing as he backed away. "I am known as sorcerer. Wielder of dark magic. River witch. But to you, I will soon be nothing. You, who are the result of my sister's and Sinh's betrayal of me. The product of their lies. And won't it be fitting to send you back to them not as their son, but as something else entirely?"

Again on her pinched face was the look of a wildcat, fierce and hungry, poised to spring. Bao stumbled and fell, bringing his bundle down with him. "You're my aunt? And my parents are still alive?" he breathed, hardly daring to believe his own words. But despite his fear and confusion, a quiet note of hope sang within him. "Why did none of you ever come to find me?"

"Enough lies!" the woman—his aunt—shouted, extending her right hand, palm outward.

On the ground, Bao felt a powerful tug between his ribs like fingers reaching inside of him, pulling out the threads of his being. He sucked in a sharp breath as the feeling intensified from a dull ache into a sharp, excruciating pain. "Please stop!" he begged, shielding his chest with one arm. The bamboo flute was still clutched in his fingers.

"I have no wish to see my family again," she said, drawing a knife from her tunic. "I want to be left alone, and you will be the message I send back to my sister."

"Don't kill me," Bao begged. His chest felt like it was on fire, like every rib was being pulled out of him one by one. "Have mercy on me, if I really am your nephew."

The woman knelt beside him and yanked the flute from his fingers, then cut the palm of his hand with her blade. She wrapped his bloody hand around the instrument once more. "Blood magic is a powerful gift for those who want it, like my sister," she said as the dark drops seeped into the holes of the flute. "But it's a curse for those who don't. She never understood why I hated my abilities. She took it as a personal insult that the gods favored me with our ancestors' powers."

The tight, unbearable pain in Bao's chest faded, but in its place was a disorienting feeling of lightness. It felt as though any second, his arms and legs might lift off the ground and he would be flung into the heavens with no ballast. "What are you doing to me?" he choked out.

"I am cursing you, dear nephew." The witch's mouth curved humorlessly. "If it's magic my sister wants, then it's magic she will have. This enchantment can only be broken by love, *real* love, from someone you love in return. And it must be broken before the full moon in two weeks, or it will be permanent. Listen closely, for this is the last time I ever plan to see you."

"You're punishing the wrong person," he said weakly, his free hand scrabbling for her arm, the vines on the ground, a boulder . . . anything to keep him from floating into the sky.

"First, you cannot be apart from your flute or you will die," she said, pushing away his desperate hand. In the darkness, the outline of Bao's body had become filmy and insubstantial, like fog. "Second, you will lose your form as you're doing now, and the person you love must bring you back with a touch. But doing this will cost them, and tie them to you and the spell. I can't imagine your mother would risk herself like that to save you, but we will see, won't we?"

Bao felt the overpowering urge to close his eyes and go to sleep, but a small voice in his mind told him fiercely to hang on. "Please . . ."

"The only way to shatter this enchantment is for her to make a declaration of love before the full moon." The woman bared her teeth. "Easy to do, but she must *mean* it with all of her heart and soul. If she succeeds, it will be the first time my sister has ever loved anyone more than herself. If she doesn't, well . . . I hope you really enjoy that flute as much as you seem to."

Before Bao could say or do anything else, the witch lifted him in her arms in one smooth movement, as though he weighed nothing. She carried him over to the rowboat and laid him inside with his belongings, then bent over the crack with the tree resin, patching up the damage.

Bao tried to lift his head, but as light as he had been a moment before, his body now felt heavy and weighed down. The world around him seemed to be expanding—or was he growing smaller? The pulling sensation in his ribs returned with a vengeance and Bao screamed as he shrank and shrank until he had fallen right into one of the holes of the bamboo flute.

"Help me!" he shrieked, but the words came out low and reedy, like the notes played on his instrument. He could no longer flail his limbs, for he had lost them; he had become one with the flute itself. He felt the coarse wood of the boat beneath him, rocking gently in the water, and the hot, damp breeze play over his bamboo skin.

This is another dream, he told himself frantically. *I am asleep and dreaming in the boat.* Any second now, he would awaken and find himself floating south.

The river witch's gaunt face hovered over him. "What a pity," she said, and he felt the vibration of her voice in the wood of the boat. "The first time I've seen you since you were a baby, and we couldn't reunite as nephew and aunt. Goodbye, Bao. I can only hope that your mother has changed, and that she loves you as she has never loved me."

"Wait! Stop!" Bao wanted to shout, but again his voice came out as low, reedy notes.

The woman closed her eyes and leaned over him, whispering words in a language he did not recognize. And then, with a powerful push, she sent the vessel onto the water and spoke in a soft, solemn voice: "Return from whence you came." And despite the fact that no one was rowing, the boat began to move at a steady, even pace, drifting away from the riverbank.

The last thing Bao saw of the witch was the infinite sorrow in her eyes.

8

Lan sat by the window, watching the sun drape a red-gold veil over the mountains as it descended. The river bustled with activity as fishermen rowed home with the day's catch and market vendors ferried empty baskets to be filled again for the next morning. Almost eighteen years had she looked upon these men, women, and children who lived and worked and passed by her home every day, and yet she had never cared to speak to any of them. She had never wondered about their lives or pondered their hardships or sadnesses. As she looked out, she saw a young boatman glide past her window, using a long pole to propel his vessel. The mere sight of him was enough to make her heart pick up and her shame return, though she knew it wasn't Bao. He clearly was not coming back, and she would never have a chance to apologize.

Sighing, Lan turned away. Her maid was dusting the lacquered surfaces in the room even though they were already clean, and Lan knew Chau was only doing so to keep her company. It was the sort of thing the girl had done frequently throughout the years, but today it struck Lan that she had always taken the maid's kindnesses for granted.

"Chau?" Lan asked tentatively, and the other girl looked up. She had a round, friendly face that was quick to smile, and it was one of the reasons Lady Vu had hired her for Lan on the spot. "Are you happy here?"

Chau tilted her head, confused. "Miss?"

"Do you like working here? You can tell me honestly and I won't be angry."

"You and Lady Vu have always been kind and fair to me, and I wouldn't work anywhere else. That's the honest truth." Chau's eyes grew round. "Are *you* unhappy with *me*, miss?"

"Of course not!" Lan said hastily. "I want to keep you with me always."

"Then why do you ask this, after so many years together?"

Lan fiddled with the hem of her *ao dai*, which today was the color of leaves in summer. "I just wondered," she said. "It's been bothering me since . . . since Bao. I said some horrible things to him, as you know, and I've been wondering whether I believe them somewhere deep down."

"You were heartbroken," Chau said gently, "and you didn't mean to take your anger out on him. Anyone with sense would know that, miss. And anyone who knows you knows you have a good heart."

"Thank you," Lan whispered, wiping her eyes. She gave a rueful laugh at the pity on the maid's face. "I have been pathetic, haven't I?"

Chau shook her head. "I just don't like to see you sad, that's all."

Lan rose and squeezed the other girl's hand. "This will be over sometime."

Yesterday, Chau had helped her return all of Tam's gifts to the Huynhs. Madam Huynh had not been back to visit Lady Vu, but Master Huynh had come the day before, chastened and apologetic, and had shut himself up with Minister Vu for an hour. He had done his best to make amends, but Lan knew the rift between their families would be irrevocable. According to Master Huynh, Tam had gone to stay with his uncle indefinitely, and Lan had not heard one word from him. *Likely because Bao isn't here to write the notes for him*, she thought bitterly, and accepted that it was better this way. She would have burned anything Tam had sent her, anyway.

Later, when faithful Chau had left and Lan was getting ready for bed, she went to close the shutters over her window. For the past two nights, the sight of the empty river had hurt her, and she had found herself closing her eyes so she wouldn't have to see the boatman's absence: the Tam she had imagined, and the Bao who had come in reality. *You'll have to get used to it sometime*, she chided herself, and looked out at the water as she closed the shutters.

An empty rowboat sat exactly where Bao's had been all those nights.

Lan's foolish heart leapt into her throat, though reason told her it couldn't have belonged to him. It had been three days since her parents had told her of his departure, and he was surely long gone by now. But the boat looked so familiar . . .

She chewed on her lip. She could send servants to investigate, but she would feel silly for disturbing the whole household if the boat turned out to belong to some passerby. And if she went herself, and if it *was* Bao's boat, she might be able to apologize to him at last.

Lan pulled on slippers and a yellow silk robe and tiptoed downstairs, letting herself out through the front gate. She glanced back at the house, but all of the windows were dark. With any luck, she could find Bao, say what she needed to say, and return without anyone noticing. She both hoped for and dreaded the meeting, knowing he must still be angry, but she couldn't let him go again without knowing how sorry she felt.

The grass tickled her feet as she hurried down the hill. The boat was just far enough out that she had to get into the water up to her ankles and pull it in. It was made of cheap but sturdy gray-brown wood, with two planks for seats and a pair of oars balanced on either side. Lan ran her fingers over the edge, wondering how to tell if it belonged to Bao, when the moon emerged from behind a cloud and illuminated the interior of the boat.

Beneath the seat lay a crudely carved flute. Lan picked it up eagerly. It was light as a feather, with irregularly spaced holes and a mouthpiece that had been worn down over time, but the bamboo was shiny from frequent cleaning. She felt sure now that the boat was Bao's, but she couldn't fathom why he had abandoned it . . . until a sudden terrifying thought occurred to her.

Her eyes fell upon the river. She felt cold all over at the thought of Bao having done anything to hurt himself because of *her*. A sob of panic built in her chest. She struggled to calm down, but still a few hot tears slipped from her face and onto the flute in her trembling hands.

"Why are you crying?"

Lan shrieked as Bao appeared in front of her. "You're alive!" she cried, the joy and relief in her voice so palpable as to be unladylike, but she couldn't have cared less in the moment. "Thank the gods you're all right! I was so worried. I thought . . ."

He didn't respond or look at her. Instead, he trained his gaze somewhere over the top of her head, and her gut clenched at the thought that this time, it wasn't out of shyness, but anger.

She took a tentative step toward him. There was something different about him—but then Bao had always been different from the men she knew. Where her father and brothers were small and stocky, Bao was lean and lanky, towering over everyone else. His skin, too, was darker and his hair longer, and she felt an irrational impulse to brush it out of his eyes and feel the softness of it in her fingers. She remembered, with sudden clarity, how she had stumbled against him at tea and grasped his arm for balance. She had never touched any man like that before.

Lan's cheeks burned at the memory. She gazed up at him, suddenly shy. "I wanted to find you the other day, but my parents said you had left town."

"Why, when you had made it clear you didn't want to see me ever again?" Though Bao's words seemed bitter, he spoke in a strained, fearful voice. Any apology Lan had intended to make died in her throat at the sight of the sheer terror in his eyes.

"Are you all right?" she asked. "What's wrong?"

He swallowed hard. "You wouldn't believe me if I told you."

"Try me." She studied him. There was definitely something strange about his appearance tonight—the outline of his body seemed to shimmer in the darkness, but perhaps it was a trick of the moonlight. "Maybe I can help you."

He looked around nervously, his shoulders wavering like smoke. "How on earth did I end up back *here*, of all places? I thought she was sending me south."

"Who?" Lan asked, baffled.

Bao met her eyes at last, almost defiantly. "The river witch."

She pressed her lips together to keep from saying anything she might regret. She knew he had to be mocking her out of revenge, and yet his expression was as serious as death. Perhaps he had fallen out of his boat and had hit his head.

"I *knew* you wouldn't believe me," he said, shaking his head in frustration despite her tactful silence. "To have *you* of all people find me in this condition—"

"I didn't say anything!"

"You didn't have to. You think I'm mad. It's written all over your face!"

"Just tell me what happened."

Bao clenched his jaw. "I was going south to start a new life. I half joked to a friend that I was going to find the river witch, so she could erase all of my memories of . . ." He didn't finish the sentence. "I didn't even believe in her, not completely. I thought she was only a folktale. But somehow my boat took me to her and she cast an enchantment on me."

"The river witch cast a spell on you," Lan said carefully. She wondered if she would have time to call someone from the house to help her. Clearly, Bao had not returned in his right mind. But he was watching her, so she kept her face neutral and asked, "Why? Did she do it for pure enjoyment, as Bà nội used to say whenever she told me that story?"

"She claimed to be my aunt, and she knew about a birthmark I have." Bao lifted one hand to his shoulder and winced, then looked down at his palm, where Lan saw a long, shallow cut. "She claimed that my mother had stolen my father from her, and she wanted to take revenge by enchanting me. She shrank me somehow, made me filmy like smoke. I fell inside *that*."

Lan followed his gaze to the flute in her hands.

"And then she commanded my boat to return to where it had come from." He drew his thick brows together, his face dawning with understanding. "*That's* why I'm here! She accused me of luring her home on behalf of my mother—she thought I would go back to the Gray City. But this was my home. You picked up the flute and I turned back into myself."

He shuddered, and he looked so intensely frightened that Lan couldn't help believing him. At least, she believed that *he* believed what he was telling her. "All right," she said, trying to keep him calm. "Don't worry. We can figure this out."

"What is there to figure out?" Bao's voice rose slightly with hysteria. "The spell must be broken before the next full moon, or I'll be forever trapped inside the flute. She said I can't be apart from it, and I will lose my physical form unless someone I love touches me. But that will tie them to the enchantment, too. And to fix it all, they must declare their love for me."

Lan lifted her eyebrows. It sounded so convoluted that she wondered, disturbed, whether it could really be true. "What did she mean about you losing your physical form?"

"Isn't it obvious? Look at me!" He gestured frantically at his own body, which looked like a column of smoke in the dark whenever he moved.

Still confused, she poked him with the flute. Or rather, she attempted to do so, because as soon as the instrument touched his chest, it went right through his body. They both stared at the spot where it should have made contact with him.

"What is this?" Lan whispered. The panic on his face mirrored her own as she tried once more to poke him with the flute. Again, the bamboo passed through him as though he was air. He flinched when she reached for him with her free hand. The air around him was warm, but when her fingers came close to his chest, she felt a gust of pure, terrifying cold. "Are you a ghost?"

"It's the spell. Do you believe me now?" he asked hopelessly. "The witch said my mother would be able to break the spell. But if she's been alive all this time, why didn't she ever try to find me? Surely that means she doesn't love me, so she couldn't help me anyway."

Lan's heart gave a tug at the devastation in his voice. "Don't think like that. You don't know that for sure." She stared at him in fearful wonder. Even with protective parents who never allowed talk of the Serpent God, she knew from books that spells and magic wielders existed, but it had all seemed like mere stories, far away from the realities of her own life. "I believe you," she said tentatively. "At least, I think I do. When is the next full moon?"

Bao's shoulders slumped. "Two weeks. Barely enough time for me to get to the Gray City. And if she was deceiving me and my mother doesn't live there, I will have wasted all of that time. And yet the witch knew my name . . ." He touched his shoulder again. Lan watched his fingers make contact, and it gave her an idea.

She reached for him again. He didn't stop her, so she pushed through the cold and laid her hand upon his chest. Slowly, the chill dissipated and the shimmering around the edge of his body vanished. His muscles tensed where she touched him, but his face was full of revelation. His wide, shocked eyes locked on hers, and his chest rose and fell beneath her fingers with his quickened breath. She could feel his heart galloping against her bare skin as they looked at each other. Hastily, they broke apart, Bao stepping backward and Lan removing her hand.

Lan looked down at her fingers, aghast. "I did it. I brought you back to your physical form, but how? You said the witch told you it had to be someone you loved . . . oh." Blood rushed to her cheeks as Bao turned away, but not before she saw the pained look on his face. "Bao, I apologize for what I said the other day. I spoke to you out of anger and hurt toward someone else, and it was wrong of me. I deeply regret the awful things I said."

"Are aristocrats capable of regret? That's new to me." He kept his back turned and his voice was taut, like a rope about to snap in half. But Lan ached at the sadness she heard, too—the sadness *she* had caused. She laid her hand on his back, now warm and solid, but this time he jerked away. "Please," he said in a strangled voice, "please, Miss Vu. Don't touch me."

For some reason, that hurt more than his rejecting her touch: his reversion to addressing her formally after her given name, Lan, had slipped from his lips that terrible day he had told her he loved her. *He certainly doesn't anymore*, she thought, and the hurt sharpened. "I can't change what I did or said," she told him. "I can only tell you how desperately sorry I am."

Bao turned around, but still didn't look at her. "I think you mean it," he said gruffly, "but you're not apologizing for me."

"What on earth do you mean?"

"You're apologizing for yourself. You've been consumed by guilt for days, something you're not accustomed to feeling. You want to say sorry and have me absolve you, and then we can part ways forever and you'll sleep well again. You can go back to your life of painted fans and expensive weddings, and you won't ever have to care what becomes of me."

"This is what you think of me?" Lan whispered. Every muscle in her body had frozen during his speech, and now she fairly shook with cold.

"It is, now that I know the truth."

"And what is the truth?" she asked, though she didn't want to know.

"I thought you were perfect." He looked over her head, a muscle working in his jaw. "I thought if I ever married, I would want someone who was just like you. Well, that's changed."

The cold seeped into her gut, filling her with shame and hurt and rising anger. "It is not my fault you made me into some ideal that never existed," she told him, struggling to keep calm. "It is not my fault you created some version of me that I wasn't."

"The way you did to Tam?"

"Don't *ever* speak that name to me!" she half shouted, half sobbed. "I never want to hear about him again!" Her shoulders shook as she fought to regain control, telling herself that Bao was mostly scared and upset about the enchantment. He was only doing to her what she had already done to him—venting his feelings, except Lan actually deserved his anger. She took a few deep breaths before she spoke again. "Whatever you may think of me, I did you wrong. I wish to make amends."

"How?" he asked, running a hand over his exhausted face.

Another memory flashed through Lan's mind: a small Bao, unkempt in hand-me-downs, standing in the courtyard while Tam and her brothers teased him. Everything about the other boys, from their clothing to their well-fed bodies, had an air of being cared for, and little Bao ran a skinny hand over his face, already conscious of being different. He had always been held apart when he had only ever wanted to belong. *And in my anger toward him, I emphasized that isolation more*, Lan realized.

"I'm coming with you." She spoke quickly, before she could change her mind—before she realized the absurd impossibility of her decision. "To the Gray City to find your mother, or wherever your search takes you. You shouldn't be alone, and you won't be. I'm going to stay with you until you figure out how to break this spell. I mean every word."

Bao's stunned eyes met hers. "I—I can't ask you to do that for me."

It was a rash decision. Impulsive. It was everything her parents had taught her *not* to be or do, and yet with each passing second, Lan knew it was the right thing to do. "You didn't ask me. I offered," she pointed out. "Let this be my way of showing you how truly sorry I am."

He rubbed his face again, and when his hand fell away, Lan saw the utter relief he was trying to hide. "The road is dangerous. It's swarming with soldiers."

"And bandits smuggling black spice. My father told me, and he also forbade me to go south unless I got the Commander of the Great Forest to escort me. His exact words," Lan added, and detected the corner of Bao's mouth lifting ever so slightly. "But I accept this danger, and should anything happen to me, you are not to be blamed. So don't worry about that."

He raised an eyebrow. "How will you ensure that I won't be blamed?"

"I'll leave a message telling my parents I left of my own volition. They know I'm strong-willed," she said, and again, the corner of Bao's mouth twitched. "And I can also keep you from turning into a ghost, or a spirit, or whatever that witch did to you. I'll let your mother break the actual spell, of course, if she can," she added hastily, seeing the pain flash across his face again. "But I can help you in the meantime. Do you accept?"

Hesitantly, he held out his hand for the flute. When Lan placed it in his palm, it stayed there. Bao's shoulders relaxed, but his face remained troubled. "It's not just the road I'm worried about. The witch said that the person who touches me will tie themselves to the spell, too, and I don't know what that means. I don't know . . . what might happen to you."

A pang of anxiety vibrated in Lan's gut like a plucked string. But it was too late to go back, and she wanted—*needed*—to do this, if only to show them both that she wasn't a terrible person. "I guess we'll find out soon enough," she replied, with more courage than she felt.

After a long pause, Bao said, "Thank you. I accept your help."

"Good," Lan said, releasing a breath of relief. She glanced over her shoulder at the dark windows of her house, dreading the thought of her parents finding nothing but an empty bed and a note detailing her plans to help rid Bao of his spell. Her mother would likely be more concerned about the fact that Lan was traveling alone with a young man than the fact that the young man was cursed, but it couldn't be helped. "I need to get some clothes and shoes. And something to eat on the journey. Are you able to eat food, in your . . . your condition?"

Bao's stomach rumbled in response. He blushed to the roots of his hair and nearly dropped the flute.

Lan laughed. That was one thing the spell hadn't changed about him—his awkwardness. "I'll see what I can find in the kitchen. You'll be all right for a bit, won't you? I don't want to tempt fate, but I don't know if anything worse could happen to you in the next ten minutes."

She was rewarded by another slight upward tug of Bao's lips, and she was a bit discomfited by how badly she wanted to make him smile. She told herself that she just didn't want him to be angry with her, and she was disoriented by this confusing whirlwind of a night. Her whole world felt as though it had been turned upside down, thanks to the reappearance of this boy she had hurt, who loved her.

Somehow, though, Lan felt sure her grandmother would approve of her decision to help. *I'm going on an adventure at last, Bà nội,* she thought, looking up at the sky. *Just like we always talked about.* The stars seemed to twinkle down at her, putting purpose and certainty into her steps as she hurried back up to her silent house.

9

Bao watched Lan disappear through the gate and let out a slow breath, trying to calm himself down. For as long as he could remember, he had experienced what he called *terrors*—moments in which fear filled his nerves like lightning, his breaths came too fast, and his heart raced like an out-of-control horse, making him light-headed. When the river witch had trapped him inside the flute and pushed his boat adrift, he had panicked to a degree he had never felt before. The enchantment had taken away his body, but it hadn't affected his mind. In the past, the only cure had been to think, to plan, and to prepare himself, and that was what Bao had tried to do, helpless in the river's current.

But the more he had tried to be calm, the more his anxiety had worsened. What would he do if the boat really was going to the Gray City? How would he find his mother if he was a flute? And even if he got his body back, would he simply march in and ask if anyone had lost a son nineteen years ago? What if his mother didn't even want to know him?

And then the boat had brought him here, back to the girl he never wanted to see again.

Bao looked up at the house, turning the flute over and over in his hands. Maybe Lan wasn't coming back. Maybe she had decided that he was mad or that helping him was too much trouble, and she would leave him alone out here. He would sink inside the flute forever, and he would never know what it was like to be loved, to have a family, or to be a physician in his own right. *This isn't helping*, he chided himself as beads of sweat slipped down his temple.

He wiped his face and noticed the edges of his fingers glimmering. He was fading again. "Gods help me," he choked out, kneeling in the grass before the panic overtook him. He wished he had never come back. He wished Lan hadn't been so decent, and that he didn't have to accept her help. Lan, who was now his only chance, and who would never think of him as anything but a lowly peasant.

Here she came, hurrying down the slope with a rough cloth sack over one shoulder. The pale yellow robe she had worn earlier was gone, for which Bao was thankful—the thin, translucent silk had clung to her in ways that he found much too distracting. She now had on a plain over-dress and loose pants of cheap tan-colored cloth, and on her feet were a pair of rough shoes that were slightly too big. Her long, luxuriant hair had been woven into a simple braid.

Her distress was evident when she saw the condition he was in. She dropped the sack and knelt beside him. "Bao, I know you asked me not to touch you, but . . ."

"Just do it, please," he said hoarsely. He felt the same sharp tug between his ribs and a disorienting lightness, as though he might float away. His fingers scrabbled for grass, for rocks, for anything to keep him on earth . . . and found Lan's knee. It was wrong to touch someone who was not his betrothed in this way, not to mention a woman far above his station, and he wanted to pull away in horror. But his hand seemed locked in place, drawn to her warmth and vitality.

Lan laid her hand on his shoulder, just below his birthmark, where she had touched him that day at tea. His pain dissipated at once, and he could feel every pebble and dip in the ground as his body sank back into the earth. He released a breath and heard Lan do the same. He dreaded the moment when they would break apart and he would no longer feel her anchoring touch.

"Is that better?" she asked.

Bao looked into her wide, soft eyes and saw the star-filled river reflected in them. "Yes, thank you," he said, and pulled away roughly, ignoring the twinge he felt when he saw hurt flicker across her face.

She patted the cloth sack beside her. "I brought enough food for a few days, and money, too. We'll likely need to buy more provisions if we're going all the way to the Gray City."

"We're not going to the Gray City," he said. "At least, not right away— not if I can get back to the witch and persuade her to lift the spell. It could save us a long journey."

Lan shrugged. "All we can do is try. And I'm rather good at getting people to do what I want them to, so this witch doesn't stand a chance," she said, giving him a lopsided smile that made his traitorous heart skip a beat. "Get in the boat. I'll row."

"You?" he scoffed. "Do you even know how?"

"Of course," she said, looking apprehensively at the oars. "You move *those* around."

Bao bit his lip to keep from laughing or saying anything rude. "Let me row. It'll be faster if I do it."

"You're right." Lan gazed up at the moon and its light skimmed down the curve of her throat. "But I'd like to try, just for a minute or two. I think Bà nội would have found it funny."

He watched her watching the moon and thought of how the twinkling-eyed old woman, who had always been kind to him, had possessed a spark of mischief he never would have imagined in someone like her. She and Lan had loved each other desperately—that much was clear from all the times he had seen their heads bent close together, wrapped in a world that had no room for anyone else. And now her grandmother was gone forever.

"Of course," he said, then cursed his own sentimentality when Lan grinned at him, her face blooming like a rose. All she deserved was his civility and politeness; he didn't need to make her happy, too, not after how awful she had been to him.

Bao tucked her sack next to his and carefully put the flute away. Then he held the vessel steady for her to get in and climbed in after her, face-to-face. The boat, which had always felt spacious, now seemed cramped with two people, especially when one was as tall as he was. No matter how he folded his legs, he couldn't seem to avoid touching hers.

Lan watched him struggle with barely concealed amusement. "Comfortable?"

He gritted his teeth. "Not particularly."

"Well, at least we know you won't lose your form while you're in contact with me. We can't have you falling through the boat." Knee pressed firmly against his, she took an oar in each hand and began flailing them in the water. But despite all her effort, the boat moved only about five inches from shore.

"You're holding them wrong. Move your hands here and rotate the paddles more slowly," he told her. "Push them both at the same time. Your shoulders should be moving forward."

After a few more tries, she got the gist and managed to propel the boat several feet down the river, looking pleased with herself. But Bao saw that her rowing was already getting weaker. At this rate, they would arrive in time to die of old age. She panted, brushing a lock of shining hair out of her eyes and looking elegant even in her plain clothing. There was something about the way nobles carried themselves, Bao thought. Every move they made and every word they spoke indicated that the world belonged to them, while people like him struggled from birth to death and would never be good enough. He had been mad to think Lan could ever love him.

"All right, that's enough," Bao said curtly, his irritation rising once more. "Otherwise you'll be in a lot of pain later, and there won't be any servants to give you a massage."

She lifted her eyebrows at his tone, but handed the oars over without argument and rose to switch seats with him. The vessel rocked with her movement, and Bao was forced to give her his hand to keep her from toppling overboard. Her braid tickled his face, smelling of *hoa mai*, and the memory of kissing the yellow flowers she had thrown was so overpowering he had to catch his breath. He took her vacated seat and began to row, trying with all of his might to think about something, anything else.

"I always thought the river witch was a silly folktale," she said conversationally. "Something my grandmother told me whenever she wanted me to behave."

"Not everything is about you," Bao said, before he could bite back the comment.

Lan looked at him, her lips curving downward. "You don't have to be so unpleasant."

"I'm sorry." He exhaled. "I just . . . I don't know how to behave toward you anymore. I didn't think I would ever have to see you again after what happened. I need time."

"It was one moment, Bao. One mistake. It doesn't shape my character."

"It shaped mine," he said, so low he wasn't sure if she had heard him. He tried to keep his gaze on the quiet huts along the river, but his eyes kept wanting to return to her. She had turned away, giving him a perfect view of her profile: soft, long-lashed eyes, an endearingly flat nose, and full lips. He had spent eight years memorizing her face from afar, and now she was here with him—but not in any way his lovesick self had dreamed. "Why did you love him?"

Lan's eyes snapped back to him. "What?"

Heat rushed into Bao's face when he realized he had asked the question out loud. "Sorry, I forgot you didn't want to talk about Tam," he muttered, and then wanted to kick himself for saying the name when it had upset her earlier.

She was silent for so long that he thought she wouldn't answer. "Because I thought he was perfect," she said at last. "He was exactly the kind of person my parents hoped I would marry, and the first boy who ever paid attention to me. He liked me, once. He gave me gifts and wrote me messages." She angled a glance at Bao. "He even played me songs on his flute."

"But that was years ago," Bao said, frustrated. "Despite all the notes and gifts, you must have sensed that he had lost interest when he stopped visiting. And still you thought he cared enough to come to you on the river every night." He looked at her, but she kept her eyes on the dark shapes of the limestone mountains, her shoulders tense. *Good, I can rattle her the way she does me*, he thought, then felt ashamed of his own childish satisfaction.

Lan's lips tightened. "Let's just get to the witch, all right? We don't need to talk."

"You were the one who started the conversation." He tried not to flinch at the glare she gave him. "I'm sorry. I really am grateful that you're coming to help me."

"Thank you for saying so," she said loftily.

They both fell silent, and Bao tried to concentrate on rowing. The faster he got them to the witch, the less time he would have to spend in this mire of confusion—this mingled anger and shame, this inability to stop feeling Lan's hand pressed over his heart. But it was just as Lan had said: the fact that they were stuck sitting so close together on this boat was helping to stave off the curse. He felt no phantom tug beneath his heart, no unbearable lightness. He thought again of the witch's eyes on his birthmark. It was so much easier to dismiss her as a ranting, confused woman than to accept that she had been telling the truth: that all this time, his family—his *mother*—had been alive. They simply hadn't wanted him.

"It would be nice if you could stop thinking terrible things about me," Lan said.

Bao blinked and came out of his reverie. "I'm not thinking terrible things about you."

"You're glowering. I can *hear* you thinking them."

He tried to give her a derisive snort, but ended up inducing a coughing fit.

She watched him thump his chest, amused. "And do me the courtesy of responding when I speak, instead of making noises like an outraged farm animal."

"Is a farm animal more highly ranked than a peasant?" Bao asked, before he could help himself. Why, why, why couldn't he stop jabbing at her? He wished he could go back to being shy, tripping over his feet, and dropping things in her presence.

Lan threw her hands up. "You stubborn ox! Stop reminding me of what I said that day."

"I can't forget it. It pains me to think I could spend my whole life working until my back broke, and people like you and Madam Huynh would still look down on me."

"That isn't fair. Don't assume that what she thinks is what I think." She crossed her arms. "Ba admires you, and he taught me well. I've never looked down on you."

"In all the years I came to your house with Tam, did you ever think of me as a friend?"

"Well, no," Lan admitted. "But you were always so shy and quiet."

"I was lesser to you because I wasn't Huynh's son." Bao hated the way his voice cracked with emotion as he spoke.

"You were never *lesser* to me, Bao," Lan insisted. "But you were different, and Madam Huynh encouraged us to play with Tam, not you. I was too little to know any better than to listen to her."

Bao snorted again, and she looked sharply at him. "That sound was for her," he clarified.

Lan's lips curved in agreement. "Awful woman."

"I don't see what shame there is in working for Master Huynh. I may never be a court physician, but it makes me happy to serve others, no matter who they are." His heart ached, thinking of the people in the river market. They didn't own fine porcelain or wear silks, but they were honest and good and he was proud to call them his friends.

"There is no shame. And I'm sorry to have listened to that evil woman."

Bao sighed. "You don't have to keep apologizing to me."

"How else will I make you stop hating me?"

He glanced at her. "I don't hate you. Not really," he said gruffly.

This time, it was Lan's turn to look away first.

Bao rowed on through the night and all the next day, stopping only once or twice so that they could get out and stretch their legs. He had been making more of an effort to be polite, and Lan had responded in kind, resulting in a stiff formality he felt was worse than all the years in which she had ignored him. But he told himself that they were traveling only as business partners of a sort, and nothing more. Lan would make amends by helping him, and by allowing her to do so, he would break the witch's spell *and* let her go.

Lan, too, seemed to be keeping her mind on the enchantment. "What is the birthmark the river witch saw on your shoulder?" she asked that evening, as the heavy-headed trees cast long fingers of shadow over their boat. The birds had stopped singing, and the thick smell of moss and rotten fish had risen up once more.

"It's in the shape of the number three," he told her, maneuvering around a fallen branch.

"That's a bad-luck number," she said, curling her lip. "Ba won't even have any paintings in the house that show three people. Once, he commissioned some artwork from a foreign artist for my brother's wedding. It was a beautiful scene of the garden at His Majesty's palace, but it showed three court ladies, and Ba returned it to the painter to have it fixed."

"What did the painter do?" Bao asked. "Add in another person?"

"He turned one of the ladies into a big, leafy tree. It was lucky she was already wearing green," Lan said, and a laugh escaped Bao, surprising them both. "It's going to be all right, you know. Don't worry so much. We'll find your witch soon and have the spell lifted in no time."

"I'm not worried."

"You keep running your hand over your face," she said with a small smile. "You always used to do that when you were little and you were anxious about something."

Bao lifted his eyes, thunderstruck by the revelation that she knew this about him, and nearly crashed into the same rock he had the first time he had come. It was only with a reflexive movement of his oars that he avoided damaging his boat again. "We're here," he said, his heart picking up as he recognized the dark shapes of the huts. "She lives in that one."

"They all look empty," Lan said, chewing on her lower lip.

"They did the other day, too." He rowed them to shore and jumped out, grimacing at the soreness in his legs from being cramped for so long. He held the boat steady for Lan, who didn't move from her seat. Her eyes darted from the shadows in the bushes to the shabby, abandoned homes, and Bao felt a twinge of pity. "Listen, you don't have to come with me. You've done enough by coming this far, and you know how to row now, so take my boat and go home."

She looked at him, wide-eyed. "But I promised to stay."

"You don't need to make amends anymore. I—I forgive you." He held his breath in the charged silence, waiting for her answer.

"It doesn't feel right to just leave you here alone," she argued. "And I can't take your boat. What if you need to go on to the Gray City after all? What if you start fading again?"

"I'll figure something out."

"No," Lan said decisively, "I'm going to stay until you get this cleared up."

Bao felt like he could dance, right then and there, but instead he gave a casual shrug, as though it didn't matter to him and Lan might do as she pleased. And then he took a step back and promptly fell over something large and bulky, landing hard on his elbow. A branch smacked him in the face. He heard Lan laughing, and he almost wished he could sink into the flute once more.

"Are you hurt?" She got out of the boat, grinning. But her mirth quickly turned into an expression of horror. "Bao . . . *look*."

A body lay perfectly still in the shadow of the bushes. That was what Bao had tripped over, but neither of them had seen it in the dark. It was a man in his mid-to-late thirties, with sun-browned skin and scars etched all over his sharp cheekbones. He wore a sleeveless tunic embroidered with an insignia Bao did not recognize: a crimson flower surrounded by leaves. Bao pressed two fingers to the man's throat, but there was no pulse. "Dead," he uttered, and Lan backed away with a soft cry. "But he hasn't been here long. His body is still warm."

"How did he die?"

Bao studied the belt around the man's waist, which held two daggers and the scabbard for a missing sword. He grunted as he rolled the body onto its side. "He's been stabbed in the back."

"The witch?"

He examined the man's wounds as Lan coughed, looking sick. "He was stabbed multiple times. Deep, forceful cuts, and they didn't miss a single organ. Whoever killed him both meant to and knew how." He looked in the direction of the witch's hut, but it was still silent. Surely she would have heard them talking and come out by now.

Lan pointed to a great black circle on the corpse's left arm. "What is this marking?"

"That's the brand of a criminal," Bao said, shocked. "This man was an inmate of the Iron Palace, the jail in the Surjalana desert where they put those who commit awful deeds. Master Huynh had me read a volume written by a physician who specialized in treating those prisoners."

"Why would anyone treat them?"

"They're used for manual labor. Maybe this man's sentence had ended." Bao got to his feet grimly. "Let's go see if the witch is home."

As before, he gathered his belongings from the boat and Lan did the same, trailing after him as he approached the woman's door. But no one responded to his knock, and when Bao threw the door open, they found the place empty. There was nothing inside but a crooked table, a single wood bench, and a bed covered with rags. Bao's attention was attracted by a small fire in the corner. A pot of what looked like a thin stew was beginning to boil.

"She was here not long ago," Lan whispered. "Where do you think she went?"

A twig cracked outside, but Bao had no time to turn before he felt something sharp dig into his back. "And who might you be?" asked a deep, rough, accented voice.

10

Lan shrieked at the sight of a spear, long and lethal and tipped with pure silver, held by an armored man. His breastplate was emblazoned with a dragon clutching a forest within its talons, the symbol of the Kingdom of the Great Forest. That explained his accent when speaking the language of the Sacred Grasslands. No sooner had Lan ascertained this than a second, shorter soldier materialized from the shadows, holding a torch and pointing another spear at her.

"Please," she begged, showing the men her weaponless hands. "We're only simple fishing folk. We came from the river market to the north." She heard Bao's barely audible groan and wondered, too late, if she ought to have adopted more of a village accent. But perhaps two men of the Great Forest wouldn't know the difference.

"They're just children, Commander," the short soldier murmured, lowering his spear.

"Children who happen to be near a gang of smugglers. There's more to this story," the other man said.

"Commander?" Lan squeaked. "As in Commander Wei, leader of Empress Jade's army?" She goggled at the heroic figure who had been the topic of so many stories and ballads she had read over the years.

"You're rather knowledgeable for simple fishing folk." The man was armed to the teeth—Lan took note of his beautiful sword, which had rice flowers carved into the hilt—but he did not wear a helmet like his companion, and his shaven head gleamed in the torchlight. He had a sharp, handsome face, though his mouth was hard and unsmiling. Lan could tell that he was the sort of man who would be suspicious of even a toddler found on the premises. "I'm going to give you one more chance to tell me who you are. Choose your words wisely."

Lan swallowed hard, knowing the man could gut Bao like a catfish in seconds. "Please, sir," she said, adopting her most polite tone, "we don't know anything about smugglers. My father is Minister Vu, a former official in the court of the Sacred Grasslands. He wouldn't let me go south to visit my aunt because of the conflict there. So it's unlikely I would have anything to do with smuggling." She gave Commander Wei the smile that had always gotten her out of all sorts of trouble.

But instead of being disarmed, the Commander only stared coldly back at her. "Why are you traveling south, then, if your father has forbidden it?"

She fiddled with the hem of her overdress. "He doesn't know I'm gone. My friend here is ill and appeared unexpectedly. I'm helping him look for the woman who can cure him."

"Has the illness affected his tongue?" Commander Wei barked. "Turn around and speak, young man. Who are you?"

Bao obeyed, trembling. "My name is Bao. I'm the apprentice to a physician local to the river market, but he can't help me," he added hastily, seeing the Commander's mouth open to ask the question. "I'm not so much ill as . . . cursed. The woman who lives in this hut is a witch, and she placed me under a spell that I'm trying to break." He winced and looked at the Commander out of one eye, as though expecting to be speared for the sheer absurdity of his explanation.

But Commander Wei lowered the weapon instead. "A witch," he repeated. "Go on."

"She trapped me inside a flute," Bao went on, looking at Lan, who tried to give him an encouraging nod. "It will become permanent unless the spell is broken before the next full moon. Sir, I know how ridiculous I sound. If I were you, I would think I was crazy or lying. But I'm telling you the truth. We need to wait here until the witch comes back."

After a tense moment, the Commander said, "I don't think you're crazy or lying. But I'm afraid I have bad news. My men managed to intercept and kill most of the smugglers, but some evaded capture and took your witch friend with them."

"Took her?" Bao echoed, horrified. "Where?"

"My men saw that her hands and feet were bound, so she may be a prisoner. She won't be coming back for some time, if ever. We assume they've gone back to the Gray City."

Lan exchanged glances with Bao. If the witch *had* told Bao the truth, then perhaps her sister had paid men to forcefully bring her home. "We need to go after them at once!" she cried. "We've already lost time standing here. If Bao's mother summoned her back . . ." At once, she realized her mistake as the Commander's attention sharpened.

"Bao's *mother*?" He turned on Bao. "You are of the Gray City?"

"I don't know for sure, sir. I'm an orphan—or at least, I thought I was for my whole life—and I haven't lived in the south since I was ten," Bao said helplessly. "The witch claimed to be my aunt and said that my mother lived in the Gray City, but we only have her word to go on."

"A band of smugglers conveys a wagonload of black spice to sell up north, and you two happen to be in the same place at the same time? And one of you is from the Gray City as well?" Commander Wei shook his head grimly and grasped Bao's arm. They were the same height, but the Commander appeared twice as large to Lan in his ferocious armor. "That does it. I'm taking the two of you in for further questioning."

"Please, we don't know anything!" Lan cried, panicking, as the shorter soldier took her arm none too gently. "I told you the truth about who we are!"

"And if we verify that successfully, once the Empress has had a look at you, we will let you go," the Commander answered, striding off without another word.

The Empress. Lan swallowed hard as the soldier steered her through the trees. *What have you gotten yourself into this time, Vu Lan?* She remembered her father joking that she could go south as long as Commander Wei escorted her, and felt a ripple of hysterical laughter in her throat. She wondered if she would ever see her parents again. She imagined being clapped into chains, like that dead man must have been when he was in the Iron Palace . . . or worse . . .

The short soldier yanked her through the underbrush. Twigs and branches scratched her face as they followed Bao and Commander Wei for several long minutes. Lan was beginning to wonder if they would ever emerge when the line of thick trees and bushes ended. An open field stood before them, littered with bodies like the one she and Bao had discovered—except some of them were still moving, groaning and dying all over the grass.

"Gods above us," Lan whispered, her knees shaking. She had never seen death in all her life, excepting her grandmother, who had passed peacefully in her sleep, and now she'd had more than her fill in just an hour's time. There was a metallic tang to the air, sharp and sour, and an aroma like burned, spoiled meat, making her stomach turn violently.

A few of the dying men wore the armor of the Great Forest, but the vast majority wore rags or tunics stitched with a single crimson flower. Armored officers bent to examine the fallen, turning over bodies and calling to each other. One of them ran up to the Commander and saluted.

"What news?" Commander Wei asked.

"It's as you suspected, sir," the officer said. "At least half of these smugglers have the brand of the Iron Palace on them. The Gray City is employing not only foreign pirates, but convicts and murderers. Some of them are even proudly wearing Mistress Vy's mark. The sheer arrogance of displaying their affiliation when half the continent is ready to declare war on them." He glanced disgustedly at a nearby body draped in the crimson flower emblem.

The Commander listened, still gripping Bao's arm. "Send missives to the kings of the Sacred Grasslands and Dagovad at once. I will notify Empress Jade. And burn all these bodies."

"Yes, sir." The officer strode off, barking commands at the others.

Lan stumbled on the uneven terrain and made the mistake of looking down. The grass was covered in slick, dark liquid, and she gulped and looked quickly away before the torchlight could illuminate it. "Where are you taking us?" she demanded of the soldier who was leading her. "Commander Wei mentioned the Empress. Are we going to the Great Forest?"

Apparently, the Commander had sharper ears than a rabbit and had heard her query. "We're not taking you to the Imperial City," he said over his shoulder. "Her Majesty is waiting at an estate nearby."

Lan perked up. Her father had many friends among the nobles of this region, and if one of them vouched for her, the Empress would surely let her and Bao go. "Which one?"

But the Commander was busy instructing another officer who had approached. "I don't want their hands bound yet, but don't let them out of your sight," he said, pushing Bao toward the soldier. "Put them together on one horse and lead it. We should have plenty, now that . . ." He trailed off, his eyes on the open field littered with the bodies of his men.

The soldiers led Lan and Bao toward an enormous gray stallion. Her father owned several beautiful horses, but none so big as this one. It tossed its magnificent head and exchanged a look of mutual distrust with Lan as she came close to Bao, relieved to see him looking as solid as he had been all the way down the river. "Are you all right?" she asked.

"Fine. You?" Bao returned, and she shrugged. "Have you ever ridden before?"

"Of course not. My mother thinks it an unladylike activity. What about you?"

"I've taken the Huynhs' mare out on errands, but I've never ridden a war horse before." Bao eyed the saddle, with its multiple straps and buckles and hidden pockets, with trepidation. "It looks ten times bigger and higher off the ground. But I can go in front, if you like."

"Be my guest," she said as one of the soldiers boosted Bao onto the stallion's back.

The soldier lifted Lan up behind Bao, with one leg on each side. "Hold on tight," he said mockingly as he walked away. "The Commander might decide to make you walk if you fall."

"Great lumbering oaf," Lan muttered. She shifted in the stiff, uncomfortable saddle and nearly slid right off the other side. She grabbed Bao around the middle to keep from tumbling to the ground and felt him tense at her touch. "Sorry."

"It's all right," he said shortly.

She put her hands on her legs, which seemed like a safe spot, but the horse decided to shift its weight at that moment and she had to grab hold of Bao once more. They sat in silence as the soldiers hurried around them, saddling horses, sheathing weapons, and carrying bodies. Lan saw that Bao was gripping the horse's mane so tightly with one hand that his knuckles had turned white. He ran his free hand over his face, a gesture that was quickly becoming familiar to her. She opened her mouth to say something reassuring, but she knew that nothing would comfort him.

"I'm going to make the Empress believe me and let us go," she said at last.

"The way you made Commander Wei believe you?"

Lan decided to ignore that jab. Bao was trapped, he was scared, and they were losing ground on the witch with every minute. She would be irritable in his place, too. "I don't know why I couldn't charm him. I spoke to him the way I do to my parents whenever I want something and it always works. I even smiled at him! But he insists on thinking I'm a smuggler."

"I'm fairly certain no one on earth could think you were capable of smuggling."

"Why not?" she asked, a bit offended.

"The way you talk. And the way you're gripping me right now," Bao answered, and she loosened up a bit. "They just want to make sure we don't know more than we're telling them."

"Well, apparently the Empress is at an estate somewhere, and if the owners know my father, they'll send us on our way. Maybe they'll even let us borrow a carriage for the journey."

"You're very optimistic."

"We shouldn't lose hope. Not yet," she said. "And at least you're going to stay solid, and you won't be frightening the wits out of this horse by slipping through it like smoke."

Bao gave a short laugh and relaxed a bit more in her hands. "Maybe if I did that, it would take off running and you could escape from these soldiers. You could get home."

"I told you. I'm not going anywhere until the spell is broken," Lan said. "I gave you my word and I'm going to see it through."

"Thank you. I'm glad you're here," Bao said quietly, and she smiled when she saw the tips of his ears turn bright red. He cleared his throat. "Is my flute still safe?"

Lan checked through his sack, which had been secured to the saddle alongside hers. "Yes. Don't worry. I'll tuck it at the bottom so it doesn't fall out." She pushed the instrument beneath a spare tunic and heard a crumpling noise. It was a piece of paper, and on it she caught the words *You crossed the grass and the wind kissed every blade*. Heat flooded her face as she cinched the sack shut and glanced at Bao, but he was distracted, watching two soldiers argue nearby.

He had been so angry with her, angry enough and hurt enough to leave the river market behind for a new life. He had told her that he had hoped never to see her again—and yet he had brought with him the lyrics to the song he had written for her.

Tam would never have done such a thing. She knew that now. Tam was bold and reckless and handsome; he would have swung himself onto this war horse and pointed it at the highest fence he could find. He would have laughed at the sentimentality of carrying around songs and love letters. He would never have sat on the river, gathering each and every flower she threw because he didn't want to miss a single one, the way Bao had every night for weeks.

When Bao had asked her why she had loved Tam, she had said that Tam was the first boy who paid attention to her. But Bao, she reflected, had been the first boy to ever tell her he loved her. She looked at the expanse of Bao's back in front of her, at her hands still on his waist.

"Are you all right?" Bao asked suddenly, and she gave a guilty jump. "You haven't said anything in five minutes and it's a bit unsettling."

Lan chuckled. "I do like to talk. It makes me feel better."

"Don't hold back because of me," he said, and she wondered if that was his way of saying that her talking made him feel better, too.

Around them, Commander Wei's men had finished the grisly task of burning the corpses and mounted their own horses. Eight soldiers surrounded a large wooden cart carrying something bulky, concealed beneath a thick canvas cloth and strapped down securely with rope. Together, Lan and Bao watched the cart roll by to the front of the procession.

"Is that the black spice they confiscated from the smugglers?" she asked, craning her neck. "I want to see what has caused such a fuss."

"I don't know much more about it than you do," Bao admitted. "Aside from the fact that it comes in the form of incense, and that the Gray City gave Empress Xifeng wagonloads of it when she reigned over Feng Lu."

The words sparked a memory in Lan's mind. "My brother said the Gray City has always been good at flattering whoever is in power. They gave black spice to the barbarian kings who ruled over them once, too," she said, as an officer stalked around the cart in front of them, checking the ropes. "He said an epidemic killed the barbarians. Do you know anything about that?"

"A bit. They were ambitious pirates who swept out of the Shadow Sea and took over the Unclaimed Lands for a century," Bao said. "It's said that the Dragon Lords sent down a vicious plague to liberate Feng Lu of their hold. But this happened seventy years ago, and the physicians of that time didn't keep good records, so no one knows much about the nature of the disease."

"Do you think it was something like bloodpox?"

Bao shrugged. "Whatever it was, it spread fast. It emptied the Unclaimed Lands within a month, and Dagovad and the Sacred Grasslands were free to go back to fighting over them."

The horses pulling the wagon of black spice began to drag it forward and, one by one, the soldiers of Commander Wei's company followed behind it. Lan noticed the first touches of light appearing in the east as the new day dawned. Soon, the Vu household would bustle with activity, and her parents would find her gone. She hoped the note she had left would be sufficient, and that they wouldn't send out a search party. She didn't want to know what Lady Vu would say if she knew Lan was straddling a horse with a young man, surrounded by a hundred other men.

A mounted soldier came and tugged on the lead rope attached to their stallion, pulling it after his own, and they trailed after the group with Commander Wei at the head. The open field became rolling plains of bright green-gold grass, swaying gently under the brightening sky. Farms and estates dotted the land, and here and there teams of oxen tilled the earth. Lan, who had never been far from home, found it rapturously beautiful.

The procession rode for about an hour, and when the sun had fully risen, they came to a black metal gate surrounding an immense plot of land. Through the bars, Lan glimpsed a garden shaded by towering cypress trees and a building of shining dark wood, the shutters thrown open to the sweet-smelling air and light. Commander Wei spoke to the guards at the gate, and once they were allowed inside, the soldiers led the wagon toward that building.

Instead of following his men, the Commander himself took the lead rope on Bao and Lan's horse. "The soldiers are encamped there," he said, nodding at the neat wooden building. "You're coming with me to the house, where Her Majesty is staying."

"That's not the house?" Bao asked incredulously.

Lan laughed. "They probably use that for storage, or extra accommodations as they are now. No one with a property this lovely would live in such a drab little structure," she said, and she was soon proven right when the family home appeared before them.

This building was made in the style of the palace of the Sacred Grasslands, with bright mahogany beams and red lacquered pillars holding up curving roofs. Walkways hung with climbing vines connected the upper levels of the buildings together. Lan thought it was similar to how her own family's house was laid out, with three sections around a central courtyard, but this home was at least five times grander. Whoever lived here must be important indeed.

In the courtyard, lined with pale gray tiles and containing a sparkling pond full of orange fish, servants hurried forth to help them off their horses. They were accompanied by two captains in the armor of the Great Forest, who came out of the house to bow low to their Commander.

"Her Majesty awaits you in the rose antechamber, sir," one of the captains said, glancing at Lan and Bao with surprise. "Are these the smugglers?"

"No, we found them nearby," Commander Wei said. "I'm taking them to Empress Jade for further questioning. Lead the way."

They entered the house and found themselves in a bright room full of elegant scrolls and priceless vases. Carved rosewood embellishments hung all along the walls, matching the furniture, and over each doorway hung white lanterns painted with red peonies. Lan stopped to admire them, thinking how much her mother would love these.

"Come along," Commander Wei said impatiently. "Let's not keep Her Majesty waiting."

"I'm sorry, sir," she said, scurrying to catch up. "Those lights reminded me of the old folktale about the thousand lanterns. My grandmother told me that each winter on Empress Jade's birthday, the people of the Great Forest hang lanterns in the trees to honor her family. I always begged to go and see it, but my parents said I was too delicate to travel as a child."

To her surprise, Lan saw the Commander's face soften. "It's been a tradition for the past eight years, since Her Majesty took the throne. It's quite a sight to see." He glanced at her. "You seem in good health now. Minister Vu still hasn't taken you?"

"I haven't asked my father to go for years now," Lan said, surprised by the realization. "I suppose I've been too busy worrying about other things." *Like getting married*, she thought. She wondered when that had happened—when she had stopped wanting to see Empress Jade's lanterns and started caring more about wedding clothes.

"Well, we all grow up sometime," Commander Wei said, some of his gruffness returning as he strode ahead with his men, leading Lan and Bao down an elegant corridor.

"This family, whoever they are, must be well connected," Lan said to Bao in a low voice.

"Better connected than your family?"

Lan stifled a laugh. "My family can't compare to this. I wouldn't be surprised if these people were kin to the king of the Grasslands himself, with a guest like Empress Jade."

"So you are to them as I am to you?"

She raised her eyebrows at him in delight. "Bao, was that a joke? Take care or we might end up being friends before we even get to the witch."

Bao blushed and ducked his head, and then they were ushered into the room in which the Empress of the Great Forest awaited them.

11

The rose antechamber was decorated in warm pink tones, with chairs upholstered in silk from the Great Forest and tables inlaid with pearls from Kamatsu. It was a room her mother would have adored, which made Lan feel a bit more at home.

Lan had expected Empress Jade, descendant of the Dragon King, to be a magnificent, powerful-looking person. As such, she was stunned to see a small-framed, delicate young woman sitting at the mahogany tea table in flowing robes of deep red silk. Commander Wei bowed low to the Empress and the man beside her, and Lan was astonished to see Her Majesty incline her head back. She had never imagined a monarch showing respect to anyone, let alone the man who merely commanded her army. Lan nudged Bao, who stood flustered and staring, to bow with her.

"I'm glad you're back safely, Wei," Empress Jade said, with an affectionate smile at the Commander. She was in her mid-twenties but looked much younger, with a round, sweet face and wide, expressive eyes. She wore no ornamentation except for a few gold hairpins and a gold ring or two on the hand that rested on her heavily pregnant belly. "What have you to report?"

"Your Majesty, we intercepted a wagonload of black spice," the Commander said, his back impeccably straight as he addressed her. "The information from our scouts proved to be correct, and we were able to ambush the bandits before they went on to Surjalana."

"Well done." The Empress turned to the man sitting with her. "You were right. To think a whole wagonload could have slipped through our fingers if not for the scouts. These smugglers would have been deep in the desert in a matter of days, selling their wares legally."

The man furrowed his brow in agreement. "The river road is the fastest route north from the Gray City," he said, then looked at the Commander. "This is welcome news indeed, but I'm afraid there will be many more attempts in the future. The king of Surjalana refuses to join in our efforts to outlaw black spice entirely, and so the smugglers will continue going north to sell it. I suppose they aren't called the *lawless marble cities* for nothing."

Lan recognized the man speaking as Lord Koichi, the Empress's husband and head of her royal cabinet of ministers. He was one of the handsomest men she had ever seen, with a sweep of jet-black hair over a strong forehead and chiseled jaw. His feet rested on a high brocade footstool that had been provided for his comfort, as a person of short stature. She remembered asking her father why Lord Koichi hadn't become Emperor after his wedding, and her father had explained that it was because Empress Jade was the one who had descended from the ruling family *and* had chosen to rule in her own right. "*He supports his wife in her choice, and in all other aspects,*" Minister Vu had said with a hint of admiration. "*The man has no interest in power.*"

Now she listened as Commander Wei continued giving his report to the royal couple.

"The smugglers must have expected an attack, because they were well armed and fought viciously," he said. "I lost several good men, but I would have lost many more if it hadn't been for one of Lord Nguyen's new explosives. It's fortunate that the nobleman is on our side and not the Gray City's, despite all of their efforts. I must admit, Your Majesty, that I had the audacity to doubt his word and yours when he gifted them as weapons to our army."

"Caution is a virtue," Empress Jade reassured him. "But I'm glad the nobleman's new weapons were able to help you." Her eyes moved to Lan and Bao, and Lan felt a nervous jolt as she lowered her gaze with respect. Her mother had taught her all of the necessary etiquette, but it all flew right out of Lan's head as the Empress studied them. "You say you captured none of the smugglers alive, Wei. Who are these young people behind you?"

"I found them hiding nearby, Your Majesty. They claim to be citizens of the Sacred Grasslands, and as such, would fall under their king's jurisdiction, but I discovered that the boy is originally from the Gray City." Commander Wei's stern gaze swept over them. "They were also searching for a woman taken to the city by the surviving bandits, which concerned me."

Lan kept her eyes lowered and heard Bao's intake of breath as Empress Jade rose and approached them. *If only Ba and Mama could see me now,* she thought, feeling awed. *I'm standing before the woman who brought down the scourge of the empire.* Lan had been ten years old when the Great Battle had happened, and had listened hungrily to all the details when her father and older brothers had discussed it.

Empress Jade's family had once reigned over all five kingdoms of

Feng Lu: the Great Forest, the Sacred Grasslands, Kamatsu, Dagovad, and Surjalana. After Jade's mother had died, her father the Emperor had wed Xifeng, a woman of legendary beauty and cruelty who had nearly sent Feng Lu into devastation. Eight years ago, at barely eighteen, Jade had gone on a quest to summon the Dragon Lords, the gods who had created the continent, to defeat Xifeng, and had subsequently disbanded the empire to render all of the kingdoms free and independent.

A smell of orange blossoms and white jasmine followed the Empress as she stood in front of Lan and Bao. But when Lan allowed herself a quick glance upward, she saw that Her Majesty was not looking at her, but at Bao.

"Young man, what has happened to you?" Empress Jade asked, and Bao's head snapped up, astonished. "Years ago, when I undertook my quest, I came across a ghost who was holding on to a crane-maiden's cloak, and I saw, too, my mother and my eldest brother, Fu, long after they had passed from this life. You are not a spirit, and yet I have seen too many people not of this world to mistake your strange form. Please tell me your story."

Lan looked at Bao in shock, but saw none of the fading or glimmering she had witnessed at first. "You're able to see that, Your Majesty?" she asked, remembering too late that she ought not to have spoken unless addressed directly by the Empress. She felt her cheeks warm under the Commander's stern gaze, but Empress Jade did not seem to mind.

"I can see it," she said, scrutinizing Bao. "There is an odd transparent quality to your skin that reminds me of when I saw my brother. What is your name?"

Bao blinked at the Empress in silence, and for a moment, Lan worried that he might be too anxious to speak. But at last, he said haltingly, "My name is Bao. I was apprentice to a physician near the river market, more than a day's journey north of here. A witch placed a spell on me, and we were looking for her to remove it when the Commander found us."

"A spell?" the Empress asked. But Bao opened and closed his mouth, and his face reddened under her gentle scrutiny, so she turned her attention to Lan, who introduced herself and briefly explained the details of the enchantment. "I know your father, Minister Vu. I had the honor of meeting him years ago. But you say that this witch is Bao's aunt? And that Bao's family may still be in the Gray City? Do you know who they are?"

"He's never met them, Your Majesty," Lan said, and Bao threw her a look of gratitude. "He believed himself to be an orphan all his life, and though he knows he has come from the southern Grasslands, this is the first he's heard of any connection to the Gray City."

The Empress looked up at Bao's shy, earnest face. "It seems your destiny lies there if you are to find this woman. A witch, you say. I know of good magic, like that of the benevolent healers in the mountain villages of Dagovad. My heart-sister, Wren, has told me much about them. She arrived here late last night," she added, looking at Commander Wei, who gave her a slight bow of acknowledgment. "And I know of dark magic, used to manipulate or intimidate. There are rumors of some in the Gray City who still uphold the teachings of the Serpent God and use blood magic, as my stepmother, Xifeng, did, illegal as it may be. But there is no proof."

Out of the corner of her eye, Lan saw Commander Wei grimace at the name, and she recalled a romantic poem she had once read. Her mother had never approved of the ballads over which Lan's cousins swooned, so Lan had devoured them in secret, her favorite being the star-crossed romance of Commander Wei and Empress Xifeng. He had grown up with Xifeng and had been the one to take her life during the

Great Battle, and the romance and the heartbreak of it all had appealed greatly to Lan.

"The witch *did* take some of my blood. She cut my hand," Bao said, looking frightened.

"Did she burn anything that looked like incense?" the Commander asked in a sharp voice, a muscle twitching in his jaw. "Black sticks that smell strongly of earth? Those who employ dark magic use them for their spells the way most people use incense for prayer."

Bao shook his head. "No, sir."

"How long have you lived in the river market?" Empress Jade asked him.

"Eight years, Your Majesty. I've gone from family to family since I was two, and a merchant took me north when I was eleven. Master Huynh, the physician for whom I worked, can attest to that. As can Miss Vu," Bao added, looking at Lan, and she nodded at the Empress.

"I don't believe these young people are working with the Gray City in any way. But you did right in bringing them before me," Empress Jade told Commander Wei, then looked at Lan and Bao. "You are fortunate to be here. It is inevitable that war be declared on the Gray City, I'm afraid, but we will give them one last chance to meet our terms. The Commander leaves tomorrow to negotiate with their leader, Mistress Vy, and aid our allies in the Unclaimed Lands. He and his men will also escort Lady Yen, the daughter of my friends who own this house, to her betrothed. You will be safe if you accompany them in your search for the witch."

"Thank you, Your Majesty," Lan said gratefully. "May I send a message to my father to let him know that Commander Wei will be taking us south?"

The Empress nodded her consent. "Of course."

"Jade and I want to inspect the black spice you brought back, Wei,"

Lord Koichi spoke, as he climbed down from his chair to stand beside the Commander. "I'm curious to see if Mistress Vy is selling the incense only or increasing production of the stronger form of the drug."

"I think your curiosity will be satisfied," Commander Wei said grimly. "For my part, I would rather see it destroyed than learn anything more about it. I've heard of too many cases of illness and addiction and ruined families, but you shall see the supply with your own eyes, if you wish."

Bao had been listening with intent interest. "If it's all right with you and Her Majesty, sir, I—I would like to go, too," he stammered. "A colleague of Master Huynh suggested that there might be a treatment for bloodpox made from the same poppy. I'd like to see how it works."

"You may both come, if you like," Empress Jade told him and Lan, and she and her husband trailed after Commander Wei and his captains.

"This will be a rare opportunity to learn," Bao told Lan in a low voice, his face flushed and excited.

Lan noticed that the outline of his body was starting to fade. "The spell is taking hold again," she said, and he paled as she placed a hand on his back. "It took longer this time. When I first found you, you started fading within minutes after I touched you."

"Perhaps it has something to do with . . . with . . ." Bao's ears turned bright pink. "I was in contact with you for a long time in the boat, and we rode here together on one horse."

Lan mulled this over. "And you think the longer we're in contact, the longer this effect of the curse stays away? That would seem to make sense."

"It hasn't done anything to you, has it?" Bao asked, concerned. "The witch said whoever brought my form back would be tied to the spell, too, but you haven't been fading."

"I haven't noticed anything different." She sighed as they followed the others out into the elegant, well-lit corridor. "The sooner we find this witch, the better. It's a stroke of luck that Commander Wei will let us travel south with him, so let's hope those smugglers really were taking that woman back to the Gray City. I don't know what we'll do if she went elsewhere."

Bao bit his lip. "It's our best chance. We have less than two weeks left."

Two women joined them in the courtyard, both appearing to be in their late twenties or early thirties. One had an exquisite face and a dainty figure, and Lan was drawn at once to the work of art she wore: flowing robes in the style of the Great Forest court ladies, hand-painted with a design of white cranes taking flight. Lan admired her with all her heart: she seemed like the sort of elegant, well-bred lady that Lan's mother hoped she would become.

Empress Jade introduced her to Lan and Bao. "Lady Yen is the daughter of Lord and Lady Phan, who have kindly allowed me to encamp here at their summer home," she said. "Tomorrow, she will travel south with Commander Wei. She is to be Lord Nguyen's bride."

"Oh!" Lan exclaimed, and then it was her turn to blush to the roots of her hair as everyone looked at her. "I apologize. My father is friends with Lord Nguyen and I remember him talking about the upcoming marriage. Please accept my congratulations and best wishes."

Lan hadn't thought it possible, but Lady Yen was even lovelier when she smiled. "Thank you, Miss Vu. I'm grateful to Her Majesty for approving this union that has pleased my parents, and for giving me such a grand escort to my husband's estate," she said, glancing at the Commander, who stared straight ahead and maintained his stiff, formal posture. But Lan was interested to see a slight pink color enter his cheeks.

"And this," Empress Jade said, putting an arm around the second woman who had joined them, "is my dear Wren, a lieutenant in the Crimson Army. She will join your journey south."

Lan's attention shifted at once. Unlike talk of the Serpent God, the Crimson Army *was* a topic allowed at home by her parents, and she had hungrily absorbed every detail about the fierce female warriors who lived in the mountains of Dagovad. She knew that the Crimson Army had been invaluable in the defeat of Empress Jade's wicked stepmother, and that Wren had gone on the quest with the Empress and Lord Koichi.

Where Lady Yen was soft and round, Wren seemed all angles and lines, tall and thick with muscle. Both her fine black clothes and the weapons around her sturdy waist looked to be of the highest quality. But despite her dangerous reputation, Wren was all smiles as she embraced the Empress and Lord Koichi. "I don't dare hug *you*, sir," she told Commander Wei, "so I'll simply nod and tell you how gray your hair has gotten since I saw you last."

"And I'll tell *you* that you are as impudent as ever," he said loftily.

"I didn't say gray was a *bad* look on you," Wren pointed out, and Lan stared in surprise as the Commander reached out and folded the lieutenant in a gruff one-armed hug. "So, we're off to the southern Grasslands tomorrow. One hears of nothing else but the Gray City these days—except for the topic of bloodpox, which has reached the kingdom of Dagovad at last."

"Is everyone in the Crimson Army safe?" Empress Jade asked, alarmed.

"Yes, thank the gods. But Sparrow tells me not a day goes by at court without someone lobbying for the legalization of black spice. There's some rumor that it could treat bloodpox." Wren rolled her eyes. "As though Mistress Vy needs any more encouragement to keep producing that nightmare drug behind the walls of her city."

"No one in that family has ever needed encouragement," Commander

Wei said with disgust, as he gave orders for the wagon of black spice to be brought before the Empress. "Mistress Vy's ancestor didn't hesitate to make a profit when he first discovered the uses of the poppy, nor did his witch of a wife, who helped him create the first formula for black spice."

Bao looked at Lan, his face troubled. "What is it?" she whispered, but he shook his head.

"But you must remember that my own ancestor, who was Emperor then, honored that family and gave them leave to perform their research," Empress Jade said, watching as a pair of horses pulled a large, bulky wagon toward them. "Even Xifeng supported them by using their incense. Things have only changed for the worse in the past eight years, with so many families in ruin."

"Mistress Vy still has support from some nobles even today," Lord Koichi put in. "She's tried many times to enlist Lord Nguyen's help. She has never shown any interest in meeting our terms, which is why I think Wei's trip south to negotiate will really be the first step in the war."

The Empress placed a hand on his shoulder. "But it must be done nonetheless. Even she deserves one more chance."

Lan listened with growing unease. As reluctant as her father had been to let her go before, she felt sure he would summon a battalion to bring her home if he knew she was going straight into a potential war zone. But she looked at Bao's worried face and knew she could not leave him alone, not even with an armed escort.

Soldiers pulled the confiscated wagon in front of Empress Jade and lifted the canvas, revealing a wealth of materials: bundles of jet-black incense sticks, piles of pots of waxy balm, and jars of black powder. Lan noticed a powerful, earthy scent like that of a rotting swamp and fought the urge to cover her nose.

"Are the waxes and powders also black spice, Your Majesty?" she asked.

Empress Jade gave a grim nod, holding her belly with both hands as though protecting her baby from the drug. "All of it is, my young friend. In the past decade or so, the Gray City developed a balm to be applied to the skin as well as a powder that can be smoked in a pipe, which is the strongest, most intense form there is."

"There's your proof, Koichi," the Commander said, and the Empress's husband nodded, circling the wagon with a frown. Bao followed suit, his keen eyes roving over the supply and his awkwardness slipping from him like a cloak. As Lan watched him study the contents, his intelligent face bright with curiosity, she thought she could see what her father liked so much in him.

Wren and Empress Jade stood talking in low voices while Lady Yen hung back, looking a bit disturbed. Lan opened her mouth to speak to her, but caught sight of Commander Wei. His attention was not on the black spice, but on the noblewoman, and his expression had a hungry intensity to it. Yen glanced at him, seeming to feel his gaze, and they looked at each other for a second, no more. But in that briefest of exchanges, Lan could have sworn she saw the air move between them. It fascinated her, this charge in the air that vanished as soon as the stare was broken, and she wondered if such a spark had ever existed between her and Tam.

Lan turned back and gave a start when she caught Bao watching her from the other side of the wagon. He looked away quickly when Lord Koichi told him, "We can demonstrate the incense for you, but I think my wife and Lady Yen had better return to the house. Would you like to go with them, Lan?"

"I'd like to stay, sir," Lan said, peeking at Commander Wei to see if he would follow the noblewoman. But he remained in place, casting a look like thunder on the wagon of black spice.

"Well, in that case . . ." Lord Koichi handed her a strip of brown cloth that had a loop of ribbon sewn onto each side. Lan looked around at the others and saw that the Commander had slipped each loop over his ears, turning the cloth into a sort of protective mask. "This is meant to keep the black spice from affecting you. The seamstresses have been kept busy mass-producing these for the army of the Great Forest, as well as those of Dagovad and the Grasslands."

"Will Mistress Vy be using black spice as a weapon, then, sir? If it comes to war?" Lan asked, meaning it as a joke, but Lord Koichi answered seriously.

"You are more right than you think, Miss Vu. It was how Xifeng fought in the Great Battle—with bundles of incense that she lit against my wife's forces."

Lan shivered a bit as she put the mask on, again catching Bao's eye as one of the soldiers struck a sulfur match and applied the flame to the tip of an incense stick. For a moment, nothing happened, and then an enormous gray-black plume emerged. Lan took an involuntary step backward, shocked by how much smoke could come from one of the slender sticks. She watched the soldier press his free hand over his mask, keeping it securely in place, and hold the stick as far from his body as possible.

"Evil substance," Commander Wei muttered, his voice muffled behind the mask.

Lord Koichi and Wren moved deftly out of the path of the smoke. "All that is needed," the Empress's husband told Bao, "is to inhale the plumes for a minute or two and the effects will be felt. It's said to induce a feeling of calmness and well-being, and may relieve pain in some. But severe addiction is a cost that far outweighs the benefits."

Lan saw that Bao's face was pale beneath his mask, and the shadows under his eyes were pronounced than ever. "Sir," she said in alarm, looking at Commander Wei, but he had already seen Bao's pallor and begun moving toward him.

"What's wrong? Is it the spell?" the Commander demanded, but Bao did not answer. He stared blankly into empty space, his eyes unfocused and red-rimmed. His knees began to shake, and both the Commander and Lord Koichi helped him onto the ground.

"Put it out at once," Lord Koichi ordered the soldier who held the incense stick. It took a few moments for the residual smoke to clear, and then Bao blinked rapidly up at them all.

"What happened?" he gasped. "I . . . I felt so faint."

Lan rushed to his side, waving away the last tendrils of black spice. She knelt beside him and felt his damp, clammy forehead. "You're not fading," she said. "Are you in pain?"

"It wasn't the spell. I—I think it was the incense. But how could it have been, when I was wearing this, like all of you?" Bao slipped off his mask and looked at it helplessly.

"It seems you're a bit more sensitive to black spice than the rest of us," Lord Koichi told him, patting his shoulder. "How are you feeling now? Dizzy? Sick?"

But Commander Wei was watching Bao sharply. "You saw something," he said, and it was a statement, not a question. "The black spice gave you a vision. What did you see?"

Bao's face, which had begun regaining a bit of color, blanched once more. "I—I didn't see anything much. Just a hole in the ground, in a beautiful garden. I didn't know what it meant," he said, and Lan squeezed his shoulder, feeling his distress. "There was a hot spring there . . . and a mirror made of water."

Commander Wei froze, and Wren and Lord Koichi exchanged glances full of meaning.

"What does it mean?" Lan demanded, for it was clear that they all understood something she and Bao did not. "Why did Bao have this vision when none of us did?"

"There was a woman kneeling by the spring," Bao went on, before any of them could answer Lan's questions. Perspiration beaded his forehead and upper lip. "She had pale, pale skin and lips as red as blood. Eyes that lifted at the corners. She spoke to the water."

The Commander stared at him, shocked. "Who was she?"

"Wei," Wren said, a hint of warning in her voice.

"Who was she?" he repeated, and Bao quaked under the strength of his stare.

"I don't know," Bao said helplessly. And then his eyes widened. "I saw you, too, sir. But you were much younger, possibly my own age. I don't know. I have an awful headache."

"You're all right," Lan said soothingly, as he turned his desperate gaze to her. She looked up at Commander Wei, whose face looked ashen. "Sir, I don't think he meant to offend you. He doesn't know what's saying . . . He's overtired; he hasn't had any rest in a few days . . ."

"Slowly now, my young friend," Wren said briskly, helping Bao to his feet. "You and Miss Vu should return to the house, and we will talk about this later."

"That's enough for now," Lord Koichi said to the soldiers. "Ensure that this wagon is locked up until we can determine how best to destroy its contents."

Lan took Bao's arm. His face was wan and weary as they said their goodbyes to Lord Koichi, Wren, and Commander Wei and headed back toward the Phans' house.

"It was the strangest thing," Bao muttered to Lan. "Like dreaming wide awake. I had the mask on, but I could smell the black spice so strongly. I saw Commander Wei embracing this woman. I tried to look away, but I couldn't. He was so much younger, and she was so beautiful."

"It must have been Xifeng. That's why he looked so disturbed," Lan said quietly.

Bao stopped and leaned against a pillar for a moment, his breath ragged. "I had another vision, too. And it might prove what I've been afraid of since the Commander said that Mistress Vy's ancestor married a witch." He took a deep breath. "I've been dreaming for some time about a woman in a field, standing outside a great city of stone. She is searching for me and calling my name, but the second she finds me, I always wake up."

Lan listened, a growing knot of tension forming in her gut.

"This time, it wasn't a dream," Bao said, his lips trembling. "I saw her again . . . and I heard her speak. She told me she was my mother. She looked so important and regal—tall like me, with iron-gray hair. She smiled and said that my aunt had come home, and so would I. Lan," he added, forgetting to address her formally in his fear, "I think Mistress Vy of the Gray City is my mother. And I think that the river witch must truly be my aunt."

A trickle of cold slipped down Lan's spine. From everything she had heard of the Gray City and its enigmatic leader, they were by all intents and purposes malicious and profane. She could see on Bao's face the same consternation—that he could be so closely related to the very woman against whom Empress Jade and two other kings wished to declare war. But son or not, she knew he could not be anything like Mistress Vy; she could imagine no one more different from shy, retiring Bao, with his awkward ways and love of learning.

"All right," she said, full of pity for his distress. She put a hand on his shoulder, and it felt almost natural to comfort him with touch, the same way she had brought him back from the curse. "Let's think about this some more and keep it to ourselves for now. We won't tell anyone else yet, especially the Commander."

Bao nodded, clearly relieved. "He won't be pleased. And he'll trust us even less. Maybe he won't even want to take us south anymore."

"He doesn't have to know yet," Lan said firmly. "We will both get some rest, and tomorrow we'll finish what we set out to do."

12

Bao lay on a cloud, and as he watched the stars wheeling overhead, he saw images in the light they cast: Commander Wei standing over the body of the beautiful, dead Xifeng; the poppy fields ablaze with light outside a vast and unknowable city; and the woman who searched the fields for Bao, calling his name as she wandered through the tall grass. The cloud spun him ever higher into the sky, and soon he would leave earth behind for all time . . .

Someone was shaking him. He saw a beloved face, a pair of wide eyes, rose-pink lips pleading with him to wake up, please wake up. Suddenly, the drowsiness and the lightness left him, and Bao blinked and found himself in a grand bedchamber, lying on a thick bed filled with swan feathers. It took him a moment to remember where he was: Lord and Lady Phan's home, where Empress Jade was staying. The first rays of dawn were creeping through the open shutters, along with a pleasant breeze. He turned his head slowly, disoriented, taking in the delicate paintings and the stacks of books on the rosewood table, and finally Lan kneeling beside him.

"Thank the gods," she sobbed. Both of her hands were gripping his right arm so tightly, her fingers had left marks in his skin. "I thought I was too late."

Bao stared at her in confusion, then jerked backward. It had been a warm night and he had slept half-naked. "Lan!" he cried, again forgetting to address her in a formal manner. He yanked the light blanket up to his neck, covering his bare chest. "What are you doing in here?"

"What am I *doing*?" she half shouted, and he saw with surprise that she had tears running down her face. "I was saving your life! Commander Wei, Wren, Lady Yen, the soldiers . . . All of them are in the courtyard getting ready to leave, and I was out there waiting for you and you never came. So I went to find you, and a good thing, too. You were almost gone!" She fell back on the floor, her face pale except for two spots of red, panting as she stared angrily at him.

"Gone?" Bao repeated. He took in her disheveled hair and her nostrils flaring, and realized how frightened she had been. "Do you mean I was fading?"

"What else would I mean?" she demanded. She took in a few deep breaths and wiped her face. "I came in and I could barely see you lying there. I thought the bed was empty at first. Your body was almost gone. Completely disappeared."

He lifted the blanket cautiously, so she wouldn't see anything of his chest, and looked down at himself. He was as solid as ever, but a moment ago . . . Bao thought of that sensation of floating on the cloud and leaving the earth behind. "I didn't know," he said, feeling foolish. "I guess it was because I had spent so long alone in here . . ." He felt blood rush to his cheeks at the implication that she should have stayed with him. "That is, I meant—"

"Save your breath, Bao." Lan seemed to have recovered somewhat.

She stood up and smoothed her hair, and he noticed a little trickle of perspiration along one temple. She had been truly worried about him—terrified, even. "Hurry up and get ready. Everyone's waiting outside, and the sooner we find this stupid witch, the better."

Bao nodded, still clutching the blanket to his neck, frozen with shock at almost having vanished entirely, flustered that Lan had seen him almost naked, and embarrassed that he hadn't immediately realized what had happened. A small thread of panic, too, had blossomed in his gut at the thought of stern Commander Wei waiting on him. Why was Lan still standing here, glaring at him? He couldn't think what he had done wrong.

"Well?" she asked. "Isn't there anything you want to say to me for my trouble?"

"Um . . ." Bao's mind felt as though it was moving at half its usual speed. "I'm sorry."

Lan threw her hands up in the air, exasperated, and stomped out of the bedchamber. Perhaps it wasn't what she had wanted him to say—but there was no time to linger on it, not with everyone waiting. Bao hurled himself out of bed and dressed as quickly as he could. He counted in his head as he gathered his belongings, trying to figure out how many more nights he had until the full moon. *Ten*, he thought, biting down hard on the inside of his cheek. Just over a week until the enchantment was permanent.

All at once, his thoughts came like fire-tipped arrows, reminding him of everything he would never do if he failed to break the spell. He would never row his boat or see his friends at the river market again, never see joy in the faces of a patient's family when he helped them, never carry a small son or daughter in his arms, never kiss Lan . . .

He was feeling faint again. He took a moment to breathe deeply before running out to the courtyard. Commander Wei and a dozen Imperial soldiers were readying the horses, four of which had been designated for Wren, Bao, Lan, and Lady Yen. Bao had expected Lady Yen to take a palanquin, but supposed that she hadn't wanted one since everyone else was riding.

"Want a boost onto your horse?" Wren asked. She stood almost eye to eye with him and was dressed all in black, as she had been the day before. He marveled at the strength in her hands as she lifted him onto a calm chestnut mare.

Bao thanked her and looked around for Lan, who wore a simple blue tunic and matching pants and gripped the reins of a bay mare. She glowered at him when he rode over. "I'm sorry I didn't say thank you earlier, Miss Vu. I didn't quite know what was happening."

Lan's lips pressed tightly together. "You gave me the fright of my life. But I'm sure it was much scarier for you," she said, looking at him sidelong.

"It was. I'm grateful to you," he said, and her face softened a bit. "I was floating . . ."

He struggled to find words to describe how it had felt to drift away from earth and then come back to her again, to a version of Lan he could never have imagined after years of adoring her from afar. There was the perfect Lan he had imagined, and the Lan who had shouted insults at him, and now this Lan, whose face had been wet with tears of worry for him. This Lan whose hands had brought him back, this Lan who cared, this Lan he was glad to have by his side.

But how could he tell her all this in words?

She was still staring at him, and Bao realized he had taken too long to continue when she turned away. Cursing his awkwardness, he watched Empress Jade, Lord Koichi, and another man come out to bid them farewell. He didn't need introductions to know that the second man was Lord Koichi's father. He was bent and gray, but had the same eyes, smile, and voice as his son. Bao wondered what it was like to have a father he resembled. He wondered if his own father was still alive, like his mother.

Mother. Short-lived as his vision had been the day before, he remembered it with sharp clarity. The woman had looked like a queen, tall and imposing, with the assuredness of a leader whose armies would follow her in death at one command. She had spoken to Bao in a voice like rich, warm honey: "I've missed you, my child, but soon we will be together once more in the Gray City. I will embrace you as your mother at long last. I am Mistress Vy, and you will come to me . . ." Bao had been drawn to her like a lonely moth to a flame he had longed for. This woman was claiming kinship with him, which no one had ever done in all his life.

Bao's attention snapped back to the present as Empress Jade came to wish them a safe journey. He bowed from the waist, watching as Her Majesty moved to hug both Wren and the Commander and marveling at the familiarity with which she treated her friends. As one, the company turned their horses out of the Phans' gates and rode back into the grasslands.

Wren pulled her sleek black horse alongside him. For some reason, Bao didn't feel at all nervous around the keen-eyed warrior. She had a kindly, straightforward manner that made him feel as though he had known her a long time. "Is your flute safe?" she asked. "Jade told me about your curse."

"I've checked my sack a thousand times to make sure it's in there," he confessed. "I don't know what would happen if I were parted from it, but I'm not eager to find out."

"May I see it?" Wren accepted the bamboo flute and examined it. Keeping her eyes on Bao, she urged her horse slightly ahead of his, still holding the instrument. "How do you feel?"

"Fine." Bao looked down at his hands and body, which were both still solid.

Wren nudged her steed until she rode abreast with Lady Yen, two horses' length ahead.

"I'm fine," Bao said again, when she glanced back at him. But this time, he felt a scratching sensation in his throat, as though from a cold, when he spoke.

The warrior nudged her horse forward so that now she rode side by side with two of the soldiers, about fifteen feet away from Bao. She looked back again, then rode forward toward the Commander, and Bao felt a sudden powerful pressure on his windpipe, like hands gripping his neck and blocking the air to his lungs. He coughed as he tried to call for Wren, but the feeling intensified until he could no longer think about anything else but getting another breath of air.

"Wren, come back!" Lan called, looking anxiously at Bao.

The minute the warrior doubled back and rode beside Bao once more, the feeling eased. "Well, you weren't joking about the curse," she said, watching him massage his neck painfully.

"I can't ever lose that flute," he wheezed, his throat as raw as though it had been scraped by a blade. "I think it might kill me. It felt like being underwater, and the flute was the surface."

Wren handed him a flask of water, which he gulped gratefully. "This witch cursed you because she was jealous of your father choosing your mother over her? Punishing their son doesn't seem right to me."

"It's not right," he agreed, handing the flask back with his thanks. He pictured again the woman in the vision: bright eyes, broad cheekbones, and a smile like the sun. He could easily imagine anyone choosing her over the sullen river witch. "She didn't think my mother could break the spell, either. She seemed to imply that my mother had never truly loved anyone."

"I wonder who your mother is. There aren't many with magical blood in Feng Lu," Wren said thoughtfully, and Bao averted his eyes. "And those visions of yours. Xifeng used to use black spice to foresee the future. I wonder if having magical blood makes you more sensitive to seeing things."

Bao frowned. "I don't have magic."

Lan, who had been listening from Wren's other side, spoke up. "She said magical *blood*, not magic. Perhaps you can carry the blood without having any powers."

"I know a woman in Dagovad who claims to be a witch," Wren said. "She ferments snakes in jars of alcohol and sells the liquid as a health tonic, which some villagers say have given them night vision or the ability to find lost things. One man claimed to be able to see the future for a short time. Perhaps your enchantment has given you the ability to have visions."

"Maybe." Bao turned his attention to the grasslands around them, pretending to admire the swaying yellow-green grass beneath the brightening sky. He hoped Wren and Lan would change the subject—it made him anxious to keep talking about the spell, and it worried him that Wren might connect him to Mistress Vy. But if the Gray City's leader and her family were known for their magical blood, it would only be a matter of time before everyone else came to that conclusion. He imagined Commander Wei treating him like the son of an enemy and ordering the soldiers to leave him behind.

If Mistress Vy truly was Bao's mother, that meant the Gray City was

Bao's true home. And it also meant that it was *his* family who was responsible for the strife on Feng Lu. They had ignored the king's orders to stop producing a dangerous drug, and they were the reason why Empress Jade was sending Commander Wei to negotiate before openly declaring war. Bao didn't know how to feel about his association to such a family, when mere days ago, he hadn't known he'd had a family at all.

He felt sick with the confusion of it all.

Lan was watching him, likely fretting over his pallor and silence. Bao knew he ought to be grateful for her concern, but he already felt trapped within the walls of his own mind—he didn't need to add worrying about someone else's fear into the bargain.

That afternoon, when they stopped to eat and rest, Bao avoided Lan and approached Commander Wei, who stood brushing his stallion's coat tenderly. He raised an eyebrow as Bao came close and asked, "What is your story, young man? I saw what black spice did to you. I knew someone once who also . . . That drug doesn't give visions to just anybody."

"Believe me, sir, I didn't want that vision," Bao told him.

All around them, their companions sat down to eat. The soldiers had packed a wagon full of food for the journey, and from the murmurs of satisfaction, it sounded as though they had done their job well. Lan's bright, rippling laugh rose above the rumble of deep voices.

The Commander gestured to the ground, and they both sat.

Bao felt the tension between them like a thick curtain and knew that his dignity would not be able to weather the Commander throwing him out of the group like a shameful traitor. It was time to be truthful. "I'm worried about my visions," he admitted. "And my connection to the Gray City. You mentioned that Mistress Vy's family had a witch in its bloodline, and the witch who cursed me may be my aunt. I'm afraid."

"I'm not going to abandon you because you might be a criminal's son,"

Commander Wei said gently, and Bao's head snapped to him in surprise. There was a wry, not unkind look on the older man's face. "I promised Empress Jade that I would take you south, and I will. Her Majesty believes you to be honest, and she also knows Minister Vu. Miss Vu told us last night that her father would gladly vouch for you. So don't worry."

"Thank you, sir," Bao said, with quiet gratitude.

"And since you weren't raised by Mistress Vy, leader of the biggest eyesore on Feng Lu, why don't you tell me who *did* raise you?"

The Commander sharpened his daggers as Bao told him about the various people with whom he had lived. The young, unmarried mother who had taken him in, thinking he would provide for her and her daughters when he grew up, but who had soon given up the arduous task of feeding three mouths. The family who had let him live on their farm until a drought had destroyed their crops. The kind old man who had taught him how to fish, but whose son's wife had evicted Bao, fearing that Bao would take precedence over her own children.

"You were only ever a knife's edge away from the work camps," the Commander said, pausing in his work to look at Bao. "It's a hard existence for any child, I imagine, being forced to shovel in the mines, work the fields, dye fabrics in stuffy buildings. Whatever use people find for those orphans after the parents die of illness . . . or black spice addiction, as so many did."

"I was fortunate to avoid the camps." Bao pulled out the flute, his grip on it tight and secure. "I also lived with an elderly couple who gave me this and showed me more kindness than I have ever known. I started to think that might be what it felt like to have a family. People who wonder about you when you're not there, and want you to be happy wherever you are."

Commander Wei's face was gentler than Bao had ever seen it. "I spent many years alone, too. My parents died when I was young, and I always dreamed of marrying one day and raising my own children."

"But that never happened?"

His silence was all the answer Bao needed. He watched the Commander's hands move deftly over the blade and couldn't help wondering about the man's love for former Empress Xifeng. What might it do to a man—not only having to see a woman he had loved die, but to be the cause of her death himself? Bao felt a surge of sympathy for the gruff, lonely soldier.

"You're fading a bit," Commander Wei said suddenly.

Bao looked down to see his hands growing filmy. "It's the spell," he said wearily.

Commander Wei placed a large, heavy hand on Bao's shoulder, but Bao's hands did not solidify as they would have done for Lan. Bao felt only a seeping dark cold in his fingers . . . and then a luxurious, joyful warmth from his other shoulder, where Lan had just placed her hand. Bao hadn't heard her approach. Her touch was sunlight pushing back the ageless cold. In his lap, his hands grew solid and heavy, and he felt himself sinking into the soft grass. She wore a little smirk as he looked up at her sheepishly.

"The witch said it would only work with someone he loves," she told Commander Wei.

"Someone he loves," the Commander said thoughtfully. "So, are the two of you . . ."

"No, sir," Bao said hastily, at the same time that Lan blurted out, "Of course not."

They looked at each other, flustered, as Commander Wei studied them with a small smile playing about his lips. But the next moment, his posture went rigid and he sheathed his blade, muttering something about checking the food supply before striding off.

Lady Yen appeared beside Lan, holding food wrapped in a cloth. "Have you had anything to eat, Bao? I brought you dried meat and fruit."

"Thank you," Bao said, surprised, not having thought she would deem him worthy of her attention. But she gave him a gracious smile and took the spot vacated by the Commander.

"When is your wedding?" Lan asked her.

"The day after I arrive at Lord Nguyen's estate. It's an unconventional wedding, without much ceremony, since it's an affair of state. Empress Jade and my parents made the match to help strengthen the Great Forest's relations with the Sacred Grasslands."

"Will Lord Nguyen bring the betrothal gifts to your parents' home, as is tradition?"

"He sent them by wagon," Lady Yen said, her smile a bit forced. "Nine wagons, in fact, full of gifts and cakes and a roast pig. It pleased my father, who didn't expect such a generous offering for a bride as old as I am. My sisters were half my age when they were wed."

"Well," Lan said politely, "I hear it is an arrangement that pleases all parties."

"It will please the parties that matter most," Lady Yen said quietly.

All around them, the soldiers got up and dusted themselves off. Commander Wei came over, looking at Lan and Bao as he spoke. "We depart in five minutes. Leave nothing behind. We have about a week's journey ahead of us, as long as we make good time."

"Surely we can wait a bit longer?" Lady Yen asked, gesturing to the half-eaten food in Bao's hands. "This young man hasn't finished his meal yet."

"He can eat while we ride," the Commander said curtly, avoiding her eyes.

"What an uncomfortable practice." Lady Yen grimaced as she rose, looking as stiff as Bao felt. None of them were used to riding so much, except, of course, Wren and the soldiers.

"Perhaps we should have taken Her Majesty's suggestion and brought you a palanquin, then," Commander Wei said tartly. "You would certainly sleep better in it than you will tonight."

Lady Yen shrugged, unperturbed by his cold manner. "I've never had trouble sleeping, and I don't intend to start now," she said, smiling up at him. "In fact, I think all of this riding will help. So let's not mention the palanquin yet again, *if* that is acceptable to you, Commander."

Commander Wei's mouth opened and closed, but no sound came out. At last, he gave a single nod and brought out his dagger, sharpening it as though his life depended upon it. Bao didn't have the heart to remind him that he had already honed the blade just moments ago.

He saw Lan watching the exchange, too, looking amused. If they had been friends, they might have discussed it and perhaps laughed at the folly of an attachment between the Commander and a *very* betrothed noblewoman who would never be free—laughed and shed a tear or two. Bao wasn't one to judge a man who loved someone he ought not to.

But he and Lan were not friends—not quite yet, not when he was obligated to her, dependent on her, and utterly unsure how to treat her—and so they each mounted their respective horses and did not speak much for the rest of the day.

13

After Lan sent a message to her parents to tell them she was safe, she had allowed herself to give in to the excitement of her quest, but the exhilaration of adventuring was wearing off quickly. She was wearing her maid's shoes, she was riding a horse—something her mother would *never* allow—and she was far from home, all of which made her feel like a different person, the type of free-spirited, courageous girl she had once dreamed of being.

But as the first day of traveling went on, Lan had to admit that that adventures weren't as comfortable as she had imagined them to be. Her backside ached from riding, her hair was matted upon her forehead, and her stomach hurt from the dried meat that apparently passed for good food among the soldiers. But despite these inconveniences, Lan vowed not to utter a single complaint, not wanting Bao to think that she regretted helping him. Deep down, she knew he was grateful to her, but it was hard to remember that whenever he snapped at her or ignored her, as he did now. He had been riding up near the Commander all afternoon.

"I think Wei is warming up to your friend," Wren commented.

"We aren't friends, really. We just grew up together," Lan told her.

Lady Yen, who was riding between them, raised an eyebrow at Lan. "Not even friends, yet you're the only one who can break his spell?"

"I haven't broken the spell. I just help ward off its effects."

Lan caught them exchanging a knowing look and turned her attention back to the road, her face hot. She knew that was the other thorn in Bao's side: the fact that he still cared about her. Whatever lingering feelings he had for her was why Lan could affect his curse at all.

Her eyes found his tall, lanky frame at the front of the procession. He rode between the Commander and another soldier, looking comfortable and confident in the saddle, his head swiveling between the two men as they talked. He was gesturing emphatically as he spoke, with none of the shy awkwardness he had around Lan. It was difficult to reconcile his quiet, red-faced self with the boatman who had come to her on the river, his flute singing her love songs over the sound of crickets, but she supposed the distance between his boat and her window had given him the confidence he lacked.

He hadn't been Tam, but he had been *there*. He had given her all he had and had cared enough for her to overcome his painful shyness. Perhaps that was part of the reason why she insisted on helping him: because he reminded her that she was worthy of love.

"Have you ever met Lord Nguyen?" Wren was asking Lady Yen.

"Once, many years ago. He's a widower much older than I am, but he seemed kind," Yen said. "He's a distant relation of my mother. Her family is from the Grasslands and as proud of it as my father's family is of being from the Great Forest. It was inevitable that one of my sisters or I would make a political marriage."

"How do you feel about marrying him?" Lan asked curiously.

"Empress Jade asked me the same question. She was the only one who cared to know if the match pleased me." Yen's eyes were far away, and a bit sad. "I told her I liked Lord Nguyen, so the marriage moved forward. That was two years ago. I keep thinking how we sometimes seal our destinies earlier than we should, before we know what we want."

Lan looked ahead at Commander Wei. He had started out riding at the front of the group, but as they traveled, she noticed that he made a point to pull back and ride alongside each of his men. He was now speaking to a pair of soldiers who were just ahead of the women.

Yen cleared her throat. "But this marriage is better than I could hope for. I'm well into my thirties, and my parents had given me up as an old maid when Lord Nguyen came along. And I'm looking forward to a quieter life in the Grasslands, away from the court of the Great Forest."

"But I'm sure you'll miss court. And some of the people, too," Wren added slyly.

She flushed. "Don't speak of that, please. That life was only ever a dream, and we mustn't shock poor Lan."

"You're talking about Commander Wei," Lan said, without missing a beat.

Wren burst out laughing. "There's no hiding this from anyone. Lan hasn't known you for a full day, and she already understands your heart better than you do."

"How did you meet?" Lan asked. "Don't soldiers and noble ladies live apart at court?"

"Far, far apart," Yen said. "But the Commander is Her Majesty's friend and attends all of her functions. We met at a banquet last year, when my little nephew fell into the decorative pond and the Commander rescued him. He had always seemed so grim to me, but I'll never forget the way he comforted the child. It was a side of him I don't think he shows to many."

Lan envisioned the romantic scene: Commander Wei wrapping his cloak around a shivering boy and gazing up at Yen, luminously beautiful in her festival silks. "And you saw more of him after that? Did you make plans to meet?"

"You're as bad as Wren!" Lady Yen scolded her, though by now she was laughing, too. "I only ever saw him and spoke to him at events. It would have been inappropriate to meet alone. I am, after all," she added, the light in her eyes fading, "betrothed to wed another."

"But it's not too late," Wren began, and Yen whirled on her.

"Are you suggesting that I go against the word of my Empress? That is treason."

"You said yourself that Her Majesty cares about your happiness."

Yen shook her head. "I'm not listening to this. Empress Jade agreed to this match because of what's happening in the Gray City. My marriage will strengthen two kingdoms and give both more power in the event of an uprising. Don't you see? I can't . . . I *couldn't* . . ."

She looked so distressed that Lan felt a stab of pity. "I knew next to nothing about the Gray City before I came," she said, changing the subject. "But I can see now why they want to become an independent kingdom, if black spice has made them so rich. And if it really *can* treat bloodpox, they'll have even more power to hold over everyone else." She glanced again at Bao. He had seemed upset after learning about his potential link to Mistress Vy, but there had been longing there, too, the hunger of a boy who had gone all his life without a mother.

"We won't let that happen," Wren promised. "Not Commander Wei and the army of the Great Forest, nor the kings of Dagovad and the

Grasslands, nor the Crimson Army. We won't let the Gray City take land or power or anything that doesn't belong to them."

"The Crimson Army? Will they be coming as well?" Lan asked.

Wren nodded. "All forces will converge outside the Gray City, to await the result of negotiations. Mistress Vy doesn't seem to be one for diplomacy."

"Lord Koichi said that she might use black spice as a weapon, just like Xifeng did in the Great War," Lan recalled. "That's why all of the cloth masks were made to protect the soldiers."

"We have to be prepared for every circumstance."

"I know that the Crimson Army paints their lips red before a battle," Lady Yen said. "How will enemies see their fearsome smiles beneath those cloth masks?"

The warrior grinned. "We haven't thought of that yet. Perhaps we'll paint some lips on the outside of the cloth masks, though I don't know how Wei would feel about that."

They looked up to see that both Commander Wei and Bao had pulled their horses to one side, waiting for the women to catch up. "Are you all right back here?" the Commander asked, moving his horse to the other side of Wren. Bao was forced to take the spot next to Lan, and she tried not to look at him to gauge his reaction.

Wren made a face at the Commander. "As you know, I killed an evil eunuch eight years ago, when I was barely twenty. Of course I'm all right."

The corner of the man's mouth lifted, and then he glanced at Yen. "And you? And Lan?"

"Fine," Lady Yen said. "Having a light-hearted conversation about the Gray City."

The Commander's mouth thinned. "I'll be glad when we destroy whatever supply of black spice and flowers that woman has been harboring inside the city walls."

"You'll do that if negotiations go poorly?" Bao asked, looking a bit disturbed.

"We'll do it either way," Commander Wei replied. "Part of the treaty Empress Jade and the other rulers hope Mistress Vy will sign calls for the complete destruction of her supplies. I'll be very much surprised if she agrees to even a compromise."

"Well, of course she won't," Bao said, annoyed, and they all looked at him. He turned red under their collective attention, but drew himself up in the saddle. "Black spice is her life's work and her family's legacy. If you get rid of it all and decimate her supply of flowers, she won't have anything left, and we'll never know if she might have had a treatment for bloodpox."

"It wouldn't matter to me," the Commander said slowly, "if black spice cured death. Even if evidence came out that it could treat disease, I care most about the proof of its harm: the intense addiction it causes, the way people turn against their own families, and the devastation it has wreaked upon the economy, with good Feng Lu gold and silver flowing into the Gray City's coffers."

Wren placed a calming hand on his arm. "The drug may have medicinal benefits, yes; no one is arguing with you there," she told Bao. "But it has done much more harm than good, and the rulers of Feng Lu—Jade included—are hesitant to allow the continued production of something that has sent so many families into ruin and populated the work camps with orphans."

"Have you given Mistress Vy a chance to show her research?" Bao challenged her, and Lan stared at him, astonished by how confrontational he was being. "Would any of you listen even if you were shown conclusive proof that the drug could help, too? What if, gods forbid, the bloodpox turned into an epidemic and you destroyed the only treatment?"

"You're a physician, Bao," Wren said calmly. "You should know there is no miracle cure. I've seen enough death and illness in my time with the Crimson Army to understand that. Has black spice ever been rumored to get rid of the bloodpox completely?"

Bao shook his head.

As Lady Yen tactfully changed the subject, Lan glanced at Bao. She pitied him, wondering if the idea of being Mistress Vy's son had made him feel obligated to be loyal to the woman already. "I think you had a good point," she told him in a soft voice, so the others wouldn't hear. "But it seems the decision has been made already, and the Commander hates anything to do with black spice, which is why he didn't listen to your defense of the Gray City."

"I wasn't defending the Gray City."

"It sounded like you were."

Bao clenched his jaw. "I was trying to think like a physician and be open-minded to remedies we don't know about yet, just like Master Huynh taught me."

She bristled at his rude tone. "Like the Commander said, they *do* know about black spice. And they know it's harmful."

"Oh, what do you know about it?" he demanded, so loudly that the others stopped conversing and stared. "What business is it of yours? Let me think what I want to and stop trying to change my mind. Stop worrying about me so much. I am tired of being your responsibility."

Lan yanked her mare to a stop, furious. "You're *tired*? You're sick of how I save your life, each and every single time you fade?" she demanded. A part of her wanted to stay calm and control herself—Bao was upset about the curse and his ties to Mistress Vy—but the other part of her had snapped. She was done being understanding. "If you're so determined to be unpleasant and ungrateful, perhaps I ought to go home and let Commander Wei take care of you and your stupid spell. Shall we see how well that works?"

As she spoke, her horse tossed its head and stamped its feet, alarmed by her loud tone. Annoyed, Lan dug her heels into the animal's side to urge it on, the way Wren had shown her. But in her inexperience, she must have done it too hard, because the mare took off at a gallop.

Lan heard the others shouting, but her limbs were frozen with terror and refused to obey her. She held on to the horse's mane for dear life as the world rocked beneath her and the grasslands and sky flew by in a manic whirl of gold and blue. Her braid came undone, with loose strands of long hair whipping at her face, and all she could think of was how slovenly she would look to her mother, if Lady Vu were here to see her die in such a spectacular fashion.

Hoofbeats thundered behind her and then a figure appeared. Through the dark curtain of her hair, Lan felt rather than saw someone grab her reins and yank back. Her horse tossed its head again, but stopped abruptly. The sudden halt sent Lan flying from the saddle and into a graceless heap in the trampled grass. She lay still with the wind knocked out of her, her elbow and knee on the left side stiff and sore from their sudden contact with the ground.

"Lan!" Her rescuer dismounted and bent down to her. It was Bao, kneeling beside her on the grass, his face stricken. "Are you all right?"

She gasped in a few shaky breaths. Her stomach felt like it was still racing ahead and hadn't stopped when the horse had. "I'm still alive."

"She's fine! Go on without us; we'll catch up," Bao shouted to the others. Lan heard Commander Wei yell something back, but couldn't distinguish the words with the ringing in her ears. Bao waved at him, then turned back to Lan. "You didn't seem to fall *very* hard—"

"Oh, yes," she said, struggling to sit up. Smears of dirt covered both knees and one side of her tunic, but she suspected her pride was wounded more than anything else. "Why stop at just a few insults? Go ahead and tell me how weak I am for being hurt by this little fall."

"I was going to say that I still want to make sure you didn't hurt yourself," he said, looking abashed. He reached tentatively for her arm, but she snatched it away.

"Stop pretending like you care, Bao. You would prefer that I had broken my neck, because it seems death is the only way you'll ever forgive me." Lan twisted away from him and watched their group ride past. Wren and Lady Yen lifted their hands and she waved back. "I'm sick of apologizing. I'm sick of your insults and petty remarks, and I'm sick of you holding one mistake over my head for the rest of my life."

For a moment, there was only silence, punctuated by Bao still trying to catch his breath.

"Why are you breathing like that when *I'm* the one who fell?" Lan turned back to see him massaging his neck again. "What happened to you? Where's the flute?"

He gestured to the sack still attached to his horse, coughing. "When you took off on the horse," he said in a strained voice, "I had the same sensation of suffocating as when Wren took the flute away. Like hands around my neck, blocking my air. That didn't happen last night, when you were in a completely different room. I think the spell is . . ."

"Progressing? Changing somehow?" she asked, and Bao nodded, still coughing. "And you don't fade so quickly anymore. We've been riding for hours and you've still got your form. So I'm the only one who can keep you from turning into a spirit, and now I'm also the only one you need to stay close to—besides the flute—or die of suffocation. And you say *you're* the one who's tired of being my responsibility?"

"Lan," he said determinedly, drawing out her name, and she hid her surprise. "I shouldn't have said that, or even thought it. I'm sorry for being awful to you. I've tried not to be, but that doesn't excuse what slips out."

Lan angled a glance at him. "You've said something like this before. You told me you needed time. But we're stuck together now, because like it or not, you would succumb to the spell if I weren't here. You would be a stick of bamboo already if not for me."

He rubbed his face, his tired eyes on the horizon. "I know. I'm a bit of a mess right now."

She gave an emphatic nod, and Bao let out a weary chuckle.

"I'm constantly thinking about everything I'll never get to do once the curse takes hold. I'm torn between believing my mother is a villain, like everyone says, and wanting to know what it's like to have family at last. And then there's you. I have no idea how to treat you."

"Like a human being?" she suggested tartly.

"But you were never *just* that to me," Bao said, blushing. "You were special. And then you told me I had never meant anything to you, and *then* you vowed to help me, and now you're around all the time and I can't be alone to think because you're always there. I have to hold on to my anger because it keeps me safe."

"Safe from what?" Lan asked softly, feeling her own anger ebb away.

He looked at her at last, and she saw, in the uncertain slant of his mouth and the tension in his shoulders, what effort it took for him to meet her gaze so directly. "Don't you know by now?" he asked, very low. His face was still as red as Empress Jade's silks, but he did not look away.

In the warmth of his eyes, Lan saw again the moon, the river, and the *hoa mai* scattered in the water like stars in the sky. She had never cared for Bao or noticed him as anything more than a bashful, quiet apprentice until the day he had confessed his feelings. She had spent years blinded by Tam's brilliance, but when that light had died out, it was as though she had found Bao standing shyly in the space left behind. Unassuming and wholly unexpected.

"I've never stopped caring for you," he said shakily. "I don't think I ever could."

"Well, then," she said, "stop taking your affection out on me."

Bao stared uncertainly, and then his shoulders sagged at the forgiveness he saw in her face. The tension dissipated like the air after a storm when he smiled, and Lan returned it after a moment. "We should get going," he said. "But first let me see if you're hurt."

"My elbow's a bit sore," she said, wincing as she offered him the arm she had landed on.

He accepted it, his hands gentle as he turned her wrist, elbow, and shoulder, scanning her face for a reaction. He shifted to take the other arm, intent and businesslike, as a young physician could only be, and Lan couldn't help smiling at his seriousness. His eyes flickered to hers self-consciously, and she shivered a bit as he released her arm, his warm fingers trailing along the length of her skin. "You might have a bruise or two tomorrow, and a bit of soreness, but nothing's broken. Which is, ah, good news," he said, some of his awkwardness returning. He rubbed the back of his neck. "How are your legs?"

Her legs were perfectly fine. Lan knew it well, because they didn't hurt one bit when she shifted on the grass. She could have told him that. Instead, she said, "I'm not sure." He was looking right at her, and she couldn't tell if he knew she was lying, but it didn't matter. She gave him a nod of consent, and he put his hands tentatively on her right leg.

She felt their warmth acutely through the cotton, as though he were touching her bare skin.

Bao glanced at her and she tried to breathe normally as he pushed her knee into a bent position. "Did that hurt at all?" he asked, and when she shook her head, he moved to her ankle. His hands did touch bare skin there, at the hem of her pants, and he gently swiveled her foot.

Lan's pulse raced and her mouth went dry, trying to stave off any inappropriate thoughts of his capable hands moving in the opposite direction from her ankle as Bao switched to her other leg. She felt every soft touch and press of his fingers in the nerves at the base of her spine.

"Nothing's broken, though you'll likely be sore for a day or two," he said, pulling away as soon as he was finished. The fingers of his left hand were relentlessly tapping his right hand, another nervous habit Lan recalled from his visits to her house. "Let me help you up."

"Thank you," Lan said, a little breathless. She took his hand and rose, knees shaking in a way that had nothing to do with her fall. He formed a step with his hands and boosted her back onto her horse, which snorted and looked unimpressed. "I think I'll be all right."

"I'm glad of it. And . . ." Bao cleared his throat. "And I'm glad I could make sure."

They rode back together and caught up to the others, unhurt and in one piece. But Lan knew, catching his eye for a moment, that everything between them had begun to change.

14

Bao struggled to sleep well for the first few nights of the journey. Each time he sank into slumber, he had feverish dreams of fields consumed by fire, scarlet flowers weeping black tears, and the parent figures who had faded in and out of his life like butterflies in summer. His mother, the person he wanted to see again the most, evaded him, lingering just beyond the edge of his mind. He felt her presence in every dream.

"Have you always slept this poorly, or is it the traveling?" Lan asked him one morning. The day had dawned fine and bright, and the company was packing up and preparing to leave.

"You heard me talking in my sleep?" he asked sheepishly. She looked fresh and pretty beside him, and he found it ironic that a spoiled minister's daughter slept better outdoors than he did. "I must be nervous about getting to the Gray City. I can't help but wonder if my mother's expecting me. The dreams feel so real, and sometimes I feel I'm betraying her by traveling with Commander Wei."

"You're not traveling with him to declare war," Lan pointed out. "You're going because you need to find the witch. Your life is at stake. Don't feel guilty about fighting for it."

He smiled at the urgency in her voice. "Thank you."

"You're welcome."

Bao pretended to be engrossed in folding his bedroll, but he watched out of the corner of his eye as she swept her long hair over one shoulder and braided it with slim, graceful hands. It would make a nice painting, he thought: a girl weaving the silken strands of her hair, with her eyes on the sunrise, surrounded by the fragrant grasslands in high summer. It would surely be a painting he would treasure forever. Lan glanced at him, and he realized he had forgotten his bedroll in favor of staring at her.

"Sorry, I was just . . ." He stood up too quickly and the bedroll slipped from his hands, unraveling itself. "I wondered if you needed help with yours."

"I think *you're* the one who might need help," she returned, laughing as she tied off her braid with a strip of cloth. She helped him fold it up, their hands brushing as she gave it to him, and Bao secured the roll to his horse, wishing he could just speak to her once without falling on his behind or dropping everything he was holding. "Will you help me up?"

Bao walked over to her horse and folded his hands, forming a step for her to use. She placed her hand on his shoulder, squeezing it in thanks when she was safely on her mare. He used a nearby boulder to mount his own steed.

"Do you have your flute?" she asked.

He checked the cloth sack hanging from his saddle. "Yes, safe and sound."

"I was listening when you told Commander Wei the other day about all the people you had lived with," Lan admitted, blushing. "I liked the story of the couple who gave you the flute. I didn't realize you had gone through so many different families."

"I never talked about it before," he said. "I didn't want people pitying me. But something about the Commander told me he wouldn't, and he would understand."

"I can't imagine what that must have been like. I'm sorry."

"I'm glad I found Master Huynh. I learned much from him," Bao told her. "But I always wished I had a father like yours, kind and generous and knowledgeable."

Lan beamed. "He is the best of fathers. And he always admired and respected you," she said. "He only ever had something complimentary to say about you. As did my grandmother."

"I liked her, too. She brought out a different side of you." Bao smiled, remembering the day they had climbed the tree at the old woman's suggestion. "You were always more daring and bold, and you stood up to your brothers and . . ." He broke off before he could say the name.

"And Tam," she finished for him, sighing. "Bà nội always encouraged me to do what I wanted while I could. *Too soon*, she would say, *you'll only do what you're supposed to do, and say what you're supposed to say.* And she was right. For a while now, I've only wanted what I thought I was supposed to want. She never liked Tam, by the way," she added, glancing at him.

Another memory came to Bao then: a spring afternoon, when the words of Lan's song had first come to him like fireflies whose light would soon be lost. He had hurried to catch them on paper, terrified they would slip away into the wind. Tam had caught him scribbling in the barn and had given him an unpleasant jolt, as though he had wandered into one of Bao's innermost dreams.

Tam had bent his elegant face over the words. "Aren't you a loyal little servant? Always ready to do whatever my parents command."

"They didn't tell me to write this. I wrote it myself."

Tam's laugh, even when harsh and unhappy, was a handsome sound. "Use that cleverness to find me a way out of this marriage, and I'll pay you five times what my father gives you now." He leaned against the wall with an easy, careless grace. "Help me escape from my shackles."

"Miss Vu isn't the monster you keep making her out to be."

"Of course not. This isn't about Lan. She's just bait that my parents are dangling in front of me to keep me obedient." Tam had tipped his head back, his long, straight nose like a blade cutting down his profile. "This is about me having a say in my own life and making my own choices, without my mother screaming at me or my father disowning me."

Ink had splattered Bao's chin. He had pressed the tip of the pen too hard into the paper. "Then tell them you want to break off the betrothal completely. They know you're unhappy, so what is the point of all this pretense? You could save me the trouble of carrying on this lie, of writing notes in your name and sending flowers that are supposed to be from you. I'm tired of hurting a girl who has never done anything wrong."

"What is the point?" Tam had echoed. "The point is that even if I break it off with Lan, my parents will find me another suitable bride. It is always what *they* want, and what *they* think best. And I must do my filial duty and bend to their will and make them happy. So why not stall? Why not string them along until I can find a chance to escape?"

"You're stringing Miss Vu along, too," Bao had pointed out furiously. "And the longer this goes on, the deeper in you'll be."

"One of these days," Tam had said, "I'm going to find a chance to escape and live life for myself. But until then, I'm not about to risk my father disowning me for embarrassing Minister Vu." And true to his word, Tam had never said anything to his parents. He had learned from a young age to pay someone else to do what he couldn't or didn't wish to, and so Lan had suffered, and Bao had suffered, and a deep rift had formed between the two families.

One of these days, Bao decided, he would tell Lan about this memory. He would find the words to let her know the depths of Tam's selfishness and cowardice, and then—with any luck—she might finally be able to let her heartache go.

They traveled all through the morning, and when the sun was at its peak in the sky, they had reached a part of the grasslands where the river returned, calm and gentle along one side of a village whose cottages rose like ruddy stones in the fields. Bao looked joyfully at the water, glad to see that it was part of *his* river, the one that had felt more like home to him than any other place. Commander Wei signaled for them all to stop and let the horses rest, and the soldiers began unloading the wagon of food as Bao slid to the ground, eager to walk along the riverbank.

"Look at this place." Wren stood with her hands on her hips, surveying the village uneasily, and when Bao followed her gaze, he saw what disturbed her. Though the homes were well made from bricks, wood, and bamboo, not a single one appeared to be occupied. There were no streams of smoke that indicated cooking, no washing hung out to dry, and no animals in the barren pens. In fact, the place seemed completely deserted.

"It looks abandoned," he said.

"It is. The question is *why*, because it's such an ideal location." Wren studied the heavy-headed fruit trees lining the river. "I suppose it's as good a place as any for us to rest and gather supplies. Only three more days before we deliver Lord Nguyen's new bride to him."

They turned to look at Yen, who stood speaking to the Commander. The man listened in silence, and after a moment, he strode to the river with his face like stone.

Wren sighed. "I told Jade it wasn't a good idea for Wei to escort Lady Yen. Well, they'll either work it out between them or keep sulking, which they're both quite good at. I'm going to go look around this village," she added, strolling off into the group of houses.

"And I am in desperate need of a bath," Lan said, looking at the river with the same yearning Bao felt. "Will you perish if I go?"

"I suppose we'll find out."

She turned to face him and began walking backward slowly, one step at a time, toward the edge of the water. The tightness in Bao's throat returned well before she reached the trees, and despite all of his efforts to fight it, the magic wrapped its fingers around his windpipe and squeezed. Dots danced in his vision as he lurched forward, gasping for air.

Lan hurried back, and the pressure eased instantaneously. "This is hopeless."

"I'm sorry," Bao said, ashamed. "Maybe you can try again and I'll find a way to—"

"Choke to death? Don't be ridiculous. You'll just have to come with me while I bathe," she said. Despite her matter-of-fact tone, two spots of pink flamed in her cheeks.

"Are you mad? I couldn't *possibly!*" he cried, aghast.

"Oh, come on." Lan grabbed his arm and started dragging him toward the water. "You'll turn your back like a gentleman, and we have a dozen chaperones here to supervise your behavior. You might as well bathe, too. The gods know you need it more than I do." She laughed at his peeved expression, then added, "Do you know, you haven't faded in over two days now?"

"No, I hadn't noticed." It was a lie, for this was the first time in over two days that Lan had touched him; how could Bao not have noticed? "The enchantment must be changing again. Before, it threatened to turn me into a spirit, and now I can't . . ." *Be apart from you*, he thought, but the words seemed too weighty and meaningful to say aloud.

"I wonder what it will do next, if I *will* be tied to it like the witch said. Perhaps we'll get to the Gray City before we have to find out," Lan said.

"Only seven days left until the full moon." He forced a smile, but it didn't lessen the weight of his words. The panic never lingered far from the surface. "The Commander says we'll be at Lord Nguyen's estate in three days, and then the city is another day after that."

"Which means we have two extra days to find the witch. Soon we will find your witch in the Gray City and the spell will be broken," Lan vowed, and he couldn't help but be heartened by her optimism. "We will fix this, and then we'll go back to normal life."

They reached the riverbank, which was lined with fragrant, shady trees.

Lan bent down and began taking off her shoes, and Bao nearly tripped over his feet in his haste to turn away. "Are you afraid you'll see my ankles and be seduced?" she joked.

"That's already happened," he replied, and then his cheeks flamed when he realized what he had said. "I meant I've already seen your ankles!"

Her laugh rippled as Bao looked around desperately. The riverbank was not a straight line, as it had been back home. This one curved and had thick patches of undergrowth, perfect for hiding one's modesty. *If one has any modesty*, he thought, ignoring Lan's smirk. He dashed into the dense shrubbery, just far enough for privacy without tempting the spell's malicious side.

"Can you still breathe?" Lan called, a grin evident in her voice.

"I'm fine." Bao waited for her to come charging through the bushes, just to make him panic, which seemed like something she would do. But there was only silence, and then a splash and a contented sigh as she slipped into the water on the other side.

Quickly, he slipped off his own clothes, taking care to place his bundle containing the flute in a safe spot before getting into the water. The river lapped at his hot, blistered skin and he closed his eyes, letting it soothe his aching body. It reminded him of afternoons off from working for Master Huynh, when he would take a dip to find relief from the hot sun.

"Nice, isn't it?" Lan's voice was so close that his eyes flew open in horror.

Instinctively, Bao scrunched up his body, a rather difficult feat with his long arms and legs. He heard her laughing, but saw nothing of her through the trees, thank the gods. He shook his head but couldn't keep from smiling. This was the bold, fearless Lan of years past who had climbed trees and played pranks on her brothers, encouraged by her delighted grandmother. He didn't know how much he had missed her. "Where are you?" he demanded.

"I'm still on my side, of course," she said, giggling.

"You are infuriating."

"No, that won't work. You can't make me apologize again."

Lan's voice was *so* close. He couldn't help peering through the undergrowth . . . to make certain she was at an appropriate distance, of course. He caught sight of a long, pale neck and the slope of a naked shoulder before he turned away, appalled at himself. *Think of anything else,* he thought, pulse thundering madly. *Think of your music.* But thinking of music only reminded him of Lan's silhouette in her bedroom window, and the silk robe clinging softly to her body when she had found him under the spell, and the feel of her legs, slender and shapely, in his hands . . .

"Why are you being so quiet?" she inquired.

"I'm *bathing,* and bathing is private." He almost wished they were fighting again.

"But isn't it communal in the river market? My father says that all of the men stop work early one day a month and jump into the water together."

"We're not *in* the river market, and you and I are—"

"Hush!" Lan hissed. "Stop talking!"

"Me?" he asked incredulously, but then he heard Commander Wei and Lady Yen's voices raised in a heated discussion. They seemed to be coming closer every minute. Bao made to get out, but froze in horror when he saw Lan peering at him through the bushes. Her eyes crinkled in amusement, and she shook her head at him, telling him to remain in place.

"I'm not a goat, Wei," Lady Yen was saying indignantly. "I'm not a sack of rice or a bag of potatoes to be thrown onto a cart and conveyed to my owner. I am a human being with thoughts and desires of my own."

"I have nothing to say about that," the Commander replied. "I am serving my Empress, who charged me with the task of bringing you safely to your husband. That's all I care about."

There was a silence, and then, in a very low voice: "You don't care about anything else?"

"I cannot tell you what you wish to hear."

"Then perhaps you'll show me?"

Through the low-hanging branches of the trees, Bao saw Lady Yen draw closer to the Commander, who did not move away. They were only ten feet from the water and would certainly notice if Bao tried to escape, but this was *not* a conversation for anyone else's ears. He found Lan's eyes, mortified, but she shook her head again, gesturing for him to stay put.

"You know what I've told you about my past," the Commander said, low and desperate.

"I don't care about Xifeng."

"Not about her," he said sharply. "I meant my childhood. My poverty. I know what it is to be hungry, to want for basic necessities, and it is something you have never known and never *will* know. Your fate is to be comfortable, and you must follow your father's wishes in order to be so."

"What about *my* wishes? Why must I forever bow my head and do what others tell me?"

Something flickered in the Commander's face—a memory, or the ghost of someone he had once known. "You would never go hungry in Lord Nguyen's house."

"And you think this is a better existence for me? Living without you?"

He remained silent.

"Will you live out your days alone? Doing what someone else commands you to?"

He turned away. "I will live as a respectable man of honor and serve my Empress."

"But why should that have to end if you are with me?" Yen cried passionately.

"If I stole the woman I loved away from her rightful husband, I would be breaking their alliance and failing in my duty. I would forfeit my position."

"You would not."

"I would lose Her Majesty's respect and the goodwill of my men. No soldier would follow a dishonorable, unprincipled man. I would be sent away."

"Empress Jade loves you! She would never do that to you!"

The Commander turned back to her. "Jade was the one who gave me this second chance. She was just eighteen when I first saw her, stumbling in the desert with dusty clothes and shorn hair, and even then I knew who she was. I owed it to her brother, who gave me my *first* chance, to serve and protect her, and I won't turn my back on my duty to them."

They stood in a charged silence, looking at each other.

"You said you loved me," Yen said.

The Commander went still. "What?"

"You said, 'If I stole the woman I *loved* away from her rightful husband.'"

His nostrils flared. "No, I didn't. You misheard me."

Yen just crossed her arms and stared back at him.

She has you there, Bao thought, smiling as he watched the flustered Commander struggle for words. He glanced through the bushes at Lan, but her eyes were on the trees, starry and unfocused as she witnessed the love story playing out before them. It reminded him of her leaning out of her window toward the river, her face alight.

"All right," the Commander said at last. "I *do* love you, you irritating woman, more than I ever thought I could love someone again. But I'm bringing you to the man you'll spend your life with, and I see no point in voicing something that can never be."

"I will not spend my life with this stranger."

He threw up his hands. "So you'll go against your family's wishes? You'll defy Her Majesty's hope for continued peace between the Great Forest and the Grasslands?"

"Oh, burn the Great Forest and the Grasslands!" Yen shouted, and Commander Wei reared back in shock. "What do I care for Feng Lu? There are plenty of other noblewomen they can find. I have my own life and happiness to worry about, and I want to share them with you."

The Commander closed his eyes.

"I know your life has been hard. But what hurts you hurts me." Yen took one of his hands in both of hers. "Before you, I was just another worthless daughter to marry off. Too old, too outspoken, too passionate to be proper. No one ever looked at me like I mattered until you."

"Yen," he said brokenly, but couldn't go on.

She wiped his wet face with the heel of her hand with infinite tenderness. "I know you're afraid. You gave your heart once, and it almost destroyed you, but I promise you that it will be different with me. I will never hurt you or turn from you the way Xifeng did."

For a tense moment, Bao thought the Commander would walk away. The man was a fighter who lived by his sword, who intimately knew death and the dark side of mankind, and yet the fear on his face was palpable. But then something broke within him, and he pulled Lady Yen close to him. His was the face of a weary sailor coming to a safe port glowing with light. Their lips met, gentle at first, and then fiercer, harder. They kissed as though each needed the other's air to survive, their bodies melding until there was no separation between their hearts.

Through the bushes, Lan jerked her head at Bao. They emerged from the water and dressed in silence on their respective sides, completely unnoticed by the lovers. Bao raised a hand to scratch his cheek and was surprised to find tears on his skin, cool in the heat of the day.

All the pain and the anger and the torture of love overwhelmed him. Ever since Lan had hurt him, he had wondered what the point was of offering his heart to someone who could push it away with both hands. But what he had just witnessed gave him the answer: it was the chance, however small, that the other person would accept his heart instead and keep it safe.

Lan met him on his side of the shrubbery, and they walked back together in silence.

People make mistakes, Bao thought. *Hearts get broken, but somehow we forget the pain. Or choose the chance of happiness in spite of the pain.*

He glanced at Lan beside him, whose head was tipped in that thoughtful way she had, her wet hair gleaming like black silk in the sunlight.

People make mistakes.

15

Lan and Bao returned to the encampment to find the Imperial soldiers hurrying about, packing the food back up and preparing the horses. Wren was nowhere to be seen, but faint voices emanated from the abandoned village.

"What's happened?" Lan asked one of the men, alarmed.

"We must leave at once," the soldier told her, tightening the saddle on his mount. "We will have to find somewhere else to camp for the night, because it turns out the village isn't empty at all. There is a woman who is deathly ill. Have you seen the Commander?"

"He's down by the river with . . . He's down by the river. Maybe I can do something to help," Bao said, straightening. "Where is this sick woman?"

The soldier shook his head, looking harassed. "That stubborn Crimson Army woman is with her, but I want everyone else out here. It's too dangerous. I think it's bloodpox."

No sooner had he finished speaking than Bao dove for the cottages without hesitation. Lan watched him go with a surge of admiration. She didn't know many people who would so willingly plunge into danger to help a complete stranger. "He's had experience with bloodpox," she told the soldier, who looked nettled at Bao's disregard for his warning, and went to find her waterskin. Her throat itched terribly, likely because of the dusty air, but the sensation did not go away even after drinking. She coughed and coughed, remembering that Bao had done so when they were separated, and nearly dropped the waterskin in her realization.

Bao had run off to help the sick woman, forgetting about the enchantment. Earlier, he had described it as feeling like hands gripping his throat, and there *was* an odd tightness around Lan's neck. This, then, was how the magic would entrap her—a punishment for trying to save Bao's life. Would she also be stuck in the flute if they failed to break the spell? She cursed the witch's pettiness as she hurried toward the cottages in search of Bao, coughing as she ran.

The village looked abandoned, but still the back of her neck crawled with the feeling of being watched. She shivered as a curtain moved at one of the windows, barely imperceptible, and a sliver of a face disappeared beyond her view. She cleared her dry throat and spotted Bao kneeling in front of a cottage, gasping for air, his face pale. She ran to him, aching at the sight of him in so much pain, and the look in his eyes could have stopped her heart: there was such desperation and joy and relief. He gazed at her as though he hadn't seen her in years.

"I'm here," she managed to say as the pressure around her own throat eased. She put her hands on either side of his face. "I'm here, Bao."

"It was stupid of me," he croaked. His hands found her elbows and slid upward, leaving a tingling trail of warmth in their wake as he wrapped his fingers over hers. "I forgot. But you . . . you didn't feel it, too, did you?" For she was also gulping in great breaths of air.

"I think we've found out what the witch meant." Lan forced a laugh.

"This is all my fault," he said, his eyes full of regret.

"*I* chose to help you."

Shyly, Bao moved one of his hands to her face and tenderly tucked a strand of hair behind her ear. She lowered her hands to his shoulders and felt the pulse in his neck fluttering against her fingers. The urge to press her lips to it was overwhelming. She knew now that she had never, ever felt this for Tam—this delightful, almost painful longing. She looked up into Bao's warm, kind eyes, wishing she could express it in words.

But he was already getting up and pulling her to her feet, too. "They're over here," he said, and would have let go, but Lan held on to his hand. He looked down at their joined fingers, then up at her, and something sparked in his eyes. They walked over to the cottage together and peered inside to see a motley gathering of people: Wren standing warily beside two Imperial soldiers, one of them bleeding from a gash on his forehead, and a fierce girl of about eleven gripping a cooking pan, which was presumably what had injured him. The sick woman lay motionless on a small bed, and a young man bent over her, wiping the perspiration from her face.

Bao squeezed Lan's hand and went inside to speak with the man for several tense minutes. Lan stayed by the door, resisting the impulse to cover her nose at the thick, sour-sweet smell of the shabby cottage.

The sick woman was of indiscriminate age, her jet-black hair matted with sweat. She had a curious green-yellow tinge to her warm complexion and lay beneath a blanket with a messy red-brown pattern, which Lan realized with horror was large splotches of dried blood. As she watched, the woman coughed, splattering what little clean space was left on the blanket.

"I don't care what your intentions are." The young man suddenly raised his voice to Bao, and Lan's attention shifted to him. He was small and slender, but his ferocious eyes and the knife-sharp slope of his jaw made his presence seem larger. "I want you and your soldiers to go at once. Tell everyone you see of the sickness here, and maybe they'll leave us alone, too."

Footsteps sounded behind Lan, and she turned to see Commander Wei. "Bao, get away from that woman at once," he ordered. "I don't want you infecting everyone else."

"She's not contagious, even though Huy here would have me believe so," Bao said in a calm, respectful voice as he looked at the angry young man. "I know you're trying to keep your village safe, but I also know that you want to see this woman get better. Lying to me won't do any good if I'm to help."

"Nobody asked for your help!" Huy declared, and the sick woman stirred wearily.

Bao glanced at her. "She needs to rest. Let's talk outside."

As Lan stepped away from the door so that the others could come out, she noticed a small face in the window of the adjacent home. The head bobbed and disappeared. "There are other people in this village," she whispered to Wren, who gave a grim nod.

"I checked some of the houses. There are dozens of children here. They all ran when I asked where their parents were, and some of them became downright hostile." Wren gestured to the bleeding soldier, who glared at the girl with the pan. The child glowered back just as fiercely, as a pair of twin boys who resembled her scurried out from behind a barrel and ran to her side.

"She was protecting her family," Bao said softly, and the girl shot him a suspicious look.

"Why are you all here?" Huy demanded. Even his stance was defensive, with his arms crossed over his chest and his legs wide. He wore a tunic of brown hemp cloth with the sleeves cut off, revealing tawny muscles, and his trousers were of an equally cheap fabric.

The Commander drew himself to his full height. "I am Commander Wei of the Great Forest. My men and I are headed south on a mission, and we plan to encamp tonight by the river outside your village. I give you my word that no harm will come to anyone."

"I'm afraid that won't do. You cannot stay here."

"You don't own the riverbank," Commander Wei pointed out. "We will not enter your village again, but you cannot prevent us from setting up camp by the water."

"Of course not. But I *respectfully* ask you to move at least a mile south," Huy said, and he was subjected to the full brunt of Commander Wei's unyielding stare. "You should know that this village has been quarantined after thirteen deaths from bloodpox, which afflicts that woman inside. I have not fallen ill after weeks of caring for her, it's true, but I would not be so quick to dismiss the power of the disease after so many lives lost."

A ripple of uneasiness ran through the assembled company.

"You were quarantined by the king?" Wren asked.

"This village has been self-quarantined by me. Everyone within five miles knows to avoid it. I do not need any assistance, so please leave us."

"There must be something I can do to help," Bao said, his voice mild and patient. "I've seen another case of bloodpox north of here. I was with a man who suffered greatly for the final moments of his life. His symptoms had been building slowly for months."

"And did you save him?" Huy asked, with a sardonic expression.

"No," Bao said honestly. "But he was at a much later stage than the woman in there. I was a physician's apprentice, and I can make what time she has left more comfortable."

Huy took Bao in from head to toe. "There is nothing you can do that I have not thought of already," he said coldly. "I used to live in the Gray City. I watched my parents and aunt die of bloodpox, as did hundreds of other children who were shipped off to the labor camps with me."

"We have heard no reports of such widespread bloodpox," Commander Wei said sharply.

"Perhaps you hear only what Mistress Vy wishes you to hear."

"What does that mean?" Bao demanded. "That she's hushed up these illnesses?"

Huy shifted his weight, his eyes darting nervously around the silent village. "I don't know. I have nothing to do with the Gray City any longer."

At that moment, the reason for Huy's uneasiness became clear. An elderly couple came out of a cottage on the far side of the village, the man carrying a steaming pot of soup while the woman held a basket. They walked toward them, slow and bent, and only just seemed to notice the group when they drew closer. Their eyes widened in horror at the sight of the armed soldiers.

"Huy?" the old woman asked tremulously. "Have we been found out?"

Huy shook his head at her, but it was too late. Commander Wei strode forward and looked into her basket. She cowered in fear as he pulled out a bundle of black incense sticks. Lan and Bao gasped in unison. "What were you saying about having nothing to do with the Gray City?" the Commander asked Huy in a low, dangerous voice. "If that's true, why do you have black spice in your village? And how did you pay for this?"

The bravado and determination seemed to drain from Huy, leaving behind a very young, very tired man. His shoulders sagged, but he said nothing.

"A minute ago, I was ready to dismiss you as merely unfriendly. But now?" Commander Wei dropped the black spice back into the basket, disgusted. "Now I am involved, as an agent of Empress Jade, who together with your king has declared this drug illegal. You had better tell me everything before I bring you before His Majesty as a criminal."

"No, please!" the old woman quavered.

"We can't go on without him," the elderly man added, struggling under the weight of the heavy soup pot. Wordlessly, Bao stepped forward to relieve him of his burden.

"I told you," Huy said to the Commander, his face weary, "I was sent to the labor camps with the other Gray City children orphaned by bloodpox. I escaped and found this village. But people here were also falling victim to the disease, and the physician took me in as an assistant."

Lan glanced at Bao, struck by the similarity of his story to Huy's.

"That is the last we have of the black spice," Huy went on, nodding at the basket in the old woman's hands. "Years ago, the Gray City hid their drugs in towns and villages all over the Grasslands before selling them. This was one such place. As a reward for their complicity, the villagers received a percentage of the black spice to use. That was how bloodpox started."

Bao shook his head, confused. "You seem to imply that there is a link between bloodpox and the fact that the Gray City gave black spice to these villagers."

"I'm not implying it. I'm telling you straight out." Huy seemed grimly pleased that Bao understood. "The disease begins with aches, chills, and fatigue, and it ends within weeks as the person bleeds from their eyes, noses, mouths, and ears until they die. The physician and I noticed that bloodpox did not exist in this village until black spice came. We also noted that every sick person had used the drug. Black spice *causes* the bloodpox."

There was a long, shocked silence.

Huy jabbed a finger at the basket. "That is what the Gray City doesn't want you to know. That family has hushed up illnesses and deaths for generations. Mistress Vy's ancestors kept the secret of how the barbarian kings truly died out. Mistress Vy's grandmother created a variant that wiped out an entire sector of the city. And her uncle was the first one to conceive the idea of cross-breeding the poppy to another plant, but only managed to create another deadly version."

"How do you know all this?" Commander Wei demanded.

"I have friends who escaped the labor camps with me. They are more bent on revenge than I am, spying and collecting information against Mistress Vy. I care nothing for her. Since the physician died of old age, these villagers—who have been nothing but kind to me—have become my responsibility." Huy uttered a humorless laugh. "The irony is that for over a century, the Gray City has been trying to make a miracle medicine. They sell black spice in order to fund the true research: creating a variant that will end all sickness in the world."

"A noble objective, perhaps, but not at the cost of innocent lives," Bao said, his face troubled as he looked at the pot of soup in his hands, and Lan knew he was thinking of his connection to Mistress Vy.

"But if black spice causes the bloodpox, why are you bringing it to a woman ridden with the disease?" Commander Wei asked.

"We've heard rumors about a potential treatment for bloodpox," Bao mused, before Huy could answer. "You've been attempting to treat her with black spice, haven't you?"

The young man gave a tight nod. "It causes the illness, but it is also the only treatment that works for the symptoms. It keeps the patient alive and takes away her discomfort . . . for a time."

"But it doesn't cure her?" Bao guessed. "It only prolongs her life, and when the symptoms come back, they are stronger than before?"

The old woman came forward. "M-my lord," she pleaded to the Commander, "my name is Cam and this is my husband, Tao. The sick woman is our daughter. We've known Huy since he was a boy, and he was only trying to help us, and he has such a good heart, my lord . . ."

"You all know that black spice is illegal, and still you used it," the Commander said flatly.

"Huy bought us more time with our daughter, sir," Tao said in a shaky voice. "We *will* let her go; we are not so selfish as to want to prolong her suffering. But we wished to say goodbye to her properly. Please do not throw Huy in prison—he has his whole life before him. If anyone must be tried before the king, let it be me." Hearing his distress, the little girl and the twin boys clustered around him.

Lan's heart ached for them all. There would be no one left to help them without Huy, and from the way the children hugged Tao, the old couple apparently cared for the orphans of the village, too. "Please, sir," she begged Commander Wei in her turn, "the harm is done. And it isn't as though they bought the black spice; it was given to them by the Gray City. Is there truly a need to punish them further?"

After a moment, Commander Wei sighed. "I will make no decision yet," he said, but Lan could see as well as the elderly couple that pity had won out. They thanked him effusively.

"I am deeply sorry for your grief," Bao told the couple quietly. "I cannot imagine how difficult it must be for you. But I urge you to consider the Commander's words: black spice is hurting all of you more than it is helping. Even if you do nothing now, sooner or later, the supply will run out. Your daughter's suffering must end, but I want it to be clear that this is your decision to make . . . yours and hers, if she is able to communicate her wishes. No one else."

Cam, who had been crying into her husband's shoulder, looked up at Bao. "It is too cruel, the way the drug evens her breathing and takes the green tinge from her skin. She looks so healthy and lovely, lying there. But it always comes back."

"I understand," Bao said sympathetically.

"And I can't help but cling to her in those moments, and think to myself, *What if this time, the illness never comes back?*" The old woman began to cry again weakly. "I know we have to let her go, I do . . ."

"You are loving parents. Everything you are feeling is perfectly natural," Bao assured her, and Cam and Tao's faces filled with gratitude. Lan looked on, moved by their reaction to his compassion. "The soldiers will encamp outside the village tonight, and I promise they will not come in to disturb your daughter. Our company leaves at dawn. But I would like to help Huy tonight, with your permission. I can make a tonic of ginseng and mint and a few other ingredients to help relieve your daughter's pain and let her rest comfortably. May I do that?"

"Yes, of course," Tao said, glancing at his wife. "And we will . . . we will try to find the strength to say goodbye. We need to speak to our daughter about this and hear her wishes. But perhaps it's time."

Cam's face crumpled, but she nodded and gave the basket to Huy.

"Why don't you go in and see her now? I'll help you with this and leave you alone," Bao said, following the couple inside with the pot of soup. After a moment, he came back out, his face endlessly sad, and Lan went to stand by his side without a word. "We can't destroy the black spice until they've made their decision. It wouldn't be right. But I think they understand."

Huy sighed as he looked at the contents of the basket. "This was all my doing. She would have died weeks ago, but they begged me . . ."

"Didn't you hear Cam?" Bao asked him. "You gave her time with her daughter, and she's grateful to you. What's done is done."

"But the sooner we get to the Gray City, the better," Wren said fiercely. "We need to inform our allies and send a message back to Jade about the truth of Mistress Vy's doings. We have to rally our troops. It is time to fight this evil and declare war outright, and to hell with the negotiations."

A chill crawled down Lan's spine at the warrior's words. Lan had merely left home to right a wrong, but it would bring her into a conflict much bigger than herself and all of the small worries that had consumed her for nearly eighteen years.

But then a large, warm hand slipped into hers, and she looked up and saw the love in Bao's eyes—the love that had never left him, not even in his anger—and she couldn't help feeling that it might all be worth it. It wasn't just the right thing to do, because Bao's life was at stake; she knew now that even without a spell, it was what she *wanted* to do.

16

"What's that?" a little girl asked, wrinkling her nose at the bowl. "It doesn't look good."

"This tonic will help the lady sleep," Bao explained patiently, continuing to mash the mixture of herbs, berries, and river water. "And it will help make sure nothing hurts."

"How do you know what to put in it?" asked one of the twins.

"I've made this before. I worked for a physician," he explained. "That's a person who helps sick people. They teach others, like me, how to take care of anyone who isn't feeling well."

He had removed a table from one of the empty homes and pulled it in front of the sick woman's cottage, where he could work without disturbing her. Huy had helped him gather herbs and roots and other medicinal plants, and Bao had spent the better part of an hour making a variety of different tonics. Slowly, children had grown accustomed to his presence and crept out of their cottages to watch, curiosity overcoming their fear. At first, it had been only one or two of them, but now at least a dozen boys and girls surrounded him.

Bao surreptitiously studied them as he worked. They were thin and small, but relatively healthy and well cared for, probably thanks to Cam and Tao. One of the girls was coughing a bit—he would have to make a draft for her—and he noticed a shallow cut on one of the twins' arms, probably from a tree branch. "May I see?" he asked the child, who offered his arm shyly and allowed Bao to use the last of the river water to clean the wound.

Another boy who was watching crept close to Bao's side. He couldn't have been more than four or five. He beckoned for Bao to bend down and whispered, "I have one, too," offering a skinny brown arm with a much smaller cut. But Bao cleaned it nonetheless, smiling as all of the other children looked on with serious expressions. He felt like a physician surrounded by very small, businesslike apprentices. The boy whispered, "Thank you," and Bao ruffled the child's hair before peering into the cottage.

Cam was sitting by her daughter's bed and Tao stood behind her, his hands on her shoulders. The sick woman was awake, her lips cracked apart into a smile at something Cam had said. Bao drew back to give them privacy. He looked around at the houses that must have seen love and laughter once, and were now empty shells of former lives, and felt the deep, abiding loneliness he knew well. He caught sight of Lan sitting cross-legged in front of the cottage across the way. A little girl sat behind her, placidly weaving duck feathers into Lan's braid, and Bao recognized her as the child who had hit the Imperial soldier with a pan.

"Did you enjoy teaching all of those tiny physicians?" Lan asked, smiling, when he came over to sit with her. The little girl eyed Bao suspiciously, then returned to working on Lan's braid.

"I have to hold back some secrets; otherwise they would let it get to their heads." It wasn't even a good joke, but Bao felt oddly proud of himself. Speaking in complete sentences and not tripping over his feet in front of Lan would always feel like an accomplishment.

"I didn't know you were so good with children," she said. "And you were wonderful with Cam and Tao earlier. Do you think they'll destroy the black spice?"

Bao leaned his weary bones against the cottage behind them. "I hope so. I felt breathless the whole time Huy was talking, but I knew it had nothing to do with the spell and everything to do with Mistress Vy. It's unconscionable what her family has knowingly done to all of these innocent people. And I have their blood and their deeds flowing in my veins."

"Their blood, perhaps," Lan said firmly. "But not their deeds."

"But my *mother* did this. My grandparents, my ancestors. They are all complicit. I don't know how I came to be separated from them, but if I had stayed, I would have grown up in the Gray City. I would have learned their ways. Would I be working on the black spice formula now, too? Would I disregard human life in pursuit of their dream?"

"You are here now, and you recognize right from wrong."

"Maybe they did hope to create a medicine that would help others," Bao said. He was so tired. He felt exhaustion creep into his muscles, weighing him down with everything he had learned. "But they took so many lives in the process. I am a part of that family, and I am about to come home to them. There's no defending that, Lan."

"No," she said fiercely, straightening. "Even if you had stayed in the Gray City, you would have chosen differently. You would have wanted to *truly* help people, and you wouldn't have hurt anyone to do so."

Bao's face glowed. "You think this highly of me? Even though I'm just a . . ."

"Don't you dare say *peasant!*" she cried, then rolled her eyes when he grinned. She picked up a duck feather and rolled it between her fingers. "You know what I keep thinking? What a shame it was that I knew so few men outside of my family. I thought so highly of Tam, once."

He felt a pang of jealousy, seeing how it hurt her to say Tam's name even now.

"But then I leave home," Lan went on. "And I meet Commander Wei, who loves Lady Yen so, and I meet Huy, who is risking much to help these villagers. And I think back . . . and I can't imagine Tam putting anyone else first. I spent years dreaming about a selfish boy who would never love me, and all that time, out in the world, there were men like Huy and the commander. Men who care about strangers, who put other people first, always."

"It wasn't ever about you, you know," Bao said. "For Tam, I mean. It was the *idea* of you Tam didn't want. He was tired of being controlled by his family, but he was too cowardly to tell his parents straight out. So he kept stringing you and your parents along. He was just scared."

"That doesn't free him from blame. Even without all that, he never looked at me when I spoke. He always took the most comfortable chair in the room, even when elders were present. He cared about himself most of all. I keep comparing him to all the other men I meet and finding more and more in their favor. Including you." She hugged her knees and looked at him sidelong. "Especially you."

"Me?" he said offhandedly, as though his heart wasn't singing for joy. "An orphan of no account."

"An orphan of very much account indeed, as I found out."

Bao forced himself to meet her gaze, though his palms dampened and his heart beat off-kilter. He was close enough to see every eyelash she had. He wondered if she was thinking of that moment earlier, too, when the spell had nearly choked him. The feel of her hands on his face had been imprinted into his skin. He had come so close to kissing her, and he had thought—looking into her starry eyes in that moment— that she might not have pulled away if he had.

"I'm glad you came with me," he said.

"You're not just saying that because the spell might kill you without me?"

"I'm not just saying that because the spell might kill me without you."

In her laugh, Bao heard relief, and it filled his lungs like air. He felt a flurry of movement beside him and realized that the little girl's twin brothers had snuck up to his bag and started pawing through it for sweets. The bamboo flute fell out, and Bao snatched it up, quick as a flash, just as the boys reached for it eagerly. "This isn't a toy," he said gently. "It's a flute, and it's something that's very important to me."

"Will you play something?" one of the twins asked.

"What do you want to hear?"

The child thought for a moment. "Something beautiful."

"Something *fast*," his twin said, with a wide, toothless grin.

"Well, I don't know any fast songs, but I do know something I think is pretty." Bao lifted the flute to his lips, intending to play a cheerful tune he had learned long ago. But what emerged from the instrument instead were the soft, reedy notes of the melody he had written for Lan.

> *Little yellow flower,*
> *You crossed the grass and the wind kissed every blade*
> *Your feet had blessed.*
> *I see springtime in the garden of your eyes.*

He sensed her awareness beside him and her eyes on him, soft with memory. Bao gave in to the music, enjoying the perfect calm of doing something he loved and pleasing others at the same time. Across the way, Tao peered out of the sick woman's cottage with a smile, and the children who had watched Bao make tonics earlier crept back out of their cottages to listen. The melody was short, but Bao repeated it a few times as his audience grew.

Music had always been one of the ways in which he battled his terrors. His moments of panic seemed to dull whenever he picked up the flute, running his hands down the familiar worn bamboo, and found the perfect combination of breath and finger placement to make something beautiful—something he would hold on to whenever he was afraid, as he was now and had been since leaving the river witch. It gave him hope that he would find the answers he sought.

When Bao finished playing, the children clapped dutifully, their faces wreathed in smiles. "Another! Another!" they cried, but he shook his head at them, promising another song later, and they all scattered back to where they had been. The sun was setting, casting a rosy light over the village as the sky deepened into star-dappled blue-black. Bao looked at his flute in the light—his only companion for so many lonely years, and now his lifeline.

"I never thanked you for writing me that melody," Lan said.

"You're welcome."

She rested her head on her knees. "It makes me think of home. I'll be glad to see Ba and Mama again. Just think: in a few days, your spell will be broken and we'll be on our way back."

"Home." Bao rolled the word around in his mouth. "I'm not sure I have the right to use that word."

Lan lifted her head from her knees. "You're not . . . you're not thinking of staying in the Gray City? Not with everything that might happen?"

"I just don't know if the river market was ever home for me. And there's so much good I could do elsewhere," he said, aware that he hadn't answered her question. The truth was that he didn't know what to do. Family was what made a home, but family wasn't always blood—which was all he shared with Mistress Vy and the witch at the moment. "They need physicians everywhere. I felt lucky when Master Huynh took me in, but I quickly learned that healing walks hand in hand with death. There is so much sorrow in the world, and if I could ease that, if I could make my life mean something, that would be enough."

"I envy you," Lan said quietly. "For knowing what you want to do, and for having the freedom to do it. I wish . . . I wish I could go with you."

Bao's breath hitched in his throat. He felt like he was standing at the edge of a precipice, one he had looked over before and vowed never to see again. *But this time, I'm not alone,* he thought as she turned and looked straight into his eyes. It was not a dream or a wish anymore—he saw the truth of her feelings in her gaze. "I wish you could go with me, too," he whispered.

"How did you spend it?" she asked suddenly. "The money the Huynhs paid you to keep up the pretense of Tam wanting to marry me?"

"I bought medicine for the river market people. I guess it was my way of thanking the people who had been kind to me. Like Huy and these villagers."

"See? An orphan of very much account." She smiled at him, and Bao allowed himself a moment of pure, quiet joy. She had seen him—seen *him*—at last.

They heard Wren's voice outside the village, calling them to supper at the encampment, and Bao rose and dusted himself off. Lan stayed where she was, her hand outstretched for his. He pulled her up, her warm fingers fitting as perfectly in his as the bamboo flute ever had. He'd had precious little human contact in his life—he couldn't remember many of his guardians hugging him when he was a child, and certainly not dignified Master Huynh. The feel of Lan's hand in his was a foreign sensation, one that filled him with inexpressible joy.

Bao didn't want to let go before they started walking, though propriety demanded it.

Lan looked down at their joined hands, then up at his face. She didn't let go.

17

That night, Bao kept his vigil beside the sick woman's bed while everyone slept. He had persuaded Cam and Tao to get their rest, and Lan had gone to the cottage next door to stay with the little girl and her twin brothers—far enough that Bao could feel their separation acutely, but not so far that it would prevent him from doing his task. He wiped the ailing woman's forehead with cool water every now and then and monitored her breathing. Thanks to the tonic, she slept deeply, and after a few hours Bao felt himself slipping into slumber as well.

He was standing in the fields outside the Gray City again, but it felt different this time and more real than he had ever seen it. The colors were vibrant, from the bronze of the grass to the blue of the night sky and the crimson tunic worn by the woman next to him. She was almost as tall as he was, with a strong body and alert eyes. She looked like someone who would stand and fight if the sky were to fall, but there was a gentleness to her expression as she looked him.

"Hello, Bao," she said, in a low, sweet voice. "I've been waiting for you."

Bao was struck again by the reality of the scene. The wind ruffled his hair, bringing with it the sharp, salty smell of seawater, and beneath that lingered a dark scent of damp, rotten earth. The grass whispered around his legs, and when the woman—Mistress Vy—touched his arm, he felt the warmth of her fingers. It felt as though he had been plucked right out of the village by the river and deposited outside the Gray City.

"I'm not really here," he said, though it came out as more of a question.

Vy gave him a smile of infinite kindness. "You're not really here. This is a vision. All of those dreams you've had over the years have been my failed attempts to summon you, but I succeeded this time thanks to my sister's help. I'm sure this vision is clearer for you than your dreams have been." She looked him up and down with benign curiosity. "You have undoubtedly crossed paths with Huong. I can see her mark upon you."

After the initial surprise of seeing her came the memory of everything Bao knew about her and all that Huy had revealed. "Yes," he said, anger rising in him, "I have met the river witch. And I've had the privilege of being cursed by her, too, for your sake, which is why I'm coming to the Gray City to find her."

His mother's eyes fairly glowed. "We will help you when you get here," she promised. "Huong has been with me for a few days now, and I'm glad that she's home and I've finally found you. I feared I had lost you forever."

"It took you almost twenty years," he said bitterly. "Or weren't you looking at all? I suppose you were busy mixing poisonous drugs for profit?"

Vy gazed at him with disarming warmth in her eyes. "I understand your reluctance to trust me, Bao, with all that you've surely heard about me, but I'd like to tell you what happened in your past. I owe you that, at least. Will you walk with me and allow me to explain?"

Bao nodded, but he did not accept the arm she held out. As they walked toward the gates of the city, he detected a disorienting, familiar scent like dark soil after the rain. "I smell black spice," he said stiffly. "It has an effect on me that I do not like."

She laughed. "Of course it affects you. I sense that you are like me: you have no magic, but you still carry our family's blood in your veins," she said affectionately. "Do not be so quick to denounce black spice, for I used it along with Huong's magic to bring you to me tonight."

The gates before them were crafted of oak and cypress reinforced with steel, set tightly into the city wall that stretched upward fifty feet and comprised slabs of gold-veined granite. Vy signaled to the guard towers and two mammoth wheels began to spin, pulling the gates open to reveal a vast and sprawling city glowing with lanternlight.

Bao observed his mother from the corner of his eye. Her soft, serene features were lit in profile, and her plentiful iron-gray hair had been twisted into a bun, accentuating her cheekbones. The river witch had been right that Bao and Vy looked nothing alike, except perhaps for their strong chins and thin-lipped mouths. As he studied the woman, her narrow dark eyes found his.

"I know what you think of me, Bao," she said softly, "and that is why I want to show you my city in hopes that you'll think better of me along the way. I won't blame you, however, if you would rather end the vision now." She stood still, waiting for his answer as he looked through the gates at the dark winding city of homes, buildings, and markets.

This is where I was born, he thought with wonder. And as much as he did not trust her, he knew this would be a chance to find the answers for which he hungered. "How did I come to be separated from my family?" he asked. "Did you give me up?"

She smiled, catlike, pleased he hadn't demanded to end the vision, and led him through the gates. The same shining granite had been laid on the ground all through the city, and it gleamed in the lanternlight. "Huong took you away from the city without my consent," she said, as they entered a wide street lined with sloping-roofed buildings and gardens that perfumed the air. "My sister and I have never gotten along. We fought all through childhood. I was jealous of her magic, and she was jealous of my ability to make people love me—Sinh being one of them. We all grew up together, and she adored him, but he chose me for his wife."

So far, what she had said matched with what the witch had told Bao. He looked around at the silent shops and empty vendor carts, having expected the city to be teeming with people.

"This is only a vision of my city, an image I have projected into your mind, which is why we are mostly alone," Vy said, as though answering his thoughts. "Centuries ago, my ancestors sought to please the Emperors of Feng Lu, so they designed this place in homage to the Imperial City and crafted our home in the image of the palace. The shape of the Gray City, however, is all its own. It is made of concentric rings, with our home situated at its heart."

"Are any of our family still alive? Sinh, my father?"

Mistress Vy bowed her head. "They all died of bloodpox: Sinh, my parents, grandparents, and uncle, who raised Huong and me for a time," she said. "Ours is a family of visionaries, Bao, people ahead of their time, but with these gifts come hubris and carelessness. Even we are not immune to the temptation of our creation. One by one, they became addicted, whether through using the drug themselves or secondhand exposure while testing it. They all believed, with every new formula, that *this* one would be safe or that *they* could not possibly contract bloodpox, which they knew was a consequence of using black spice. I watched the people I love go through unimaginable suffering and pain, and I vowed to protect myself and avoid the temptation to which they had fallen."

"I expected you to lie," Bao said, surprised by her honesty. There was such deep-rooted pain in her voice that he couldn't help but pity her. Vy knew what it was like to be alone, too. "I thought you would tell me that everyone is wrong and that black spice is only noble and good."

"You are my son. You deserve to know the truth. And I also want you to understand what has driven me to keep producing the drug and bringing in money for my research."

They came to another pair of enormous steel-and-wood gates at the end of the street, and again, Vy signaled for them to be opened. Bao realized how impeccable the Gray City's security was, with each concentric circle of the city being surrounded by its own wall and guard towers. The next section was a smithing district, and he saw a few people bent over fires, faces intent as they hammered at weapons and wheeled swords and spears away to be stored.

Mistress Vy faced Bao, her eyes glimmering with tears. "I am consumed by the need to make my loved ones' deaths count. To ensure that they did not die in vain. I owe it to them to be single-minded, even ruthless, in my search for the ultimate medicine. And when I find it, it will eradicate bloodpox and every imaginable disease, and no one will suffer from loneliness or heartache ever again. You can understand that, can't you? Even if you don't agree?"

Bao thought of what he had told Lan about healing walking hand in hand with death. He thought of all the patients he had seen die over the years, leaving behind the husbands and wives they loved, adored children, grieving parents, bereft friends. All around her, Vy's loved ones had left this life. She had been alone, longing for a family just as he had.

She steered him through the gates. "Huong did not understand *or* agree," she said. "When you were two years old and Sinh had died after a long, drawn-out battle with bloodpox, she begged me to stop my research. We had done enough harm, she said. Was I waiting until I had lost her *and* you, too?" She had to stop speaking for a moment and struggle for composure.

"Is that what happened?" Bao asked, moved by her grief. "You refused to stop your work, and Huong took me and fled?"

"In the dead of night, without even saying goodbye. She had decided that the Gray City wasn't a good place for you, and that I wasn't a fit mother." Vy paused again, her lips trembling. "I sent out legions of guards to find the two of you, but could not. You had all but disappeared. I knew I would never get you back if I tried to pressure her. And so I stopped looking. I focused on my work, hoping she would relent and come back."

"She didn't keep me herself," Bao realized. "She took me out of the city, away from you, and then abandoned me instead of raising me herself."

"She always had some notion that our blood and our family were toxic. No doubt she had some noble intention of distancing you from anything to do with it, including herself."

"But eventually, you did decide to look for her. You sent people to bring her back to you five nights ago. I came to her home shortly after she was taken, hoping to persuade her to remove the curse," Bao explained, seeing her startled look.

"I had been redoubling my efforts to find you both in the last year or so," Mistress Vy explained. "I found Huong first, and I knew she would help me find you. I didn't want to bring her to the Gray City against her will, but I knew she wouldn't come with me any other way. She hates me, as much as I love her." She turned to face the smiths' fires, the flames flickering across her grief-stricken features. "I have been too long without family, Bao. I need you both by my side. I don't pretend to be anything other than what I am. I make no excuses for the ruined lives my family has left in its wake, but I am just one woman, and outside forces are closing in around this city our family has paid for with our lives. *Everything* we have worked for might well be destroyed, and I am so desperately close to finding the right formula."

"But how many more lives must be taken?" Bao demanded. "Your cause, your intention may be noble, but the impact is devastating."

"I don't deny the harm we have caused. Each and every life lost because of our family's work will rest on my conscience forever," Vy said, her eyes still on the flames. "But I am driven by the knowledge that with more time, I can and will save thousands of lives more."

A growing chill filled Bao's heart as he watched her. He sensed her remorse was genuine, and that the deaths of her husband and family had irrevocably marked her. And yet she refused to lay down the Gray City's legacy and end its generations of bloodshed. She would barrel steadily on in her search to save mankind—and in doing so, continue taking lives without hesitation. She was no better than a murderer, he realized, and yet he pitied her, he understood her, and he longed for her and the love she would freely give him. He felt sick with the confusion of it all.

A bell tolled somewhere in the darkness.

Mistress Vy blinked out of her reverie. "Now I have said everything I wanted to say, and it is time for us to part. I don't expect anything from you, not your love or understanding or respect. Come to my city freely, and you are welcome to stay or to go just as freely when Huong lifts the spell. You're a man now." She gave him a smile tinged with pride and sorrow. "Look how you've grown. That birthmark on your shoulder must seem very small now. I know that some believe the number three to be bad luck, but I always liked it. I was happiest when I had the three people I loved most with me—Huong, Sinh, and *you*."

Her words wrenched at Bao's heart. Even with all she was and all she had done, she was his mother, his family, for whom he had longed his entire hungry life. Tentatively, Vy reached out and laid her fingers upon his cheek, and he fought the urge to pull away.

"Goodbye, son," she said softly. "I'll see you soon."

The firelit city's winding roads and gold-veined walls began to fade as Bao felt himself wake up. He had the sensation of rising slowly to the surface, as though he had been submerged in a deep pool. And then he was back in his chair in the shabby cottage, sitting beside a sleeping woman, and the sky was still dark over the little village. The single candle he had lit was still burning, casting flickering shadows over the walls. He heard a soft noise and turned, surprised, to see that the shy little boy from earlier that day—the one who had asked Bao, in a whisper, to clean the cut on his skinny arm—curled up behind Bao's chair, fast asleep.

Quietly, Bao lifted the thin blanket on his lap and draped it over the child, watching his unconscious face. He had been that small himself, once. Motherless, wandering, starved for love as much as for food. He thought of all the families that had been broken apart because of Mistress Vy and her ruthless, unforgiving vision of a diseaseless world.

"Bao?" The door opened and the candle danced wildly in the breeze as Lan came in, her braid disheveled, her eyes shadowed but alert. On the floor, the little boy's eyes flew open and he made a sound of alarm, but she put a reassuring hand on his head and he lay quiet again.

"You should be resting," Bao whispered. He worried about the darkness under her eyes and the lines of exhaustion on her face. After a lifetime of sleeping full nights in a soft bed, he could see that traveling was taking a toll on her. "Are you all right?"

"I'm fine," she said, still stroking the child's hair. The boy's eyes were slowly closing again. "I just wanted to see how you were. I can sit up with the woman if you want some sleep."

"I dozed off a bit just now. I didn't even hear this child come in," he admitted, rubbing his eyes. He had been so engrossed in the vision—in his turmoil of guilt and pity and longing—that he had slept as deeply as the sick woman.

Lan straightened, and he saw in her eyes that she was as worried about him as he was about her. "I'll stay with you for a bit."

He drew his hand away from his face. "Because of the spell?"

"Because I want to. Do you want me to go?"

"No," he said a little too quickly, and she smiled. The candlelight blurred her—he could only just see the halo of her hair, the shine of her eyes, and the curve of her lips. "I'm glad you're here. I had a bit of a disturbing dream just now. A vision, actually."

"Was it your mother again?" Lan whispered.

His head ached, and it felt too heavy for his neck. He let it droop to his chest in answer. "She's been trying to summon me with black spice for years. She's only just now succeeded because the river witch—her sister, Huong—is with her and helped her with magic."

"What did she want?"

"To show me her city. And to tell me why I've been alone all my life." Briefly, he told her what he had learned. "I want Commander Wei to know, but I need to figure out how to tell him. You know how he gets about black spice. He doesn't think I'm a spy, but the fact that I spoke privately with Mistress Vy . . . I need to work up my courage."

Lan shook her head. "I won't say a thing. And I'm glad, at least, that they know you're coming. They'll be ready to break the spell, and then we can go home and put this behind us."

He remained silent and felt her watch him keenly.

"You can't mean to stay with her in the Gray City. Not after all this— not now, when the rulers of three kingdoms are against her and we know she's doing everything purposefully."

"I know," he said helplessly. "I don't know what to do."

"Listen to me," she said, putting a hand on his shoulder. "I know she seemed truly remorseful, and perhaps she believes she is. But if she regretted all her family has done, she wouldn't keep doing it in order to possibly *not* do it in the future. Am I making any sense?"

He let out a low, humorless laugh. "Yes."

"I know she's your mother," Lan said softly, "but I don't think she's genuinely selfless and caring like you. I care about you, Bao. I . . . I don't want to see you get hurt."

Her voice quivered as she spoke, and Bao lifted his head. Her gaze was as soft as the notes of the flute. They were almost the same height now, with her standing and him sitting. He looked steadily back at her, longer than he had ever before, thinking how much braver he was in the shadows. Brave enough to let his eyes fall to her mouth, brave enough to put his hands on her waist and pull her close to him. A little gasp escaped her, and Bao stayed still, his hands resting above her hips, giving her a chance to pull away if she wanted to.

She did not pull away. She put her hands on his shoulders, her thumbs brushing his jaw as lightly as butterflies. She bent her head down, slowly, her eyes never leaving his. Some of her hair tumbled out of its braid, covering them like a curtain. She was close enough that he could hear her heartbeat galloping with his own. He slid his hand gently up from her waist, fingers catching the edge of her tunic, lifting it to feel the warm, petal-soft skin of her back, and heard her breath hitch in her throat. Their noses touched.

The little boy sat up and began sniffling. Lan and Bao broke apart, startled, and she pushed her hair back hastily. Even in the darkness, he could see her face was flushed. He sat motionless, his pulse hammering, as she tended to the child.

"I need to . . . to go . . . but I'm scared of the dark," the boy wailed, and Lan hushed him.

"I'm going to take him out," she said breathlessly, helping the child up.

Bao cleared his throat. "Yes, that's a good idea," he said, his voice unsteady. "And you should try to sleep. Wren will call us in the morning when it's time to go."

"What about you?" she asked. "Will you be all right?"

Not without you. Come back and stay with me tonight, he wanted to say. But even the shadows couldn't make him as brave as that. "I'll be fine. I'll see you in the morning."

Lan lingered, looking at him as though she wanted to say something else, but the child whimpered. Sighing, she took him by the hand and led him out of the cottage, the tightness in Bao's throat and heart returning with every step she took away from him.

18

"I don't like the look of that sky," Lady Yen said, peering up at the gathering swirl of dark, heavy gray clouds. The group had been traveling all morning and afternoon, and had stopped briefly to eat and rest. "It's a good thing we left the village when we did."

"I'm glad, too. We can't afford to waste much more time." Lan's eyes found Bao, who had been drawn into a discussion about flute music with Wren. The kind-hearted warrior seemed to be doing her utmost to cheer him up, and though Bao was his usual polite self, Lan saw the weariness in the droop of his shoulders. He looked like he hadn't slept since leaving the village three days ago. She knew it weighed upon him, the decision to leave Cam, Tao, their daughter, and all of those children behind.

"Is Bao worried about the villagers?" Lady Yen asked gently. "From what I hear, the elderly couple has that capable young man, Huy, to help them. I'm sure they'll be all right."

"I hope so. But either way, we have to focus on getting to the Gray

City. The full moon is in only three nights." Lan glanced at the sky, which seemed to grow darker every minute. "We're going to look a bit bedraggled for Lord Nguyen, I'm afraid, if this storm breaks soon."

"I doubt he cares what people look like. He just wants us to get there safely."

Lady Yen fell silent, and Lan knew she was thinking about the moment late tonight when she would set foot upon her husband-to-be's estate. Soon she would be Lord Nguyen's wife and no longer free to feel what she did for Commander Wei. They would long for each other all the rest of their lives, trapped in separate worlds that would never overlap.

Lan had come close to a similar entrapment herself—one of her own making, from which she had been saved by an honest confession. Her eyes again found Bao, whose careworn hands were cleaning the bamboo flute.

The morning of their departure, they had all looked on as Huy destroyed the last of the black spice at Cam and Tao's request. The couple had stood watching with tears in their eyes, and then Cam had begged Bao to play a specific song for her daughter. Lan had recognized the lullaby as one her mother had sung to her, about a rabbit who had come home to find her baby gone. It was a cheerful tune because the rabbits reunited in the end, but looking at Cam's frail face and Tao's stooped shoulders, Lan knew that they had chosen it to remember happier days, singing the lullaby to their little girl, and to give them hope that one day they would be with her again.

Bao had played as Lan had never heard him play before, and she had thought what an extraordinary gift his music was. It was everything he had to offer, the very best of him. He was like his music: quiet and unassuming, with unexpected depths of beauty she might have seen if she had only taken the time to look. Afterward, he had wrapped his arms around the elderly couple and made their pain his own, and then Tao had stroked Cam's hair and Lan had had the sudden thought that Bao, too, would love his wife that much and for that long.

Now, Lan saw Bao give another weary, polite nod and wondered whether she ought to go save him from Wren's chatter. But then Commander Wei strode over and spoke to the warrior.

"I could use your opinion on something," the Commander said briskly, and Wren got up at once. "Go on over to where my stallion is tethered. I need to talk to Bao for a minute."

Bao looked up from his flute apprehensively, clearly thinking—like Lan—that the man might have found out about his conversation with Mistress Vy, but then the Commander unfolded a bundle of cloth tucked beneath his arm. It was a large, silk-lined cloak of dark green wool, with gold stitching around the collar and a metal pin.

"Wrap this around you," he told Bao gruffly. "I'm no physician, but I know the feeling of being cold when you're bone-tired. And you look bone-tired to me."

"I can't accept this, sir," Bao argued. "And you'll need it yourself, with rain coming."

"I'm lending it to you. Take it," Commander Wei said in a stern tone, then waved away Bao's thanks and returned to where Wren was waiting.

Lan got up and went over to Bao, who had gratefully wrapped the cloak around himself despite his protests. She noticed that he was shivering beneath the wool. "That was kind. Have you been promoted to Commander of the Great Forest?" she asked, longing to make him smile.

"Almost. I need to learn how to use a sword first."

She reached over and pulled the cloak tightly around him. "I should have paid attention when you were making those tonics. I could have made you something to help you sleep."

"I don't think it would do much good," he said, shivering. "Even my toes and my fingers are freezing. I feel like I can't get warm. I think it's . . . I think it's the spell. It must be changing again, progressing to a different stage. We're running out of time."

"We have enough time," Lan said, feeling a pang of worry looking at his pale face. He was almost gray with exhaustion. "I wish I could make it better."

"You are. Just by being here." He took her hand and she gasped at the iciness of his fingers. "Lan, if anything happens to me . . . if somehow, we don't get there in time . . ."

"Stop. I won't listen to that kind of talk. I didn't come all this way, sleep on the ground with roots sticking into my back, choke down disgusting dried meat, and forgo the gods know how many baths, to *fail*. I'm going to make you better, even if I have to carry you on my back all the way to the Gray City." Lan leaned her head against him and smiled when his shoulder shook weakly with laughter. "I'm not going to let anything happen to you. I promise."

Bao pressed his lips to her hair.

The rain began to fall lightly, and then in sheets. The soldiers shouted to each other as they hurried to get their horses under the shelter of the banyan trees, where Lan and Bao were already sitting. The canopy of leaves helped a bit, though a few raindrops still managed to find them. Lan hugged herself, looking up at the sky through the treetops, and Bao wrapped the Commander's cloak around her, too. He felt warm and safe against her.

"Great timing for a storm, isn't it?" Wren shouted and Lan turned, a bit dismayed to see that she had decided to join them under their tree. The Imperial soldiers were clustered under three other trees, and Commander Wei and Lady Yen had managed to find one to themselves.

The noblewoman looked as cheerful at the delay as Bao was dejected by it.

"Hopefully it stops soon so we can be on our way," Bao said, his face tight with anxiety.

Lightning cracked the sky, and several seconds later, they heard a rumble of thunder. A few of the horses whinnied, rearing up in fright at the loud noise. The Commander was jogging from tree to tree, speaking to everyone. "We may need to camp here tonight," he said loudly, to be heard over the sound of the torrential rain. "The road is going to be submerged and dangerous for the horses. We will have to be on our way tomorrow morning if this doesn't stop in an hour."

"We don't have time," Bao protested, but the Commander had already run off again.

Lan squeezed his hand. "We're going to be fine. It's just a small delay."

But it rained heavily all through the afternoon and night, and by the next morning, the skies were still pouring. At last, in the late afternoon, the sun emerged and the tired, soaked company set out again at last. Lan felt Bao's fear and worry like a second cloak wrapped around him. But she took comfort in the fact that he had slept well and dreamlessly that night. They traveled without stopping, to make up for lost time, but it was slow going on the muddy, rain-drenched roads, and it wasn't until late that evening that they arrived at Lord Nguyen's estate, a day later than anticipated.

The home was a grand and sprawling affair, with mother-of-pearl gates, gold pillars, and opulent buildings linked by courtyards, and though Lan admired it all, Bao looked without seeming to see anything. He was still shivering and wrapped in the Commander's cloak.

"I just need more sleep," he tried to reassure her. "I don't care if it's a swan-feather bed or a bamboo pallet. I could probably get the best sleep of my life right here on the marble steps." Servants came forward to take their horses as Lady Yen stood gazing over the grandeur of the courtyard. The heavy oak doors opened to reveal Lord Nguyen, a short, stout man in his fifties, dressed in finely tailored robes of slate-gray silk. He was bald, with two tufts of gray-black hair over each ear, and a bright, good-natured face. Three wrinkled, sweet-faced dogs with short white hair trailed joyfully behind him as he came out to greet the newcomers.

Lan thought of all she'd heard about this man and the deadly explosives he had created, and could not reconcile his friendly, cheerful appearance with such a dangerous invention.

He went straight to Yen, who looked startled as though she had expected him to greet the Commander first, man to man. He bowed low to her. "Welcome, my dear lady. I'm happy to see you," he said warmly. "You must be exhausted. I'll have a maid show you to your chambers."

Yen returned his bow, then introduced the group. Lan liked that he gave a slight bow of respect to each person, and when Yen introduced Lan, he brightened with recognition. Up close, she saw that his eyes were keen and sharp with intelligence. She wondered if his jovial manners were deliberate, so that anyone who underestimated him as a happy-go-lucky noble would get a surprise when he displayed his intellect.

"I have the honor of calling your esteemed father a friend," he told Lan kindly. "He must be worried about you. Would you like to send him a message to let him know you're here safely? I'll give you a chamber near Wren and Lady Yen and make sure you're given plenty of ink. A messenger will take the note as soon as you've finished." He waved away her thanks and looked at Bao. "Young man, I think you'll be more comfortable near the Commander and his men?"

"If you don't mind, sir, I'd prefer a chamber near Miss Vu," Bao said, and Lan blushed, wondering what Lord Nguyen might make of this request. She almost explained about the spell, but the nobleman only nodded at Bao without any judgment whatsoever.

"Of course. You must all be comfortable in my home. Which reminds me." He turned to Commander Wei. "I took the liberty of sending for rice wine from the Great Forest weeks ago. I thought you and your men might enjoy a taste of home before moving on again."

"That is most thoughtful of you, my lord. Thank you." Commander Wei had been silent the whole time, averting his eyes from Lady Yen, but now he looked genuinely taken aback.

Lan couldn't help smiling at how pleased Lord Nguyen looked with himself. She could see why her father liked the man so much. When the servants led Commander Wei and his men in one direction and Bao and the ladies in the other, Lan glanced back to see the nobleman petting his wrinkled dogs and speaking to them as they pressed adoringly against his legs.

"I'm glad he seems so nice, for Lady Yen's sake," Lan told Bao softly. "And that was quick thinking, asking to be near me. You need rest, and we don't want the spell disrupting it."

Bao turned bright red and nearly walked into one of Lord Nguyen's priceless vases. "I, um, had almost forgotten about the spell when I asked," he said, and Lan laughed, their shoulders bumping as they walked. "If I had my way, I wouldn't stop here at all. I would keep riding on to get to the witch, but it seemed rude to refuse Lord Nguyen's hospitality."

Lan glanced at his shadowed eyes. "Not to mention you would fall off your horse if you did any more traveling. You need rest. We'll leave for the Gray City first thing in the morning." She spoke in a voice of forced cheer, trying not to think what it would be like if he decided not to come home after they had broken the spell. She had known him for almost ten years and had wasted it all on someone else, and now they might only have a matter of days left together.

"What is it?" he asked, noticing her change in mood at once. "Why do you look so sad?"

"It's nothing," she said quickly. He had enough to worry about without her fretting, too.

Lord Nguyen's servant led them through a gilded, well-lit corridor and showed Bao to the first chamber, which contained oak tables and a massive bed piled high with brocade pillows.

"I'm going to get some sleep before supper," Bao told her, looking longingly at the bed, and she smiled as he fairly ran into the room. Her own chamber was just as comfortable and close enough to his that the spell wouldn't keep either of them from breathing. But even when they got the witch to lift the enchantment, Lan wondered if it would ever really go away, this aching feeling of loss whenever he wasn't near.

She sank into a silk chair, thinking morosely about what her parents would say if they knew how she felt about Bao now. Lady Vu would have a fit, and her father likely wouldn't approve, either, despite his affection for the young man. Lan had thrown their differences in station in Bao's face when she had spoken to him in anger, and it had been wrong of her to do so—but the divide between them *was* reality, and these slowly awakening feelings only a dream that she would have to wake up from sometime.

In the gathering darkness, Lan lifted her hand and felt tears on her face.

This journey of theirs would have an end, and that end was a parting of the ways.

19

Bao collapsed onto the bed, still wrapped in Commander Wei's thick wool cloak. He was asleep the second his head hit the pillow, and for the first time since the village, he slipped into another vision of his mother. This time, he was in a lush garden like a jungle, overrun by large leafy trees and spreading shrubs. Black spice scented the night air and beneath it, Bao smelled rain. Mistress Vy walked toward him from the black metal gate that ringed the garden.

"My son," she said, and despite his misgivings, his heart leapt at her bright, loving smile. "I've managed to call you to me again. I missed seeing you. But you look so pale and tired." Her smile fell as she reached a hand toward his cheek.

"I haven't been sleeping well," he said, again feeling both the impulse to lean into her hand and the urge to pull away. "I think the spell is taking hold."

Vy shook her head. "Huong could always be cruel with her magic, even when she was a little girl," she said, the lines around her eyes tightening.

"Don't worry. I will make her shatter the enchantment as soon as you get here. I'll take care of you, Bao."

His shoulders relaxed a bit at her words and reassuring tone. She took a seat on a stone bench and patted the spot beside her, and he sat gingerly. The vision, again, felt as real as though he were physically in the garden with her. The stone was slightly cool beneath him, and when he touched it, he felt a bit of dampness from the rain that had fallen.

"How far are you from the Gray City?" his mother asked.

Bao opened his mouth to tell her, then hesitated, remembering what he knew of Vy's failed attempts to win Lord Nguyen over to her side. He didn't wish to be involved in whatever conflict lay between his mother and the nobleman. He felt her sharp eyes on him the whole time as he struggled to come up with an answer. "Not far. We're staying at a friend's home about a day's ride away. Only two nights left before the full moon and the enchantment takes effect."

"Hasn't it already?"

"It has limited me somewhat. I can't be separated from my flute, nor can I go far from someone with whom I'm traveling. A girl named Lan." He remembered the sadness in Lan's eyes before they had parted in the corridor. Had she, too, been thinking about what would happen when the spell was broken and they had to part ways, back to their respective worlds?

"So, you have someone special to you," Mistress Vy said, smiling, but the tension around her eyes quickly returned. "All of that valuable magic in Huong's veins, and she chooses a frivolous spell pertaining to the heart. What will break it, then? Lan confessing her love to you in return?"

Bao hesitated. All through the journey, he and Lan had shared the mutual understanding that she was helping him get to the witch. Or to his mother. He had never considered—never *dared* imagine—that Lan might be the one to break the spell, after all. She cared about him; she had told him that herself. But it was too much to hope that she might, at last, return his feelings. "The witch told me it had to be a declaration of love from someone who loves me," he said at last. "She expected it to be you. She seemed to think I was living with you and accused me of luring her back for you." Bao frowned, thinking over what Huong had told him. Something didn't fit. "Why would she think I was back in the city when she was the one who took me away?"

Vy shrugged. "She must have thought I had found you and brought you back."

You, who are the result of my sister's and Sinh's betrayal of me, he remembered the witch saying to him. *The product of their lies. And won't it be fitting to send you back to them not as their son, but as something else entirely?*

"When Huong cursed me, she seemed to think Sinh was still alive. But you told me he had died of bloodpox when I was two, right before Huong took me away," Bao said, watching his mother carefully. "Why wouldn't she already know that?"

"Your aunt has clearly gone mad in all of those years of living alone," Mistress Vy said, calm and composed. "She must have forgotten that Sinh had died."

"She loved him. How could she have forgotten something like that?" Bao asked, irritated. "I think you lied to me. Tell me exactly what happened. Is my father dead or not?"

Mistress Vy's gaze on him was cool and appraising, and her loving, maternal smile was nowhere to be found. "You have a good memory, my son. Very well, then. The truth is that your father *is* dead, but not from bloodpox, like the rest of our family." She folded her hands in her lap.

"When Sinh and I married and had you, Huong was so jealous that she poisoned him against me. She filled his ears with lies, saying that I was evil and that black spice was an instrument of my malice. And then she left the city one night without saying goodbye."

"Then Sinh was still alive when she left," Bao said slowly. "And I was still with you."

"I thought our problems were over with her gone. But your father listened to her, and he betrayed me," Vy said stiffly. "Shortly after she disappeared, he took you and fled under cover of night. I sent my guards after you, but he had hidden you, and you were lost to me. They found him alone. I begged them to bring him to me alive, but in their fierce loyalty, they chose instead to punish him . . . with death."

Bao stared at her in silence.

"Listen to me, Bao," his mother said, jaw quivering. "Sinh was threatening to reveal my formula to the world. He wished to destroy my life's work and my family's legacy, all thanks to the venom Huong had spilled into his ears. My guards were protecting me as they thought best."

"Why did you lie to me?" he asked. "Why didn't you just tell me the truth?"

"Because I was afraid of what you might think of me. Driving my sister away, driving my husband away," Vy said, "my husband dying at the hands of my guards, and then losing you. But it doesn't change anything, Bao. It's still the truth: you were taken from me, and everyone I ever loved went away. But this is my chance to make things right." She moved closer to him, her eyes wide and almost feverish. "You are my son and heir, and I am leader of the Gray City, which should be a kingdom in its own right. That makes you a prince, Bao."

"It makes me no such thing," Bao said, getting up from the bench. He felt one of his terrors coming on—his breath was coming too fast, his heart was racing, and he felt as hot as though he sat in the midday sun. "You may have given birth to me, but I can make my own choices as you said the last time we met. I can choose not to *inherit* your kingdom." He imbued the final words with as much sarcasm as he could. This woman and her excuses for murder—this woman and her delusions of being a queen.

When Vy spoke, her voice was low, defeated. "I feared you would be like this. I was afraid you would think like Huong, but I expected more of you," she said. "But you'll see—you'll *both* see. In a few weeks, I will have the formula for a medicine so powerful, so effective, the Empress of the Great Forest herself will be begging me for it."

Bao whirled on her. "You've found a way to cure the bloodpox?"

The smile returned to her face, broad, beaming. "I want to celebrate this accomplishment with my family," she said longingly. "To piece together that part of my life, to forgive Huong and be forgiven by her . . . and you. You'll see, my son. I will make this all right."

In her eyes, he saw absolute conviction. Whatever his mother had done, whatever people said of her, she absolutely believed in her mission—and her right to pursue it. "You've only done what you thought was right. I believe that," he said quietly, his heart breaking. "But that doesn't change the fact that you've killed knowingly to achieve your goal, and there is nothing anyone can say to persuade you to stop. I can't trust you, I . . ."

Mistress Vy held up a hand. "Don't say it yet," she said, in a voice both commanding and cajoling. "Wait until you get to my city before you decide what to do with your heritage. Like it or not, Bao, you are a part of me. The Gray City is in your blood."

"And you lied to me about how my father died. What else have you lied about?"

A flash of anger crossed her face like lightning. "You speak to me of lying?" she asked. "You dare lecture me about untruths when *you* have been withholding information. I know, my *loyal* son, that you travel south with a company of soldiers who seek to destroy me." She lunged forward, startling him. Bao realized he was still wearing Commander Wei's cloak when Vy snatched one of the dark green folds. "Perhaps you're leading the charge yourself for Empress Jade. Perhaps I ought to bar the gates of the Gray City to you as well as them."

"Please . . ." Bao croaked, his stomach clenching with fear.

"That full moon will look lovely outside the walls of my city, when you're standing with Commander Wei and his army," she said softly. "Mark me well, Bao. I meant everything—I want our family to be reunited again. But if I discover that you are a traitor to me—son or no, blood or no, I will bar the Gray City to you. You will not be allowed to see Huong, and you had better hope that Lan loves you enough to break the spell. If she doesn't, well . . ."

In his mother's burning eyes, Bao saw the force of her conviction—the same force that enabled her to push all else aside in favor of her ambition and to overlook the deaths she caused along the way. He didn't dare hope that Lan could love him after their short time together, and no matter what, he could not place such an unfair expectation on her. Not when she had done so much for him already. If his mother barred him from entering the city, the witch's spell would take full effect. He would be trapped inside the bamboo flute forever.

Vy looked at him sharply, waiting for him to respond.

"Mother," Bao said, his mind racing to find the right words, "I am sorry I didn't tell you who I was with. But I didn't want you to think I was traveling with any other purpose aside from finding you and the witch. All I want is to break this spell. I have nothing to do with the soldiers or the war they wish to wage. I am a healer, not a warrior."

Vy's gaze moved between each of his eyes, as though determined to catch one of them in a lie. "Do you swear this upon your life?"

"I do."

After a moment, she let go of the cloak. "If you are speaking the truth, then you won't deny me the pleasure of sending an honor guard to bring you to the Gray City safe and sound. And now that I know with whom you are traveling, I know exactly where to send them," she said, tilting her head to one side. "I find Lord Nguyen to be most interesting. At first, he seems like a foolish little man, cooing over his smelly dogs. And yet the explosives he invented are one of the deadliest weapons ever made, and he has refused point-blank to pay allegiance to me or lend me any support. Perhaps my honor guard can serve a dual purpose."

"Mother, please listen," Bao said, but she continued talking as though he hadn't spoken.

"They can teach this arrogant little nobleman a lesson in what happens when you cross me. What do I care for retaliation? They are launching an attack on the Gray City either way. I'll be ready for them, won't I?" She touched Bao's cheek tenderly. "Answer your mother when she asks you a question. Won't I be ready?"

"Yes," he said, swallowing hard. He would be walking into a trap when he entered the Gray City, but there was no other option: Huong was there, and they were running out of time.

"I'll let you go now," Vy said in her gentle, motherly tone. "My guards will arrive late tomorrow morning. Until we meet again, my son."

He felt again the sensation of rising to the surface of a pool of water and saw Vy lift her hand to him in farewell, right before she disappeared and he woke up in Lord Nguyen's home.

At supper, Bao told his companions everything. He couldn't stomach more than a few bites of Lord Nguyen's delicious food, so agitated was he over the decision to reveal all. Though it was the right thing to do, he felt hopelessly guilty about betraying his own flesh and blood. Vy was his mother and Huong his aunt, and in a just world, he would stand with no one other than his family. But this was not a just world. This was a world in which his family had created chaos, and he had grown up alone and owed them nothing.

A muscle twitched in Commander Wei's jaw as he listened, but he showed no anger at having been kept in the dark. Perhaps he could see how tormented Bao felt by what had passed.

"This is a clear threat from Mistress Vy," Wren said calmly. "From what Bao tells us, I believe she is going to attack us here. She wants revenge on Lord Nguyen for not joining her."

They all glanced at Lord Nguyen, who had listened to Bao's speech with his arms crossed over his chest and his carefree, cheery demeanor darkening with each word. "I'll give the woman revenge, if that's what she wants," he said through gritted teeth. "She has always assumed that she can bully me and bend me to her will, as she has with several other nobles."

"No one who knew you would think that, my lord," Lady Yen reassured him, and for a moment his face softened and he smiled at her. Commander Wei glowered at the interaction, but said nothing. "I am not convinced it is a threat. Perhaps this honor guard really *is* just an escort for Bao, and she may be hoping it is one last chance to win you to her cause."

"She spoke like someone who has nothing to lose," Bao said, shivering. He had tried to return Commander Wei's cloak, but the man had insisted that Bao keep it, and now he was glad for its warmth. The chill seemed to seep out of his very bones. "She knows Empress Jade's forces, and those of the Grasslands and Dagovad, will descend on her city no matter what."

Commander Wei gave a grim nod. "She never intended to negotiate. I've already sent word to our allies, and they march south as we speak. Tomorrow morning, we congregate outside the walls of the city and put an end to this once and for all."

"I've heard much talk about the Gray City being impossible to breach," Lord Nguyen said, looking at Wren and the Commander. "It's supposed to have impenetrable walls."

Wren shook her head. "No city is impenetrable," she said confidently. "There are openings for sewage, delivery of goods, or escape, even. And we have the perfect weapon with which to break down those walls and destroy the gardens and the black spice inside." She raised her eyebrows at Lord Nguyen, and Bao shivered again, imagining the gold-flecked granite walls violently reduced to rubble by explosives. Everything his mother had worked for and all his family had stood for deserved to be destroyed, and yet he couldn't help but feel a pang of regret.

Beside him, Lan, who had been listening quietly, leaned her shoulder against his, and he drew warmth from her comfort. "What if Bao and I left early?" she suggested, and everyone looked at her. "If we intercepted Mistress Vy's honor guard along the way—"

"They might still insist on coming here," Wren said. "This isn't just about her wanting to reunite with her son. She wants to punish Lord Nguyen once and for all."

"We'll see about that," the nobleman said shortly. "Commander Wei, if it is appropriate, I would like to speak to you and your soldiers. Thanks to Bao, we have been forewarned about this ambush, and I have weapons to make available to your men. Shall I summon them myself?"

"Wren and I will prepare the horses and meet you in the courtyard," the Commander said, and Lord Nguyen strode purposefully out of the room. "Bao and Lan, it is too dangerous for you to accompany us to the Gray City. We will have to find some way of bringing this witch to you."

Bao opened his mouth to protest, but Lan beat him to it. "Sir, we have no time left," she said. "There's no point in worrying about our danger on the road when Bao is about to become an inanimate object permanently. We *must* go ourselves."

"When Empress Jade asked me to escort you south, she made me responsible for you," the Commander said. "If anything happened to you—"

"You gave me an order and I chose to ignore it. We have witnesses who heard me flout your authority, which means that whatever happens to me is not your fault." Lan looked deeply satisfied with herself as the Commander struggled to respond, and Bao hid a smile.

Commander Wei turned to Lady Yen in frustration. "Help me persuade them to stay here with you. I can't have them running around when war is about to break out."

"Well, I can't exactly persuade them to stay here," Lady Yen said calmly, "because I'm not staying here, either. I'm going with all of you." Her face was pale and her lips trembled, and Bao saw how much effort it took her to be brave. She lifted her chin with near-perfect composure. "I plan to tell Lord Nguyen tonight that although I deeply respect and esteem him, he will no longer be my betrothed. I will give my heart and my hand to someone else."

Bao, Lan, and Wren all looked at one another in mingled shock and amusement as the Commander's face turned white, then scarlet, then purple. His fists clenched and unclenched as he paced.

"What you propose is impossible. And now that I've met Lord Nguyen, I know he does not deserve your desertion," he said with forced calm, but his tone quickly rose in volume when he saw the determined set of her jaw. "Do you know the consequences of breaking such an alliance and betraying a powerful man like Lord Nguyen?"

Lady Yen shrugged. "I go where you go, and there's nothing you can say about it."

"You exasperating woman!" Commander Wei cried. "You cannot—"

"Wei, you should know better than to tell a woman what she can and cannot do," Wren broke in loudly. "We don't have time to argue about this. I think we *all* ought to leave tonight. Lan and Bao will ride ahead, and everyone else will follow behind. If Vy's guards make trouble and try to do anything other than escort the young people, we will intercept them before they get to Lord Nguyen and dispatch them before meeting our forces at the Gray City."

"No, you can't attack the honor guard," Bao said, panicking. "If anything happens to them, my mother will close the city to me. I'll never be free of this spell."

"You *will* be free of it," Lan told him fiercely, slipping her hand into his. "She won't have time to worry about the honor guard with the armies of three kingdoms descending upon her. And she told you herself, she wants her family reunited. She wants you there."

Wren looked at the Commander, who gave a short nod. "Then it's decided," she said.

The sound of frantic feet running down the corridor put an end to their discussion. "Sir," said a red-faced Imperial soldier, "they're here.

The men from the Gray City are waiting outside the gates. Their leader demanded to speak to you and His Lordship."

He had barely finished speaking before Wren and Commander Wei ran out of the room, their faces grim and intent. Lady Yen rose, pressing a hand to her heart as she turned to Bao. "Your mother said they wouldn't be here until the morning, didn't she?"

Bao's heart sank. "It isn't the first time she's lied to me," he said, torn between punching a wall and being sick to his stomach. He settled for resting his head in his hands again and breathing deeply, trying to keep the panic at bay. "She must have sent them early this morning, long before she spoke to me or even knew I was with Commander Wei. She always planned to ambush the Commander and Lord Nguyen here."

"Then she can't hurt them, can she?" Lan asked. "She wouldn't risk hurting you, too."

"I don't know what she would or wouldn't risk." Bao ran his hands over his face. "I don't know anything about her at all, except that she's good at lying and she will never back down. I have to go out there. I have to speak to her guards and try to get them to stand down."

Lady Yen nodded, her face white as a funeral sheet. "I'll go out there, too. I have to make sure that Wei . . . and I have to tell Lord Nguyen . . . I . . . ." Without another word, she hurried out of the room in the direction that the Commander and Wren had gone.

Bao got up from his seat and looked into Lan's desperate, worried face. "Listen to me," he said, taking her hands. "I don't want you to come with me. I can't ask you to do any more than you already have. The Gray City is going to be the most dangerous place on Feng Lu. I can't risk anything else happening to you."

"No," she agreed softly. "You can't ask me to do any more than I already have."

He could already feel the sensation of hands around his throat, depriving him of air. Though it was what he had wanted to hear, Lan's words stabbed at him like knives. He nodded, his eyes on their joined hands. "I'm sure Lord Nguyen will provide you an escort home . . ."

"You misunderstand me, Bao," she said gently. "You can't ask me because I am going with you no matter what you say. Your life is at stake. This spell will choke us to death if we are apart, but even if it didn't exist, I would still go." She removed her hands and put them on either side of his face, just as she had that day in the village. Her eyes locked onto his, wide and beautiful and honest. "I go where you go."

A tear burned down Bao's cold face as he heard in her words the ghost of Lady Yen's promise to Commander Wei. He looked at Lan in a maelstrom of overwhelming joy and fear and disbelief. "But why?" he whispered, wanting to hear her say it. *Needing* to hear her say it.

"Don't you know by now?" Lan asked tenderly. She stood on her toes, still holding his face, and brought her lips closer to his.

And then the shouting began.

Dazed, inches from the kiss he had dreamed of for years, Bao barely registered Lan pulling away. And then they were running, hand in hand, down Lord Nguyen's exquisitely decorated corridors and carved mahogany walkways and out to the courtyard. The servants, Lord Nguyen, and Lady Yen were standing on the cobblestones, looking out in terror at the black metal gate where a group of twenty mounted men waited, wielding swords and torches. The moon was bright in the heavens, an orb of pure gold just short of being a perfect sphere.

Once, Bao thought, the moon had been his conspirator, dappling the river with its loving light as he played the flute for Lan. Soon it would be his enemy. A shard of ice formed in his core and the cold seeped through his body as he wrapped the Commander's cloak more tightly around himself. His hand found the bamboo flute, which he had removed from his sack and tucked into a pocket.

"I have to go out there," he said resolutely. "Mistress Vy is my mother, and I have to make this right. I will tell them to take me to the Gray City."

"But this is my estate," Lord Nguyen said firmly, "and it is my blood Mistress Vy wants. I will be the one to greet these criminals and to send them on their way."

"Neither of you are going out there alone," Commander Wei said, standing beside his war horse. Behind him, Wren and all of the Imperial soldiers were already on horseback, their weapons held at the ready. Bao noticed that they all wore the protective cloth masks hanging around their necks, ready to use at a moment's notice. "You'll each get on horseback behind one of my men. None of Vy's guards will have a clear shot at you, and if they attack, you'll be safer that way."

"They won't have a chance to attack," the nobleman said, smirking. Bao noticed he was carrying something in a sack over his shoulder. "But we'll do as you think best, Commander."

"Do not deploy those unless I say so, my lord," Commander Wei warned, nodding at the sack. "We attack only under provocation."

Lady Yen stepped forward, her eyes darting between the two men. She twisted the hem of her simple gray tunic. "Please be careful," she begged. "Don't endanger yourselves. I don't know what I would do if anything happened."

Lord Nguyen looked at her, touched. "You worry for me that much?"

But even as he spoke, Lady Yen came close to the Commander and slipped her hand into his, turning to look at the nobleman as she did so. "I respect and admire you, Lord Nguyen," Lady Yen said gently. "I believe you are a good man, and I am proud to know you. So I do worry for you.

But I worry for others as well. A rash action on your part may put them in jeopardy."

"I see," Lord Nguyen said, his eyes on their joined hands. He pressed his lips together and looked away, back toward the Gray City guards outside the gate. Lady Yen began to say something else, perhaps to apologize, but he waved her words away with an impatient hand. Averting his eyes from her and the Commander, he allowed one of the Imperial soldiers to help him onto his horse. "Come, let us be off and deal with these people once and for all."

Without another word, Commander Wei released Lady Yen's hand and mounted his stallion. One of the soldiers offered Bao his hand, and he took it with a backward glance at Lan, swinging onto the war horse as it rode out toward the gates. Lan and Lady Yen followed close behind, standing at the gates as the group faced the enemy.

The guards of the Gray City rode steel-colored horses and wore matching iron-hued tunics and pants with a simple emblem that Bao recognized: a crimson flower with a sprinkling of leaves around its stem. The men and women did not look nearly as impressive as Commander Wei's soldiers, who were large and fearsomely trained, but the intensity in their expressions frightened Bao. He remembered that fierce, maniacal conviction in his own mother's eyes when he had spoken to her last.

The leader of the honor guard had a face like stone and a terrible, dark red scar that stretched across his face from his left eyebrow to his right cheek. "Do I address Commander Wei of the Great Forest and Lord Nguyen of the Sacred Grasslands?" the man asked crisply, and the Commander gave a single nod. "I am Captain Quang. Mistress Vy sent me to fetch her son."

Bao lifted his chin. "I am Mistress Vy's son," he said, trying to keep his voice from shaking. "And I am ready to go with you."

"And I'm going with him, as his companion on this journey," Lan said firmly.

Captain Quang's eyes skittered over her and landed on Lord Nguyen. "My lady also commands that you accompany her son back to the city, my lord. You would be a most honored guest," he said, baring a feral smile that must have hurt because of his wound. "I'm afraid you have no choice but to accept her generous invitation."

"Yet I beg to differ," Lord Nguyen said, tipping his head to one side. "I don't think your lady quite has the power to command me just yet. And I have refused her many times."

"Lord Nguyen has made his stance clear to your lady," Commander Wei spoke coldly. "There is no need to bring him into this matter again. His answer will not change."

Captain Quang's steely glare swept him from head to toe. "Interesting to see a great warrior lowering himself to be some pompous aristocrat's secretary," he said.

The Commander remained composed. "Take Vy's son to her, and that will be that."

"No, Commander," the captain said, laughing. "That will *not* be that. We know you have three armies gathering before the walls of our city. They come from the Great Forest, from the Sacred Grasslands, and from Dagovad." His eyes moved to Wren, who fixed him with a stare that Bao was surprised did not strike him dead on the spot. "Or should I say four armies? I see you have a woman of the Crimson Army with you."

"And you'll have more before the sun rises," Wren growled.

Captain Quang turned back to Lord Nguyen. "You are in high favor with the king of the Sacred Grasslands, and respected by all of the rulers of Feng Lu," he said. "Mistress Vy wants *you* to lead the negotiations. She is willing to compromise . . ."

Wren let out a huge snort, and Bao couldn't help but agree with her.

The captain's nostrils flared, but he continued speaking in a calm voice. "She is willing to compromise as long as you, Lord Nguyen, will give your word that the armies will not attack."

"You will *not* have my word," the nobleman said, holding his head high. "Mistress Vy has had many opportunities to negotiate, and she has turned them all down. I don't see any point in coming, and even if I did, I would only advise her to surrender before subjecting her people to violence. She should give in to the peaceable request of the Great Forest, Dagovad, and the Sacred Grasslands, and forfeit this nightmarish formula of hers."

"Peaceable request?" Captain Quang laughed again, and his men joined in. "You call the forces of three kingdoms converging upon our city a *peaceable* request? Nobleman or not, you aren't cut out for diplomacy or subtlety, are you?"

"She has been given many chances before," Lord Nguyen said again. "Don't pretend you are victims of senseless violence when Mistress Vy has been warned to stop producing her drugs for years, but refused to desist. It is long past time for negotiations. You have no hold on me."

The captain quirked his eyebrow. "No hold, you say? She knows Commander Wei is here to deliver your bride. I assume that is the fortunate lady there." He raised his right arm, and behind him, one of the guards lifted a crossbow to his shoulder and took aim. He was pointing straight toward Lady Yen, standing by the gates with Lan.

"No!" Bao shouted, leaping off the horse.

The crossbow fired, but the lethally sharp arrow did not hit Lan. It grazed Lady Yen's upper arm and embedded itself in the cobblestones behind her. Crying out in pain, the noblewoman sank to the ground as Bao and Lan hurried over to her. Commander Wei spun in his saddle, his eyes furious and desperate as he yanked out his sword in a great shrieking of metal. All around him, the Imperial soldiers did the same.

"My man is not going to miss next time," Captain Quang said, smirking at Lord Nguyen.

"No, my lord!" Commander Wei yelled, as the nobleman made a quick movement. "Don't do—"

But no sooner had the words left his mouth than a massive explosion erupted, sending rubble and shrapnel everywhere. Lord Nguyen had plucked a small bomb from his sack and thrown it directly at Captain Quang. Horses screamed and men collapsed, and Bao threw himself and the Commander's cloak protectively over Lan and Lady Yen, his ears ringing from the loud noise. His eyes stung from the dirt, and his nostrils burned with the smell of fire and blood. Lan was lifting her head, her gaze frantic and her lips moving, but Bao couldn't hear a single word.

Pandemonium had broken out around them. Through the ringing in his ears, he detected the sound of metal clashing and felt sick, disoriented, and deathly cold. *Focus*, he told himself sternly, ripping off cloth from the hem of his tunic and wrapping it tightly around Lady Yen's arm. It was bleeding profusely, but it was only a surface wound and had not pierced any muscle. He looked into her white face and tried to be reassuring, but the ground was tilting beneath him.

A plume of black smoke had begun to rise steadily. Bao coughed, turning to see one of the Gray City guards deploying something that very much resembled one of Lord Nguyen's bombs. But instead of exploding, it had burst open and was spitting out toxic-smelling clouds. It engulfed a masked Commander Wei, who was clashing swords with one of the enemies, and an Imperial soldier who was lying on the ground screaming, the bones in his legs shattered completely.

"Bao!" Lan yelled, her mouth still shaping words he could not hear.

She ran over to a tangle of bodies and yanked something off them. When she came back, she was wearing a cloth mask and carrying two more for Bao and Lady Yen, but it was too late.

Bao felt himself slipping into a daze. He heard Lan's muffled scream behind her mask as a Gray City guard lifted her onto his horse, and then he felt strong arms around his middle, dragging him onto a saddle. Lord Nguyen was slumped onto the back of another Gray City horse, a painful-looking lump on his forehead. And then they were galloping down the road, away from the catastrophe in front of Lord Nguyen's estate, and Bao sank into oblivion.

20

When Bao opened his eyes, he was lying on the most comfortable bed he had ever known. It was like a nest of feathers covered in peacock-blue silk, cocooning his aching body in softness, and everywhere he looked were gold brocade pillows and thick blankets. Matching silk curtains framed the bed, sweeping down to a crimson carpet that stretched to all four of the gilded walls. Bao shifted to get a better look, his body sinking even deeper into the warm feather bed. His eyes traced lazily over marble flowers and miniature trees on a mahogany stand, neatly stacked books on an ornate rosewood desk, oil paintings depicting the Surjalana desert at sunrise, and high windows looking out onto the early evening sky.

Bao sat bolt upright.

It all came back in a flash: the ambush at Lord Nguyen's estate, the clouds of black spice enveloping everyone, Commander Wei's sword ringing against the blade of a Gray City guard, Lady Yen wounded and bleeding on the ground, and Lan shouting his name. Bao rubbed his aching head, trying desperately to remember. They had been captured and taken on horseback, him and Lan and Lord Nguyen. He vaguely recalled Lan arguing with one of the guards and Lord Nguyen shouting insults as they galloped away from his estate. The journey had been long and uncomfortable, the motion of the horse jostling Bao's painful, drooping head.

Vy's men had taken them to the Gray City, of that he was certain. But where was Lan? And how long would it be before the enchantment took hold of him?

Bao jumped out of bed, fighting off a wave of mild dizziness as he searched for his flute. None of his clothes were anywhere to be seen, and he was wearing a long, loose nightshirt that did not belong to him. Something heavy swung against his chest as he moved and he looked down to see a heavy sort of amulet, bronze and rectangular in shape, with a glowing blood-red jewel in the center. He frowned and tore it off, and then immediately wished he hadn't.

Everything he had felt since the witch had cast the spell returned with a vengeance: there was a sharp, scrabbling pain in his ribs like claws groping for his heart, his windpipe tightened as though clenched between two murderous hands, and he felt so light-headed and untethered that he put out a hand and grabbed a corner of the bed to stay on the ground. Choking and gasping for air, he slid the amulet back over his head.

Breath came back to his lungs at once. He sank into the soft carpet and pressed his face against one of the embroidered crimson flowers, his heart hammering in his chest. He closed his eyes, feeling faint and dizzy, and could not find the strength to open them even when he heard someone come into the room.

"Oh, Bao!" Mistress Vy's voice said, and it was a half sob. Her next words were fainter, as though she spoke them over her shoulder. "Help me get him back into bed."

He felt hands gently lifting him from the carpet and placing him back into the cocoon of silk and feathers. Cool fingers pressed against his burning forehead, and when he opened his eyes, his mother's terrified face swam into his vision. Her hair had again been swept back at her temples, and he noticed how it was all gray around her forehead, which was creased in worry.

"Just lie still, darling," she said, stroking his hair. "I've sent for some water. I thought I could get back and explain about the charm before you woke. I'm sorry."

The room came into sharper focus, as did Mistress Vy's anxious expression. Bao looked down and saw the blood-red amulet resting on his chest. "Wh-what happened? What is this?"

"This is a charm that I had Huong make for you. When you arrived here, you were in no condition to see her, and we were worried that she might unintentionally do more harm than good, trying to break the spell when you were unconscious. So she made you a temporary charm that would offset the spell while you slept, and allow you to breathe and be apart from your flute."

"How long have I been asleep? It looks like it's almost night. Is it too late? Am I . . ."

"Do you think I would let anything happen to you? The full moon isn't until tomorrow night," Vy said. "My guards and their horses made good time, bringing you to me by afternoon. Rest assured that Huong is ready to break the spell when you have recovered."

"And Lan? Where is she?"

"She is perfectly safe and resting. She was exhausted with worry over you, but when she saw the charms Huong made for both you and her, she had a bit of food and went right to sleep. What a pretty girl she is," Vy added, her eyes crinkling at him as she smoothed his blankets.

Bao watched her fuss over him, and when a servant came in with some water, Vy took the cup and gave it to him herself. The servant had also brought a tray of dates, persimmons, and milk fruit, and Vy bustled around, humming as she cut the fruit for him and arranged it just so. She was everything pleasant and loving and motherly, and Bao had to remind himself that this was like a spell. It was magic of a sort, the way she continually made him forget what she was and how much she had already lied to him.

"Where is Lord Nguyen?" he asked.

She stopped humming. "He's here. He put up such a fight that one of my guards had to knock him out. I think he'll have a frightful head-ache when he wakes up, unfortunately."

"Why did you capture him? I thought you wanted him dead," Bao said, not touching the food she held out to him.

"What use is anyone when they're dead? Of course I wanted him alive," Mistress Vy said. "I instructed Captain Quang and his men to bring Lord Nguyen to me as a prisoner of war. He has great influence with the king of the Sacred Grasslands and Empress Jade, who took the trouble of finding him a bride. I think Her Majesty made an even better match than she had hoped—that little noblewoman fought my guards as hard as her husband-to-be did."

"You took Lady Yen, too?" Bao asked, shocked.

"To ensure that His Lordship behaves, naturally. Oh, Bao, how little you know of me," his mother said reproachfully, seeing his horror. "I'm not going to do anything to hurt them. I need them alive and safe because if I have them both, Commander Wei and his forces won't be as likely to attack the Gray City, will they?"

"I don't think either of them would want him to hold back because of them."

Mistress Vy's face darkened. "How well you seem to know these people who have no relation to you. That is exactly what Lord Nguyen was shouting before my guards subdued him. He seemed to think his own men would kill him at his command—put him out of his misery and take away my bargaining chip."

She brushed off her clothes, as though dusting away the unpleasant topic, and crossed over to the door, issuing commands to the servants waiting outside.

"The maids will bring you a fresh set of clothes while yours are being cleaned," she told Bao. "Since you're feeling better, I want to show you something. And I want to return this to you before I forget. Keep it safe for now." She pulled the bamboo flute from her pocket and gave it to him, and at once he felt a bit calmer with the familiar ridges of the instrument beneath his fingertips.

Quickly, he dressed, taking care to keep the charm around his neck, and met Vy in the corridor. "Is Lan coming with us?" he asked. "And when are we going to see the witch?"

"I told you, Lan is resting," Mistress Vy said impatiently. "I can see you're determined not to believe anything I say. I've already explained why I lied about Sinh, and as for my guards' early arrival at Lord Nguyen's estate, I wanted to catch them unaware and bring you to me as quickly as possible." She shook her head in frustration at his prolonged silence and opened a door across the hall. She motioned for him to be quiet and to look in, and Bao did so warily.

Lan was inside, sleeping on an enormous bed identical to the one in his room, except that hers had been covered in light yellow silk. Her face looked peaceful and undisturbed, and as he watched, she rolled onto her other side and began to snore gently. He couldn't help smiling, knowing how she had longed to sleep in a real bed again.

Mistress Vy closed the door gently. "Do you believe me now?" she asked, still looking annoyed. "Shall I show you where Lord Nguyen is sleeping, and then Lady Yen? Or will you allow me to show you what I wished to, and then we can go and see my sister?"

Bao's fingers closed around the amulet. He thought of how Vy had threatened to bar the gates of the city to him and decided not to antagonize her any more than he had to. "Please lead the way, Mother," he said, and her good humor returned as she led him out of the house. "Where are we in the Gray City right now?"

"This is our family home," she said, leading him down a set of stairs. "Many generations have lived here before us. We are at the very center of the Gray City, protected by three concentric rings of heavily guarded walls. I've always liked the number three, as you know." She smiled at him over her shoulder, gesturing to the ornate interior of the home.

Bao looked around politely, but instead of being impressed by the grandeur of the place, he felt ill. His skin crawled at the sight of the bronze-and-cypress furniture, the rare painted scrolls, and the jeweled trays that decorated almost every surface. He could not forget that all of this wealth had been paid for with the blood and suffering of others. Death and black spice had gilded each table and upholstered each chair in silk. And Vy had spent her life here, walking these halls, living in comfort and making excuses for the horrors she caused.

Bao felt the sudden urge to run. He would not let this cursed city or Vy enchant him, however much he felt the eerie sense of having come home at last, and how easily he could imagine living here in peace and listening to the birds sing in the willows. *The price of a life here might be my humanity*, he thought.

The guards at the main entrance bowed to Vy as she came out and she greeted them each by name, thanking them for their work. "I want to show you the garden and the infirmary, in which I think you'll have a particular interest," she told Bao.

The house was surrounded by a granite wall, a smaller replica of the enormous one that ringed the city. As in the vision, Vy called to the guards atop the towers, and they spun two wheels to open the gates. The moon shimmered gently above them as they entered the garden, which Bao recognized at once. The tangled wilderness looked and smelled exactly as it had when he had last spoken to his mother here.

"These are the flowers my uncle created." Vy gestured to a cluster of blossoms ranging from crimson to pale pink. Beneath each bloom were several round pods oozing a thick white sap. "Before the poppies that grew outside the city were destroyed, he cross-bred them with other flowers to create these. He laid the groundwork for my research into a safer, less addictive formula for black spice. My workers collect the sap, but no part of the plant is wasted."

Throughout the garden, people in nondescript gray uniforms crouched among the plants, snipping the blossoms into baskets, scraping the white sap into jars, or weeding the flower beds and clearing away dead plants. As with the guards outside her home, Mistress Vy greeted each person by name, and they bowed to her, smiling, before returning diligently to their work.

Moonlight glittered upon a large bronze statue in the center of the garden. It took Bao a minute to realize that it depicted a monstrous snake coiled at the feet of a robed man. The man's figure was unnaturally long, and Bao imagined strings dangling from his fingers to the snake as though it were a puppet. The serpent gazed upward reverently, awaiting the man's command.

"Poppies have always been associated with the Serpent God," Vy told him. "Long before my ancestors conceived of black spice, he was using these flowers to elicit visions. Combined with blood magic, poppies gave him the potential to be the greatest among the Dragon Lords." She ran her hand over the statue and Bao shuddered; the snake looked so real that he was almost terrified it would sink its fangs into her fingers.

"Blood magic is what Huong used on me," he said. "She cut my hand to cast the spell."

"Enchantments are rendered more powerful when blood is spilt. And not just any blood, but that of someone with magic in their veins." She paused, looking at him with an appraising air. "That brings me to what I wished to show you."

The rectangular garden contained a squared-off area surrounded by another black metal gate. Within this protected enclosure stood the infirmary, a pale gray stone building covered with fragrant climbing vines. The interior was clean, quiet, and well-lit, made of strong bamboo and light wood. For such a quiet building, there was an unusual number of people inside: workers in gray uniforms bustling efficiently from the top level to the ground floor, bending over pallets, spooning soup into mouths, and applying a balm to the skin that Bao recognized as a form of black spice. He scanned the patients, who were men and women of every age, but none of them looked as Khoa had before dying in the river market or the sick woman in the village.

Vy smiled at one of the workers, who bowed deeply to her. "How are you tonight, Ly?" she asked. "Is all well? How is old Master Chu?"

"Sleeping like a baby, Mistress," the worker replied, laughing. "You were right to tell us to lower his dosage. He doesn't need much more medicine. His daughter came twice today."

"That's very like Kim," Vy said affectionately. "And Thuy? How is she?"

Bao watched as his mother asked about patient after patient, and at one point, she strolled over to one of the pallets and struck up a conversation with the old woman lying there. She pressed hands, patted shoulders, and asked after spouses and children, and every single person responded to her with genuine gratitude. He saw no pretense in the way they lit up when his mother came into the room. "Who are these people?" he asked.

"They either came to the Gray City themselves or were brought here by their families or friends," Vy said softly. Her eyes rested on a young man about Bao's age, who was sleeping fitfully nearby. "They are all survivors of the bloodpox and came here at different stages. I've been treating them for weeks with my newest formula, and it has stopped everything from fever and aches to severe bleeding, with no addiction."

Bao stared at her in shock. "You've learned how to cure the bloodpox?"

"I'm being cautious, so I won't say *cure* just yet," his mother answered, but when she turned back to him, her face was like the sun. "That woman there, for example, had been given up for dead by her son when he brought her here, but she is growing stronger every day. Oh, how joyful I've been at the prospect of trying to right our family's wrongs. Do you see now why I won't surrender to Commander Wei? They don't want a compromise. They want to come into my city and destroy everything, right when I'm on the cusp of my greatest discovery."

She bent down to chat with two middle-aged women who lay on pallets, side by side.

Bao looked around the bright, clean, and cheerful room, so at odds with what he knew of the disease and the suffering outside the Gray City. He knew from experience that medicine and the act of healing were never so polished; in all his years of shadowing Master Huynh, caring for people had never looked like this. And yet he did not doubt that these people truly had been sick. Here and there he saw hints of the bloodpox: a racking, wet cough from this man here, a slight greenish tinge to the face of that woman there.

Could it be true? Bao thought in dazed wonder and disbelief. Could his mother have, at last, found the medicine for which so many lives had been lost? It didn't make up for all of the deaths her family had caused; nothing ever would. But such a breakthrough had the potential to change the face of Feng Lu forever.

Bright laughter rang out, and he turned to see one of the patients' family members embracing Mistress Vy, who spoke to the woman in a low, kind voice. Whatever might be said about the Gray City, its citizens seemed to genuinely like and respect their leader, and she cared about them. As the woman's arm moved, Bao was startled to see a large black circle tattooed upon her bare arm. "She has the mark of the Iron Palace," he said to Vy when she came back. He remembered it as the same brand he had seen on the corpse outside of the river witch's home.

"She is a former prisoner," his mother explained. "My people come from all over Feng Lu. They are what the other kingdoms might callously, wrongly consider the dregs of society: those who are forced to sell their bodies for money, street urchins with no home, reformed criminals. They come to the Gray City to find work and a second chance at life, and I give it to them."

That explained the fierce, overwhelming loyalty, Bao thought, watching some workers bow as low to Mistress Vy as though she were Empress Jade herself.

"I've worked hard to build a safe city," his mother said, beckoning him to follow her upstairs to the top level. "We built schools to educate the children of families affected; we provide jobs of all kinds and ensure that everyone here works. No one is allowed to be idle. We even developed our own printing press so that writers could share their stories and knowledge."

Bao remembered her calling him a prince. "You're a strange sort of monarch," he commented as they emerged onto a floor similar to the one below. "I don't think many rulers care to intercede into ordinary lives."

"Everyone in the Gray City matters to me. This is no kingdom where officials serve as fingers at the end of the ruler's arm and do what she isn't inclined to." She made her rounds among the patients with a nod here and a soothing word there. "A man in my place would be deemed a great leader, but *I* will spend the rest of my life trying to convince the world of my worth and the vision my family has bled for. I've made my peace with that."

They came to a row of pallets lining the far wall. The patients lying there were quieter and more subdued than the others, who called out greetings and waved their hands to Vy as she passed. Two workers in gray uniforms were moving among these patients, who all seemed to be asleep or dazed. Bao moved closer, frowning, and saw that each patient had at least one elbow resting in a curved basin. He studied the man closest to him and saw a cut in the crook of the man's arm, from which blood was flowing into the bowl.

"Why are you bleeding these people?" he asked Vy, who was watching him again with that appraising look. "Master Huynh—the physician with whom I trained—used to do this only to the sickest of his patients."

His mother took a deep breath. "This is the secret to my new formula. The medicine comprises many different ingredients, and over the years, we played with amounts and varieties and mixtures. But everything failed. Either the drug was too addictive, or it brought on the bloodpox even more quickly, or it wasn't effective at treating anything." She looked Bao directly in the eye. "All of that changed on the night I decided to use blood, about three years ago. I was thinking about how much I resented Huong for her magic and for leaving me instead of helping. But then I thought . . . I might not have her abilities, but I do have the same blood flowing through my veins. And so I added some of my blood to the formula I was working on."

Bao listened, his eyes darting from her face to the dazed patients with dawning horror.

"It didn't work right away," Vy went on. "It took me years to figure out exactly how much blood to use, and at what temperature, and when to add it, and so on and so forth. And it required a great deal more blood than I had, unfortunately." She stood scanning him, her arms crossed over her chest. "So I decided to take some of the sickest people who came to me for help and keep them alive. Safe and comfortable and well fed. And I used their blood to experiment."

He opened his mouth, but the questions refused to emerge from his dry throat.

"They consented to having their blood taken," his mother said quickly. "I told them it was for research that might help them, which was almost the truth. And over time, the formula grew more effective and less addictive, and I used some of my own blood again and saw how much more powerful it was than the others—because of that element of magic, I suspected. So what, I asked myself, could *true* magical blood do? What would happen if I bled a person who actually had magical abilities?"

"And that's why you decided to find your sister after all this time," Bao said, his voice working at last. He felt something bubbling inside him, and after a moment, he realized it was a steadily simmering rage. "That's why you finally sent your guards for Huong. Because she could be useful to you, and you could farm her for blood as you've done to all of these other people."

"I wanted to find her because I want our family to be together again. I want you and Huong to live with me." Mistress Vy placed her hands on his shoulders, and it was all Bao could do not to shove her backward. "I showed you all this because I want to be truthful with you. I want my good work to be carried on, and to see you marry Lan and have children to whom you could pass on our legacy. Join me, Bao. Help me, work with me, and never be alone again."

He reeled backward at the mention of Lan. "Do not speak that name."

"The Gray City will be the center of all power and commerce. It started with the vision of one family. *Our* family, Bao. We will save lives with our good work, you and Huong and I."

Bao gritted his teeth. "I am a physician's apprentice, and my work centers upon healing others, not wounding and using them. I will not support anything that requires such measures to be perfected."

"I treat all of my patients with care and respect. You saw that yourself," Vy said, looking bewildered by his anger. "In this building, you see with your own eyes the miracles my drug can bring about. Look at the second chance it has given to everyone. Don't be so quick to condemn something that brought us back together and may fulfill our vision forever."

"*Your* vision," Bao pointed out, clenching his fists. He tried in vain to stem his fury, but it gushed out of him like air. "Do not bring me into this. You're bleeding helpless people who don't even know exactly what you're using their blood for! You spoke of the Serpent God as though you admired him, and now I see why: you agree with his use of blood magic and black spice to hurt and manipulate people. Well, I want no part of it, Mistress Vy."

"You mean Mother," she said softly. Bao had the impression she was not only taking in every inch of his face, but his mind and heart as well. "So this is your answer, then?"

Bao looked straight into her eyes. Even now, beneath the all-consuming ire and fear he felt, he found a thread of pity for her. "There are three armies at your door. Four, if you count the Crimson Army," he said quietly. "You can't possibly believe that there is anything you can do to stop or win this battle. They are going to destroy this city. Your fantasy of us living together here and continuing to make this drug by bleeding and killing people . . . it's just that, a fantasy."

"And what of honor? What of principle?" She let her arms fall to her sides and came close to him, with pleading eyes. "Surrendering means giving up. And no one in our family has ever given up. I will hold on to my conviction and prove to everyone that I was right all along."

"You're going to lose. Don't you see?" Bao asked, frustrated. He could not save his own mother from herself—no one could, except her, and she wasn't going to do it.

An inexpressible sorrow filled her eyes, and Bao saw that she knew he was speaking the truth. Perhaps she had known all along, but her stubbornness had not allowed her to back away. Tears streamed down her face, but her voice was calm. "I think you and Huong have more in common than you realize." She wiped her eyes, her mouth twisted with the same grief Bao remembered from when she had told him of her relatives, and of Sinh. "Very well, then. You have both refused to help me, and I accept your refusal."

"I'm sorry," Bao said, and meant it.

Vy looked up at him tenderly. "So am I."

And then she ripped the charm from his neck.

21

Someone was shaking Lan. Anxious hands patted her cheeks, and a blurry, pale oval face hovered in the darkness. "Can you hear me?" the woman asked, her voice sounding as though it were coming from underwater, and then Lan felt something cold and wet splashing her nose and eyes. She gasped and jerked awake, looking around frantically.

Lady Yen sighed with relief. "You're alive! I didn't want to waste too much water, not knowing if they'll bring us more, but I'm glad that revived you. Are you all right?"

"I think so." Lan's mouth felt dry and cottony, and her temples throbbed with pain. Her back hurt, too, and she realized that she was lying on a cold, hard floor. Stone, from the feel of it. "Where on earth are we?"

"The Gray City, remember? They took us, Bao, and Lord Nguyen. Come under here and get warm." The noblewoman helped Lan sit up and wrapped a fold of her dark green cloak around her. "It's Commander Wei's cloak. They took it off Bao when we came through the gates, and I snatched it up before they could destroy it. Do you remember anything that happened?"

Lan rubbed her aching head. "Mistress Vy was waiting, and she was nothing like I had imagined," she said slowly. "I thought she would have a hard, cruel face, but she was so clearly worried about Bao. And Lord Nguyen was yelling about how this was an inconvenience and he needed to be home to feed his dogs, and a guard knocked him out." She frowned. "But then they took us to Mistress Vy's home and gave us beautiful bedchambers, and I fell asleep. I don't remember anything after that. How did we end up here?"

"They gave *you* a beautiful bedchamber," Lady Yen said wryly. "I'm sure the woman wanted Bao to think she was treating you well. She put me in here from the start."

Lan looked around them. It was a gloomy, dark room shaped like a square, and it smelled absolutely horrible. She covered her nose with a sleeve. "What is that repulsive smell?"

"We're in a dungeon of some sort. There's nothing up there except a locked door and a window that's out of reach." Lady Yen pointed at a set of stone steps and winced as her injured arm dropped back to her side. "I'll live," she added, seeing Lan's concern. "The arrow only grazed me, and Bao wrapped me up nicely before he passed out and the guards captured us. I never saw what became of Wei."

"I'm sure he's all right," Lan said, taking her hand.

The woman wiped her face with a fold of the cloak. "And I'm even more sure that Bao is all right, too. Mistress Vy wouldn't hurt her own son." She nodded at a bucket and a tray by the stairs. "And she provided enough water and dates to last the three of us for a little while."

"The three of us?" Lan repeated, startled. She followed Lady Yen's gaze to a straw pallet in the corner. A body lay there, small, motionless, and silent, and in the dim light from the window, she could just make out a cloud of pure white hair on the thin pillow.

"It appears we're sharing these grand guest apartments with Mistress Vy's sister," Lady Yen said wryly. "She and I had a nice little conversation before you were thrown in here with us. She's just as weak as you are. She could barely stay awake."

Lan stared at the tiny, pathetic outline of the river witch. Like her sister, Huong was nothing like what Lan had expected her to be. "She's the reason Bao and I are here. It's because of her that Bao might *die*. How long have we been here? Is the full moon . . . ?"

"We were captured late last night and arrived here this afternoon. There's still one more night. Oh, I almost forgot." Lady Yen nodded at Lan's neck. "Huong wanted to tell you not to take the necklace off. It's a charm that Mistress Vy bullied her into making for you and Bao."

Confused, Lan lifted her hand to the cold, heavy stone hanging from her neck.

"It keeps the spell from choking you both when you're apart," Yen explained, "but its magic only works when it's around your neck. It's meant to be a temporary solution."

"Temporary? Why didn't Vy just have her sister break the spell?"

"Because," said the river witch in a feeble voice, as she stirred on her straw pallet, "Vy is going to hold this spell over the boy's head until he does what she wants him to."

Lan's surprise gave way to hot fury. "You," she seethed. She ignored Lady Yen's attempts to hold her back as she rose to her feet. "This is all your fault! If you had only thought a little before enchanting Bao, he could be safe right now! He could be rowing his boat on the river, playing his flute, living his life . . ." She broke down crying, tears burning her cheeks.

"I'm sorry."

The apology was so unexpected that Lan stopped sobbing. "What?"

Huong shifted painfully onto her side, and when the dim light touched her face, Lan was surprised to see that she wasn't old at all, despite her white hair and the weariness in her eyes. The woman resembled Vy in her narrow eyes and strong jaw, and even Bao in her nose. "When I recognized the boy, I assumed Vy had sent him. Twenty years and my hatred was still as sharp as ever," the witch croaked. "It didn't give me time to think or question him further. I didn't know I would be giving her another bargaining chip. I'm sorry that happened."

"Bao hasn't seen his mother in seventeen years," Lan said, wiping her face. "His father took him and fled the Gray City shortly after you left, and Bao has nothing to do with her wanting you back here."

"I know all of that now," the witch said. "Vy told me the truth when her guards first dragged me here. She was rather self-righteous about it, too, telling me how sorry she was for everything and spewing nonsense about wanting us to be reunited. She hoped her honesty would persuade me to come back and help her in her work, as a good sister would do. She painted quite a lovely picture of our happy family." She snorted and tried to prop herself against the wall. Out of instinct, Lan moved forward to help her and saw a deep, dark cut in the crook of the woman's elbow.

"Why are you down here?" Lan asked in horror. "What has your sister done to you?"

Huong issued a weak, bitter laugh. "Did you expect my sister to give me a silk bed? She threw me in this prison and bled me dry, that's what she's done."

Lady Yen covered her mouth, looking sick. "That's what they say Xifeng used to do: drink the blood of maidens to absorb their beauty."

"I am far from being a maiden, and Vy isn't drinking my blood," Huong said, giving her brittle laugh again. "She's not daft enough to want beauty when power is so much more appealing. She's discovered that blood is a key ingredient in her formula for her miracle drug, and she keeps people she's been bleeding dry in that infirmary. Well, I told her exactly what I thought of her offer, and when I turned her down, she decided to see what a witch's blood can do. And here I am." She broke off into hacking coughs that shook her whole body and Lady Yen hurried to bring her water.

Lan felt the horror of it all wash over her like cold rain. "Why is she doing this?"

"Because the Gray City is her reason to live, and life without illness is the legacy she will leave behind. Her name etched into stone, when her body is long gone. Her words, not mine." A smirk flickered across the witch's face. "What scares me the most about my sister is that in her head, she *believes* she is doing good. And she will stop at nothing to achieve it, not even when defeat is facing her. Oh, yes," Huong added, "she knows she cannot win this war. But she has protective measures in place."

"Like what? Commander Wei has four armies at his back and Lord Nguyen's explosives in his arsenal. Nothing can stop him," Lady Yen said, her eyes flashing with fierce pride.

"The most important part of the Gray City is the garden. Vy fears the destruction of her plants more than death, and she knows the enemy forces will go right for them. She told me that workers have been slaving night and day to generate more incense, powders, balms . . . whatever they can make. They've amassed a huge supply of black spice and have filled three enormous ships with them. The vessels are sitting off the coast, out of harm's way and hidden from anyone on land."

Lady Yen and Lan exchanged horrified glances.

"Vy's people have transferred the bulk of the drugs and the blood they've collected there. They also brought out roots and seeds and pods, anything to ensure they can keep growing the plants long after this battle. It is the Gray City's ultimate protection."

Lady Yen looked from Lan to the witch, her breath coming fast. "Wei needs to be told about this at once. He'll be wasting his resources trying to breach the wall when they should be out at sea, attacking the ships. We can't let her win."

"We need to get out of this cell," Lan agreed, newly formed panic rising in her throat. "If Vy is willing to bleed and imprison her own sister, what is she going to do to Bao?"

Huong shrugged. "If he refuses to help her, then she's going to keep him from seeing me. Not that I can do anything about the spell, but neither of them know that."

"What?" Lan demanded. "You created the enchantment. Of course you can break it!"

"I'm the only one in my family who doesn't want to destroy humanity. I also happen to be the only one with powerful magic, and any spell I cast is permanent, no matter how much I want to undo it. I'm sorry, young woman," Huong added, and she sounded genuinely regretful, "but I cannot help you."

"But what about Vy?" Lan asked desperately. "She seems to love Bao. At least, he thinks she does." But even as she spoke, she knew they could not rely on Bao's ruthless mother. And even if the woman *did* have the power and inclination to keep him alive, she might use him as abominably as she had used her own sister. Lan sank to the floor. The revolting smell grew stronger, but she barely noticed. "There *has* to be a way. We can't have traveled all this way for nothing."

Lady Yen put a hand on Lan's shoulder and glowered at the witch.

"Why are you trapped in here if your magic is as powerful as you say? Can't you enchant your way out?"

"You may have noticed that I didn't rise to welcome you," Huong said sarcastically. "This cell is lined with iron, which blocks magic and weakens anyone whose veins carry it. Even if she had left the door up there wide open, I would still be too weak to leave."

Lan bent her head, trying to think, but it felt hopeless. She was locked in a dungeon with a useless witch while Bao was out there, being coerced into helping his murderous mother. And when the moon rose tomorrow night, he might be trapped inside the flute forever. She would never see him again, and he would never know what he had come to mean to her.

She felt both women's eyes on her and kept her head down so she wouldn't have to see their pity. As she shifted, something creaked on the ground, and she ran her hands over what felt like a metal grate. It was wet and slimy, and the awful smell was emanating from it.

"I wouldn't do that if I were you," Huong said, amused. "That's the opening to the sewer. You may have noticed the absence of a chamber pot in here . . ."

"Lan, stop touching it!" Lady Yen shrieked, looking green.

But it was a testament to how badly Lan wanted to get out that she ignored them both. "It's too late. My hands are already coated in . . ." She swallowed hard and decided not to think much more about that. Back home, she had never so much as looked at her chamber pot—it was to be used, and then taken care of by the servants. But she steeled her nerves and looked at Lady Yen with mounting excitement. "You said the door up those stairs is locked. But the sewer could be another way out of this dungeon!"

The witch barked a laugh. "I've had stomach trouble and so have the last dozen prisoners, as you can smell. I can't imagine you fine ladies going down there, not when it could be just a dead end and an empty pit." She paused. "Well, not *empty*."

"You cannot be serious, Lan," Lady Yen said weakly.

"If we get out of here," Lan said, still feeling around the edges of the grate, "we can warn Commander Wei about the ships. And we can find Bao and stay with him until he . . ." She swallowed again and gave Yen her fiercest glare. "I don't intend on rotting in here while our friends need our help, and if that means wading around in human waste, then so be it!"

There was a momentary silence. "I can tell from the way you talk that you were raised with maids and silk slippers," Huong remarked, studying Lan. "Yet you're willing to crawl through the sewers to escape?"

"I would do worse than that to get back to Bao."

A little smile touched the witch's mouth. "You love him," she said slyly. "I can hear it in your voice."

Lan's heart gave a painful clench. "I don't know anything about love. I didn't know it when it was right in front of me."

"You *do* know about it. I've seen you," Lady Yen said gently, regaining some of her color as she smiled at Lan. "I've been watching you two since we started this journey. You and Bao have something, like a link." She moved her hand in the air helplessly, trying to find words.

Lan recalled the first time she had sensed the connection between Commander Wei and Lady Yen. "A spark," she said, and the woman nodded. "Like lightning moving between you. Do Bao and I really have that? *Can* we have that after such a short time together?"

"Time doesn't matter when it comes to love," Lady Yen said. "It might come to two people who have only just met, but not to two others who have known each other for a century."

Huong watched Lan with an inscrutable expression. "You're afraid to admit you love him. But know this: Bao was born of a union between my sister and the man I loved. I wanted to punish them with a spell that can only be broken by *real* love. If you feel even a fraction of that, then you have more of a chance to save Bao than anyone else. And if he feels the same—"

"I hurt him so badly," Lan said, her eyes stinging. "Even if he still cares for me as much as he used to, I don't know if I would deserve it."

"But isn't it worth taking the chance to save him?" the witch asked. "And if you are the one who has been keeping him whole, keeping him from becoming a spirit . . ."

Lan thought of the early days of the enchantment, when Bao had faded unless she had touched him, and of the night in the village when he had pulled her to him and they had almost kissed. She was certain that those moments had not affected her alone. It was so different from what she had felt for Tam—from what she had once expected love to be. "I guess there's only one way to find out," she said, blinking away tears. "But even if we manage to get out, the place is crawling with people. How are we going to find Bao?"

"Let me worry about that," Huong said, and she sat up straighter, as though drawing strength from her own words. "Get me out of this iron cell, let my powers come back slowly, and we will find your young man. I want to see the Gray City in ruins as badly as you do, and I want my sister to answer for her crimes."

Suddenly, Lady Yen dropped to the ground beside Lan. "I'm doing this for you, Wei," she muttered through clenched teeth, and laid her hands upon the grate. For a moment, she looked like she might be sick, but then she steeled herself and began straining to lift it.

Lan helped her, ignoring the grime that coated her hands. The metal had been bolted down at one point, but the small rivets had rusted and weakened with time. With both of them applying force, the grate gave way, sending them flying back from the hole in the floor. Lan crawled back and felt the open space with her fingers, trying not to gag at the smell. It was just wide enough for her hips and shoulders to fit through.

"There must be a way out. The water in the sewers has to drain out somewhere, right?" Lan looked at Yen, who gave a bewildered shrug, and then she closed her eyes and breathed shallowly through her mouth. She had been honest with the witch: she would do far worse things if it meant getting back to Bao. The thought of telling him how she truly felt, and the risk of him not returning her feelings, made her stomach seize up as much as the smell of the sewer did. *But he already did it for me, once,* she told herself.

And so she swung her legs into the hole and braced her hands on the opening.

22

"Careful! Hold on to me." Lady Yen lay flat on the floor and held her hands out to Lan.

Lan took her hand. "It's just like getting out of a tree," she told herself. "Like the one Bao and I climbed out of." She recalled how Bà nội had cheered when they had made it to the ground safely and held her grandmother's mischievous face in her mind as she slid farther into the hole. She could see the water at the bottom. "You can let go of me. It's not that far."

Obediently, the noblewoman loosened her grip and Lan landed more quickly than she had anticipated. She sank up to her knees into water that smelled like her worst nightmare.

"Lan, are you all right?" Lady Yen called.

"I'm fine!" Lan splashed to the side, thanking each and every god that she'd had the foresight to borrow her maid's shoes instead of wearing her usual delicate slippers. "Help Huong down first." In a minute, the witch's frail body dangled from the cell. She was so light that Lan had no trouble catching her, though the impact nearly sent them both into the mess.

"Careful," Huong said, breathing hard. "Wouldn't want to dirty your noble bottom."

"It doesn't matter. I've dirtied my noble everything else," Lan pointed out.

Yen lowered herself in after them, coughing uncontrollably as she did so. "I'll be fine," she said, leaning against the wall. "I just need a moment."

Lan looked around, encouraged by how much of their surroundings she could see. There was a faint light coming from somewhere. She splashed through the long, low tunnel, trying not to look down, and in a minute, the source of the light was revealed: a metal grate much larger than the one they had come through. This one was bolted to the wall, allowing the sewage to travel outward, and the bars were so rusted that it took Lan only a few hard tugs before they came apart. She shook her fist in jubilation as Lady Yen and Huong joined her.

"You found a way out!" the noblewoman cheered.

"Quiet," the witch scolded. "I know where we are. This is a branch downstream from where the servants do the washing. We can wash there and find a change of clothes, too."

"Thank the gods," Yen muttered, allowing the older woman to lean on her.

As quietly as they could, they climbed out of the water and onto the grass, looking around for any sign of activity. They were at the bottom of a hill, over which Lan could just see the roof of a grand stone building. Clean, fresh water ran down the hill and joined the mess of sewage at the base. Huong directed them up the slope to an area where they found pails, washboards, and washing lines from which hung an array of pants, tunics, and bedding.

Lan decided that none of the hot, scented baths she had ever taken in her pampered life even came close to the feeling of dunking herself in this stream. She grinned at Lady Yen, who was trying not to shout with glee. The witch shook her head at the both of them and jerked her head toward the washing lines. Quickly, they dried off and swapped out their soiled clothing. There were two steel-colored uniforms of the Gray City for Huong and Yen, and Lan found a simple gray overdress and pants that fit her well enough.

The witch surveyed the others with approval. Away from the iron cell, her face had taken on a healthier color. "Walk with purpose and keep your heads up. You won't attract as much suspicion that way," she advised, then paused to listen, her eyes alert.

A low, rushing rumble filled the air, and within it, Lan thought she could hear many voices shouting, horses screaming, feet running, and the clashing of weapons. And then, seconds later, there was an immense roar, like a clap of thunder, except that it shook the earth.

"The battle has been raging all this time," Lady Yen said, looking at Lan with mingled fear and hope. "That must have been one of Lord Nguyen's explosives detonating. The Commander's forces are blasting their way through the walls of the city."

Lan felt cold all over, even though she knew it was their allies charging toward them. War had only ever seemed to be fiction, an element in old stories and her father's discussions, but here she was in a city under attack—and the object of destruction, Mistress Vy's gardens, was just on the other side of a high granite wall. "How are we going to have time to find Bao *and* warn Commander Wei about the ships?" she asked anxiously.

Lady Yen's eyes glittered. "We split up. I will find a way to get out toward them and locate Wren or the Commander, or someone who can give them this information."

"Are you mad?" Lan cried. "You can't just walk out into the midst of a battle! You'll be killed, especially wearing a uniform of the Gray City!"

But Yen thrust a bundle of soaked, dark green cloth under her nose. "There was no way I was leaving the Commander's cloak behind in that smelly dungeon. I washed it as best I could just now, and I will show it to our allies to prove my identity. There's no other way, Lan. You don't need me to help with Bao, and I want to do this."

Lan took in her defiant expression and sighed. "How are you going to get out there?"

"It's an old city, and I didn't grow up here for nothing. There are many tunnels and passageways, and with any luck, Vy hasn't changed most of them," Huong said, and Yen listened intently as she explained multiple routes and the weakest points of the city walls. The noblewoman repeated it back until Huong was satisfied.

Lan threw her arms around Lady Yen, blinking away tears. "Please be careful. And promise you will come back here safely."

The woman hugged her back but made no such promise. "I'm glad I met you, Lan. I'm not afraid, but if anything happens to me, find the Commander when it's over. Tell him he'll always be the only one I love, will you? Go save the one you love, and I will try to do the same."

And then she was gone, just as another explosion rocked the city. The sound of it rang in Lan's ears for several seconds afterward. It seemed to be a bit closer than the last.

"It's awful," Lan whispered. "I can't believe Vy didn't even try to compromise. She put her city and all of her people in danger, and for what?"

Huong's lips thinned. "My sister always prided herself on never being tempted to use the drug herself. But she is addicted to it, in her own way. The obsession took root in her mind . . . in *all* of their minds, everyone in my family. And nothing will pull that poisoned root out." She touched

Lan's shoulder. "Come on, this way. Bao may still be somewhere inside Vy's house."

They dashed down the slope in the direction of the sewer, and Lan realized that the house—the grand stone building she had seen atop the hill—had been built directly over the dungeon where they had been. They had never left the building at all; she and Bao had been in the same place. Her hand found the blood-red charm at her neck as Huong led her up a shallower slope. The woman's energy seemed to grow higher the longer she was out of the iron cell.

"We're near the kitchens," the witch panted. "The windows are always left open."

Lan saw two bamboo panels pushed outward as they approached the building, letting out clouds of fragrant steam. Just as they fled past the window, a pair of round eyes looked out at them. A servant girl of about fifteen stood over a huge pot of soup. She paused in the middle of wiping her sweaty face to stare back at Lan. "What are you doing?" she cried, so loudly that three others—a woman holding a vegetable knife and two men plucking feathers from chickens—gathered around her to look at Lan and Huong.

"I'm . . . I'm just . . ." Lan stammered, unable to come up with a story. But it turned out she didn't need to, because the young girl's eyes crossed and she fell to the floor in a dead faint. The woman rushed over and met the same fate, dropping to her knees as her knife clattered harmlessly away, and then the two men followed in a great whirlwind of chicken feathers. Lan spun to see Huong's gleeful smile.

"It's a simple trick," the witch assured her as they hurried through the kitchen.

"I can't believe they were cooking in the middle of a battle."

"My older sister is in a constant state of denial," Huong panted, as they raced out of the corridor and down a set of stone stairs. "And as much as she claims to love her people, they suffer because of it. I'm sure there are maids airing out the beds, too, like nothing will happen."

They returned to the dungeon beneath Vy's house and searched the cells, all of which were empty, to Lan's surprise and relief. She recognized the one from which they had escaped when she saw the metal grate carelessly tossed to one side. "Maybe Bao and Lord Nguyen are in the bedchambers upstairs," she said hopefully.

In the corridor, they came face-to-face with two guards: a muscular woman and a bearded man holding a sword. The witch closed her eyes and concentrated, but unlike the people in the kitchen, the guards were unaffected by her magic and advancing fast.

"He's carrying iron, and she must be wearing it somewhere on her person. A clever precaution from Vy," Huong muttered, then shut her eyes and focused again.

"What are you two doing up here?" roared the female guard. But before she could get any closer to them, an enormous blue-and-white porcelain vase slipped off a nearby table and crashed into her head, sending her sprawling on the ground. Her companion dodged the shards and tackled Huong to the floor. The witch shrieked in pain as he wrenched her arm.

The vase had knocked over a chair, breaking off a few of the legs. Lan hurried over and seized one. "I'm sorry!" she shrieked at the male guard before swinging the chair leg into his face. It knocked him off the witch, giving Huong enough time to regain her concentration and send the rest of the heavy chair right at his head.

"Do you apologize to everyone you attack?" the witch asked, as they stood surveying the damage: two crumpled bodies, a shattered chair, and a mess of priceless porcelain.

"I don't make a habit of knocking people out with furniture," Lan retorted.

Footsteps sounded down the opposite corridor. Huong seized Lan and propelled her up another flight of stairs. "We'll have to split up and look into each bedchamber. I'll do this side," the witch said breathlessly. "Shout if you see anyone. Or apologize and then hit them."

Lan grimaced at the broken chair leg in her hand and ran from door to door. Her heart leapt with every handle she turned, hoping to see Bao safe and well, but all of the rooms were empty, including the one with the yellow silk bed where Vy had put her at first. She heard a cry at the end of the corridor and turned to see the witch fighting off a pair of maids.

"I'm fine!" Huong shouted, when Lan ran to help her. "Go check that door!"

Obediently, Lan pushed open the final bedchamber and saw Lord Nguyen lying prone on the bed. "Wake up, my lord!" she cried, shaking his shoulder, but he only mumbled and rolled onto his side. She looked around desperately and saw a pitcher half-full of water, which she tossed at his face. The nobleman sat bolt upright, sputtering.

"This is preposterous treatment!" he shouted, and then he saw Lan and calmed down. "Oh, it's you, Miss Vu. Are you all right? What's happened?"

Huong came into the room. "There's no time to explain," she said, looking harried. "One of the maids got away and she's calling for help. We have to go *now*."

Lan helped Lord Nguyen to his feet, and he wiped his bald head, looking a bit dazed. "Bao's not here," she said anxiously. "Where do you think Vy is keeping him?"

"I have an idea. Let's go." The witch led them to a bedchamber across the hall, shutting the door behind them. An enormous crimson rug covered the floor of the entire room, and there were books and priceless figurines on shining wood tables, but Huong seemed to be most interested in an oil painting that hung on the wall. It depicted a desert scene.

"Who is this woman?" Lord Nguyen asked Lan. He had a steadily growing purple bruise on his forehead, where Vy's guards had knocked him out earlier.

Lan gave him a brief explanation as Huong continued studying the painting. She wondered if the witch had gone a little mad until she saw her press on an almost imperceptible button on the frame of the painting. The wall on which the artwork hung slid backward several inches, and the witch began pushing it with all her strength. Lord Nguyen and Lan jumped forward to help, revealing a secret passageway.

"My ancestors built this house in the style of the Imperial Palace," Huong said, panting as they all got in and pushed the wall back in place. "And so they imitated the Emperors of Feng Lu by installing nooks and crannies all over. This one leads below the garden and into the infirmary. I think that's where my sister may be hiding out with Bao."

"Your sister is insane," Lord Nguyen puffed, wiping the sweat from his face as they ran. "She can't possibly believe that she'll win this battle."

Outside, they heard another massive explosion. The passageway trembled, shaking dust and cobwebs onto them. "Not this battle, perhaps, but possibly the war," Huong said darkly, and at the nobleman's puzzled expression, Lan explained about the ships.

"Let's hope Lady Yen gets to the Commander, then," he said.

Lan glanced at him, wondering if he was thinking about his betrothed holding hands with Commander Wei, but there was no more time to talk. Huong pushed open a section of the wall and they found themselves in a clean, well-lit building full of pallets. There were perhaps thirty or forty people lying on the pallets, and they all looked at the new arrivals in shock. Lan realized that they had gone through the wall in the bed-chamber and emerged through yet another wall.

"Where is Mistress Vy?" Huong demanded, scanning their faces.

"She's in the garden," said one of the workers, a young woman with a heart-shaped face. She put her hands on her hips. "Who are you?"

"Where is her son, Bao?" the witch persisted, ignoring the question.

"The young man who came in with her? I'm not sure. They went upstairs, but I didn't see him leave when she did . . ."

Neither Lan nor Huong waited to hear her finish her sentence. They were already running for the stairs. *I'm coming, Bao*, Lan thought. The upper level had another thirty or forty patients, most of them sleeping as more gray-uniformed workers moved in between their pallets. Several of the workers came forward, protesting and trying to block their way, but Huong made short work of them, employing the same trick she had used on the people in the kitchens. On the stairs, Lan heard Lord Nguyen dealing with the young woman downstairs.

"Bao!" she called desperately, but none of the faces staring up at her from the pallets were his. They were men and women, young and old, some still clinging to the pallor of sickness. And then, at the far wall, she saw a row of beds where the patients' elbows hung over basins. She realized, shocked, that all of them had deep cuts in the crooks of their arms, just as Huong had. These were the patients that Vy was bleeding for her formula.

They looked weakly at Lan as she ran past, studying their faces. Finally, she came to the last bed along the wall and saw a familiar long, lanky figure, lying with arms and legs tied to the bed frame.

"Bao!" she cried, running over to him.

Bao did not awaken, but continued to lie spread-eagled. The sleeves of his tunic had been rolled above his elbows, and a deep red stain had seeped through the cloths wrapped around the crooks of his arms. His face was expressionless, and his head lolled limply over one shoulder. The bamboo flute lay beside him on the bed, barely visible in the gathering shadows.

"Please be alive," Lan pleaded, throwing all propriety to the winds as she climbed onto the bed with him. "Bao, wake up. I'm here with your aunt Huong. Can you hear me?"

But Bao did not move. His skin was ice-cold, and when Lan's hand brushed the flute, she realized that it was as warm as his body should have been. She felt for a pulse in his wrists and his neck and pressed her ear against his chest, but there was nothing—no pulse, no heartbeat.

"No, no, no!" She grabbed his shoulders and shook him, but his head only rolled limply from side to side. No breath emerged from his nose or mouth. "Huong! Huong, please help!" But the witch did not respond, and downstairs, Lan heard Lord Nguyen yelling and the unmistakable sound of Huong fending off Vy's guards and workers with her magic.

Lan was on her own, and she was too late.

She pressed her lips to Bao's cold forehead, shoulders shaking with sobs. "Come back to me," she whispered, her heart shattering. In all the time they had traveled together, she'd had so many opportunities to tell him what she felt: how she respected him, how much his kindness and compassion moved her, and how easily she could see why her father and grandmother had admired him. The world had denied him much, but he had always given generously of himself. She wanted to tell him that being loved by someone with a heart as beautiful as his had been the greatest honor, and now she might not ever have the chance.

Lan buried her face in his pillow and sobbed with heartbreak and frustration. They had wasted precious time searching Vy's house, and the evil woman had been hiding him here all along. If only they had come sooner. If only Bao had never left the river market. If only Lan had loved him from the beginning.

What has passed is past.

She heard the words as clearly as though her grandmother had spoken them into her ear. She lifted her tearful face and realized suddenly that Bao wasn't wearing the charm Huong had made for him. She looked around the bed in a frenzy, but saw nothing, and so she stripped her own amulet from her chest and slid the chain over his head. She held her breath, waiting for something—anything—to happen to him or to her.

"Bao, please," Lan begged. It hurt too much to look at his lifeless face, so she curled up beside him with her cheek over his silent heart. "I'm sorry I wasted so much time. I'm sorry I never saw how wonderful you were. This past week has been . . ." She broke off, overcome with tears. She could not possibly put into words the storm of feelings inside her. But she had to try, just in case somewhere deep inside him was a spark of life listening to her. "Love isn't waiting for someone to remember me. Love isn't dreaming about them all alone. Love is talking together, forgiving each other, finding common threads in the lives we want. I've learned that now. You taught me."

She wrapped her arms around his cold body, wishing he would hold her back. She would give anything for just one minute of their eyes meeting, hands touching, and hearts stirring again.

But he wasn't moving, and when she blinked away her tears, she saw that he was fading.

The flute grew even warmer in her hand, pulling the life from him. She wanted to destroy it, to break it in two, for what it had done to him. "Forgive me for my cowardice," she told him, her voice breaking, "but the last time I gave my heart, I was badly hurt. I was afraid I had lost your good opinion forever. I was afraid that once I told you how I felt, you would turn away from me. I was afraid I would only ever be a memory to you."

The outline of Bao's body grew fainter, even though she was holding on to him with all her strength. Sobs shook Lan's body. The full moon wasn't until tomorrow night, but whatever had happened to him— whether it was Vy bleeding him or the charm being lost—was bringing the spell to completion. She had run out of time.

Lan's head sank back onto his chest. She would stay with him until it was over; she would hold him and talk to him and give him what comfort she could, if he could even hear or feel any of it. "I shouted at your aunt in the prison, you know," she whispered. "I told her off for casting the spell on you, for putting you in this situation. But now I realize that if she hadn't done that, you would have gone off forever. You would never have come back to me."

Outside, another explosion went off, and the building shivered around them.

She wiped her eyes. "It turns out the witch gave me a second chance. And if it weren't for her, I wouldn't have lost my heart to you. Bao, don't go. Don't let those nights on the river be the last time we were happy. I want new nights with you." She had never imagined such fierceness in herself, but her vow came out like a battle cry. "You have my whole heart, and no witch and no enchantment will ever take that from you. I love you."

"Little yellow flower," Bao whispered. "You crossed the grass . . ."

Lan's head snapped up. He was pale, so pale and weak, but his red-rimmed eyes had cracked open and the corners of his mouth lifted as he looked at her. "Bao?" she asked shakily. His breath stirred the hairs around her face. Beneath her fingers, his heart began to beat a faint rhythm. She choked back a sob, praying with everything in her that she wasn't imagining this—that this wasn't some sort of dream concocted by her hopeful, broken heart.

"Am I in the heavens?" he asked. "Will I be able to see earth from here?"

"No," she said, laughing through her tears, "you are still on earth. With me." She felt him growing warmer in her arms, felt his hand stroking her braid. She uttered a prayer of thanks to every god in the heavens. They had given Bao back to her; they had given her yet another chance. The skin beneath his eyes was so thin, she could see his fragile purple veins. He murmured her name, and she held on to him even more tightly, daring death to take him from her.

"I heard what you said," he said, his eyes glistening.

She drank in his gaze, for he was looking at her like she was home at the end of a long day. She felt as breathless as if she had run a great distance, and exhilarated and overwhelmed and shy. "And you'll forgive me for everything?"

"There's nothing left to forgive," Bao told her, with the kindness she now knew was as much a part of his gentle soul as his music. And then, weak as he was, weary and drained of blood as he was, he lifted his head and kissed her. His lips were ice-cold, but Lan kept her hands on either side of his face and kissed him harder. Something like a warm summer wind rose from the bamboo flute, but Lan kept holding on, and slowly Bao's mouth grew warm beneath hers.

"I love you, too," he said, muffled against her kiss, and she pulled away to see him beaming up at her. His eyes grew bright and vibrant again, and his skin pink and full of life. When she touched the bamboo flute in his hands, it was as cold as he had been a moment earlier.

They looked at each other for a long, silent moment, and then they both broke down into tears. Bao wrapped his arms around her, and she buried her face into his neck and wept and wept. Lan knew that at that very moment a great battle raged outside the walls of the city. But she didn't care.

All she cared about was that she had found a home for her heart at last, and she would never let him go.

23

The smell of war hung in the air as Bao and Lan hurried out of the infirmary, hand in hand. Behind them, the patients called out querulously and the workers magicked by the witch were recovering, but Bao was focused on the scene before them. Iron lanterns glowed all around the poppy garden, making it look malignant and otherworldly as the acrid scent of smoke, rubble, and death circled the ravaged bushes in a dense fog. The place was teeming with soldiers: men in the shining armor of the Great Forest, the Sacred Grasslands, and Dagovad, and the black-garbed women of the Crimson Army, their lips blood-red beneath their sheer masks. They bent over fallen allies, tied up prisoners, cleared away broken stone and shattered trees to make paths, and pulled up every last remaining plant by the roots, to be burned in massive piles.

An enormous hole gaped in the wall separating the garden from the outer districts, giving Bao a clear view of the wreckage: blackened buildings, some still aflame; people running through columns of smoke;

overturned wagons and destroyed goods; and bodies everywhere. The Gray City lay in ruins, exhaling plumes of devastation into the night sky.

Bao was more than familiar with the tang of sweat and blood and vomit in his line of work, but seeing the absolute horror that humans could enact upon their own kind made him physically recoil. "It's over. Vy lost, as she knew she would," he said, heartache and relief warring within him. This battle and defeat were inevitable and necessary to rid Feng Lu of his family's bloody legacy. For centuries, the Gray City had bided its time like a poisonous mushroom while weaker kings turned a blind eye, and it had grasped for power under the guise of benevolence and humanity. Yet Bao couldn't help feeling a sense of loss.

"It's all right to be sad," Lan told him softly, arms tightening around him. "I feel it, too."

He kissed the top of her head. "I'm going to see if I can help," he said, hurrying over to a group of Crimson Army warriors. His throat didn't clench at leaving Lan's side, but he felt her absence just the same. He searched the warriors' faces for Wren as they carried several fallen soldiers to a cleared space by the wall, but did not see her. "What can I do?"

"Whatever you see that needs to be done. There are supplies on that wagon if you need them," one of the women answered, before hurrying off.

He hurried over to the wagon, which had clearly been lifted from the infirmary and contained bottles of ointment, splints, needles and thread, buckets of clean water, and cloths. He grabbed what he needed and got to work, helping those who had suffered the greatest injuries. He set bones and stitched wounds almost mechanically, feeling grateful for the years of training he had received from Master Huynh. Lan had found Lord Nguyen safe and unharmed, and the two of them stayed close to Bao, assisting him when he needed it and giving blankets and water to the injured soldiers.

Someone knelt beside him as he finished dressing a wound. "The river witch!" he exclaimed, recognizing her face. She looked different from when he had seen her last: stronger and healthier, her narrow eyes ablaze with purpose under her cloud of stark-white hair.

"That's Huong to you," the woman said tartly. "I may not have been there for most of your life, but I am still your aunt, and you should show me some respect." Her eyes fell upon Lan's charm hanging from his neck. "I owe you an apology, Bao. I punished you when I wanted to hurt someone else. I'm truly glad that you broke the spell."

Bao searched within himself for anger, but could not find it, for in the weeks he had spent looking for this woman, he had found something precious instead. "I forgive you," he said, and realized that he meant it. "And truthfully, it was Lan who broke the spell."

They turned to watch her and Lord Nguyen working together on one of the soldiers, wiping his forehead and tucking a blanket around his shivering body. "I wouldn't have gotten out of your mother's dungeon without Lan's help," Huong said, smirking. "She and Lady Yen helped free me by jumping into the sewer in human filth up to their knees."

Lan came over to them for more water, and Bao grinned at her, she of the silk slippers and gold hairpins. "The daughter of a king's minister wading through a sewer?" he asked.

"Sometimes, the daughter of a king's minister does what she can with what she has," Lan replied haughtily, and returned to the soldier. It took all of Bao's willpower not to throw himself at her and kiss her right then and there.

"I see Vy got a bit of blood from you, too," the witch said softly, laying her hand upon his elbow, which was still wrapped in bloody cloth. She shut her eyes for a moment, her lips forming imperceptible words, and when she looked back at Bao, the pain and itching from the cuts Vy had made were gone. "Strange how much I wanted to see her fall and the city destroyed, and now that it has happened, I feel more empty than overjoyed."

"I feel the same," Bao admitted, with a heavy sigh. "Where is she?"

Huong's eyes slid past him, and he turned to see two soldiers of the Great Forest marching a prisoner out of the infirmary, followed by a short, powerfully built man with a blue-black beard. The woman's hands were bound tightly behind her, but still she held her head high like a queen, her eyes flashing as she surveyed the destruction. Mistress Vy's gaze landed on her sister and her son, and slowly they rose and came to meet her.

"I am General Yee, the Commander's second in command," said the bearded man, regarding Huong and Bao with keen eyes. "We found this woman hiding in a secret room on the upper level of the infirmary. Commander Wei gave me the power to order her immediate execution as a treasonous criminal, but she claims she is your kin. I felt it right to allow you a chance to speak before she meets her fate."

"Thank you, General," Huong said, her eyes never leaving her sister.

Vy lifted her chin. "So, you made it out at last. I suppose I shouldn't have doubted you. You've proven before what a slippery snake you are. And I see that my son managed to survive the curse you laid upon him." Her heavy-lidded gaze moved to Bao, and he forced himself to face her without flinching. "I'm surprised to see you both so solemn and not celebrating my defeat."

"We are your only living family," Bao said, startled by the ferocity in his own voice. "For better or for worse, you are my *mother*. The fact that you think I should be joyful about seeing you brought low and your city razed to the ground shows that you know nothing about me."

"Save your breath, nephew," the witch told him. "She has always believed other people to be as callous and petty as she herself is. She doesn't understand pity or compassion."

Vy spat at her sister's face. "Save your pity and compassion. And if you're hoping for a flowery apology or explanation, I have none. I fought for what I believed in. I kept my people happy and upheld my family's values, and when I die, I will have lived my life for a noble cause. How have you lived yours? Bitterly, with your tail tucked between your legs like the coward you are. I sought to save all of humanity, and you sought to soothe your wounded pride."

"You speak the truth," Huong said, wiping her face. "But I would rather die a coward than a self-righteous murderer. Everything you've said sounds a lot like the nonsense Xifeng spouted when she was trying to justify the means by which she secured her rule."

"There is no comparison between Xifeng and me," Mistress Vy said in her calm, low voice. "She was a senseless, depraved woman obsessed with her own beauty. I was creating something greater than myself, a medicine that would decimate illness and outlive us all."

Bao listened in disbelief. He had yearned for this woman all his life and dreamed of her as a kind, loving mother, but it had been no more than a lonely child's fancy. Even after all the death and destruction that her ambition had caused, she still had the nerve to think of herself as some kind of hero. "The roots of your intention may have been good," he said quietly. "But you chose to water them with blood. I wish you had listened to me, Mother. I wish you had surrendered and found another way to help, one that would neither hurt nor kill others. I would have supported you if you had. We might have had a home; we . . ." His throat thickened with tears, and he blinked, looking away.

"I'm sorry to disappoint you, my son," Mistress Vy said, her voice no longer as steady as it had been a moment before. "But you are a fool for wishing I were anyone other than myself."

He swallowed hard. "I wonder if you said that to my father before you had your guards kill him," he said, his heart aching. "I wonder if you ever asked yourself why both he and your sister wanted to leave you. I wonder if it ever hurt you to know that the life you chose meant that you would always be alone. I think I will always miss you, but maybe that's better than having you."

Mistress Vy's eyes glistened for a moment as she looked at him in silence.

Huong put her hand on Bao's shoulder. "It's over now. But I'm not certain she deserves death," she said, looking at the General. "I want her to rot in a prison somewhere, haunted by the misery of her own failure. I would like to speak to Commander Wei about this."

"You may get your chance sooner than you think," the man replied, nodding behind her.

A group of soldiers were marching in tight formation through the smoking gap in the wall, pulling a wagon slowly after them. Several of them were women of the Crimson Army, and Bao recognized Wren walking at the front. Her eyes met Bao's, but she did not return his smile. As she came closer, he saw that her face was drawn with grief and worry. "General Yee," she said, and the man came forward, his brow furrowed. "The Commander . . . he fell . . ."

Behind her, on the wagon pulled by the soldiers, Bao saw two bodies. One of them wore the armor of the Great Forest, dented and stained black with smoke and char. The firelight gleamed off the man's shaven head and the sharp slopes of his nose and jaw.

"No!" Lan cried, and she and Lord Nguyen hurried forward. "Commander Wei and . . . and Lady Yen, no!"

The second body was small and slender, draped in what Bao recognized as the cloak that the Commander had lent him. Long black hair streamed out around a thin, drawn face, eyes closed.

Bao ran to the wagon with the General right behind him.

"They're still alive, sir, but barely," one of the soldiers reported. "Lady Yen came with a piece of intelligence she acquired from someone named Huong. Three ships had been moored off the coast all this time, loaded with a protected supply of drugs and the plants used to make them. The Commander took a company of men and women with him at once to sink the vessels."

General Yee gave a curt nod. "Go on."

"The ships were manned by Gray City guards and rigged with poison. Bombs containing a potent formulation of the drug, which took out more than half of the Commander's people," the soldier said. "Commander Wei was badly hurt in the skirmish, as was Her Ladyship, who insisted on coming with him, but our forces still managed to destroy two of the vessels."

"And the third?" the General asked sharply.

"It escaped, but our forces are trailing it and hope to overtake it before dawn. It will be found and burned, just like the others."

The whole time they had been talking, Bao had climbed onto the wagon to assess the couple's injuries. Lady Yen had a shallow cut on her arm and a mean-looking bruise on her forehead, suggesting she had been knocked unconscious, but Bao was glad to see that she was breathing normally. Commander Wei, however, had a deep cut running from his temple to his neck and a deep sword wound in his right side. Judging from the way it was bleeding, Bao did not think it had struck any important organs, but this was not a job for a physician's apprentice, and he told Wren as much when she leaned over the wagon anxiously.

"The Imperial war surgeon is working in one of the outer rings of the city," one of the soldiers said, overhearing Bao. "He's been sent for at once and will be here shortly."

"I'll help him when he comes, but until then, I'll do what I can. Will you help me remove his armor, Wren?" Bao asked, and together they gently stripped the Commander of his heavy breastplate and weapons, laying them to one side.

"What supplies can I bring you from the wagon?" Lan asked. Her lips had turned white at the sight of all the Commander's blood, but her face was alert and voice steady, and Bao loved her all the more for it. She ran off as soon as he named what he required and he tried to stanch the Commander's bleeding, pressing a cloth into the man's side.

Beside him, Lady Yen was beginning to stir.

"Perhaps we ought to move her before she sees him," Bao suggested to Wren and the soldiers, but it was already too late, for the noblewoman's eyes had opened, and the first thing she saw was Commander Wei, lying prone and bleeding profusely beside her.

"No," Lady Yen whispered. "Wei . . ." She tried to sit up and closed her eyes against the dizziness, her face green.

"Don't move, Yen. You've had quite a head injury," Wren advised, but the noblewoman ignored her warning and slid closer to the Commander, her eyes brimming with tears.

"It's better if you don't look, Lady Yen," Bao told her, as she gasped at the cloths in his hands, stained bright red from pressing against Commander Wei's side. "He's alive, and a war surgeon is coming. Don't worry." But he knew he might as well have told the moon to stop shining, for the woman was sobbing brokenly as she looked at the Commander's motionless face. Lan ran back with all of the items Bao had asked for, and their eyes met, remembering the similar moment they had shared in the infirmary.

Bao began dressing the wound as best he could, holding it together before the surgeon came, and saw Lord Nguyen appear at his elbow. His face held nothing but genuine sorrow as he watched the woman he should have married embracing her lover, and he rose even more highly in Bao's estimation when he asked, "Is there anything I can do to help?"

"Perhaps you could bring some water for Lady Yen," he said, and Lord Nguyen nodded and moved off at once as Bao ripped up cloth after cloth. He heard Lady Yen gasp and looked up to see the Commander's eyes fluttering open. His gaze swept from Bao to the noblewoman lying beside him, her hair streaming around them both.

"I knew you wouldn't dare leave me, Wei," Lady Yen said fiercely, choking on a sob. "I knew you wouldn't dare go without telling me what you owe me."

"What could I possibly owe you?" the Commander whispered.

"I told you I loved you, over and over again. You owe me a declaration of love in return."

Bao kept his eyes on the man's wounds, as though that would give the couple a semblance of privacy, but it was no use: all eyes were riveted on the scene before them, from the General and the soldiers to Huong, Vy, and Lord Nguyen, who returned with a bucket of water.

Commander Wei made a low, gritty wheezing noise, and Bao panicked, wondering if his lungs had been punctured. But then he realized that the man was trying to laugh. "I didn't think I needed to tell you," he said to Lady Yen. "I thought you knew I couldn't live without you. That I would lose a part of myself when I brought you to your husband."

Yen laid a tender hand upon the Commander's bleeding face. "I'm not going anywhere. I am never leaving you, because *you* will be my husband and no other." She looked around for Lord Nguyen, her eyes full of apology. "I was fortunate to have made a good match. I was paired with a kind, good, and honorable man who would have treated me well and done his best to make me happy. I am sorry to hurt him and to break my promise to him—"

"You are hurting no one," Lord Nguyen said with quiet, gentle dignity. "You gave your heart to a worthy man, and far be it from me to stand between you. I may be disappointed, but I do not consider myself wronged." He reddened at the glowing look she gave him in response, and Lan came close and put her arm around her father's esteemed friend.

"And your parents?" the Commander whispered.

"I am no longer under their care, and they haven't any right to be upset if Lord Nguyen is so generous," Yen said, with another warm look at her former betrothed. "But even if they were, it wouldn't matter to me. I love you, Wei, and I will be your wife no matter what." She kissed Commander Wei's forehead, and he closed his eyes with an expression of perfect joy.

"Here's Lo now," General Yee said suddenly as a pair of soldiers led a harried-looking man in his thirties toward the wagon.

Bao respectfully climbed off the wagon to make room for the Imperial war surgeon as the man bent to examine Commander Wei's wound. "There's a bit of internal bleeding, but not much," he said after a long moment. "I'm going to need him moved indoors, where there's more light. But he's going to survive this. Whoever dressed this wound did well."

"It was this young man, Lo," the General said, and the surgeon turned to look at Bao with approval. "He's a physician's apprentice."

"I can give you a hand, sir, with whatever you need to do," Bao offered. "The infirmary is just that way, and I know for a fact that there is at least one empty pallet." He caught Lan's eye where she was still standing beside Lord Nguyen, and they shared a smile.

"Very good," the surgeon said, directing the soldiers to pull the wagon forward.

Commander Wei grimaced as the wheels began to move and caught sight of Bao. "It seems you found your witch. Has the spell been broken?" he asked weakly.

"Yes, sir," Bao said, grinning, as Lan came forward to stand beside him. "And I've found something very dear to me besides."

Commander Wei's eyes softened on the two of them, and as he was wheeled away with Yen holding his hand, Bao saw the smile widen on his rough, war-hardened face, like the beacon of a man he had once been and might still be again. "Make sure you don't lose it," he told Bao.

"I won't. And sir?" Bao asked, keeping pace with the wagon. "The witch . . . that is, my aunt and I would appreciate being able to decide Mistress Vy's fate. With your permission."

"You have it," the Commander said, and Bao bent at the waist with respect as the soldiers and surgeon conveyed him inside to the infirmary.

Bao looked back at his mother, who was still standing between the captains and guarded by General Yee. She had been quiet and resigned the whole time, her shoulders sagging with exhaustion. He guessed that she had not allowed herself to feel tired for a very long time. "You heard the Commander," Bao said to the witch. "The decision lies with us. What do you think should happen to her?"

Huong looked at him, her eyes clear and sharp. "I think you have an idea."

"We won't fight cruelty with cruelty," he said, turning to look at their family home beyond the garden. "Nor will we reward her deeds with death. My ancestors modeled the Gray City after the Imperial City, and their house after the Imperial Palace. Perhaps another palace—the Iron Palace of Surjalana—will serve my mother well as her home. She will make herself useful there." Each word tasted bitter on his tongue as he met his mother's shadowed eyes.

"Do you find pleasure in this fitting end for me?" Mistress Vy asked. "Do you enjoy thinking of me living out my days in the desert and serving a sentence that will never end?"

Bao did not rise to her bait. "Please take her to the dungeon, General, and we will make arrangements to send her away in the morning," he said, and the man nodded and marched the former leader of the Gray City back to her own home. And despite his conviction that he had done right, he couldn't help the stab of guilt he felt when he saw his mother stumble between the captains, looking small and pathetic. "That's the last of my family," he said, forcing a laugh.

"Not quite the last," the witch said quietly, looking up into his face. "I'm proud of you, Bao. You've handled this situation with grace. I know how much it hurts to have to turn your back on Vy, but we will do it together, and we will do it without conscience."

Bao had never thought he would willingly embrace the witch who had cursed him, but he did so now, folding his long arms around her frail body. He felt her hugging him back.

"Without conscience," he agreed.

24

Commander Wei's injuries were not life-threatening, but it still took the surgeon hours to fix the damage that had been done. Bao stayed the whole time, watching, learning, and doing what he could to assist. At his request, the Gray City workers who remained in the infirmary had pulled in an extra pallet for Lady Yen so she could be close to the Commander. In fact, the workers did everything Bao requested and seemed to look to him for their orders.

"It's because you're Vy's rightful heir," Huong told him matter-of-factly. They were sitting on the steps of the infirmary together, watching the dawn slowly seep into the sky like bright ink. The surgeon had insisted that Bao get some rest, but he hadn't felt tired and had decided to keep his aunt company. "The city has fallen, but it's still a city. It's home for the people here, and they need a leader to help them rebuild. Who better than Mistress Vy's son?"

"What about Mistress Vy's sister?" Bao suggested.

The witch laughed, a surprisingly pleasant sound. "I don't want this and I never did. Power is not for me. I want a quiet life," she said, looking at him. In the light of the sunrise, she looked younger and happier, and Bao thought he could imagine the girl she had been when she had left the Gray City behind. "But you . . . I could see the makings of a kind and fair leader in you, if you wished to be one. If you don't choose a different life, that is."

Bao followed her gaze to a clearing in the garden, just outside the infirmary, where the Gray City workers had moved some of the healthier patients to make room for injured soldiers. Lan, who had helped take care of the wounded all night, had fallen asleep on one of the pallets, her cheek pillowed on her hand.

"I know, Auntie Huong," he said softly, and the witch smiled at the term of endearment. "It's one thing to fall in love on a journey, far away from home. But out there, in the real world, she's the only daughter of Minister Vu, and I'm . . ." He trailed off, chuckling as he remembered how Lan had cried, *Don't you dare say peasant!*

"You are a physician's apprentice. And from what I saw last night, you're well on your way to becoming a full physician one day. The Gray City could use a leader like you, nephew. You could build a new life and a home here, with Lan."

Bao's heart sank. "But I'm still the son of a treacherous, power-hungry traitor. Minister and Lady Vu would never approve of our union."

"You think far too little of yourself, Bao. Yes, Vy was a traitor, but she was the leader of a great city, and you are the next of kin."

"She called me a prince," he said, shaking his head.

"Well, and why not? She always did think of herself as a queen." Huong snorted. "But what I'm trying to say is that you are someone. You have talent and aspiration and somewhere to go in life, and Lan clearly thinks you're a worthy partner, no matter what her parents may have to say. If Lady Yen can defy the expectations set for her, why can't your girl?"

Bao couldn't help it—his smile grew wider and wider all through her speech, and his face glowed. All his life, he had dreamed of having family who cared enough to build him up, and now he was sitting with an aunt who believed in him. "Thank you," he said softly, and Huong beamed at him. On the horizon, the sun was ascending over a city of smoke and ruin. But it was a new day, and as Bao had found out, a lot could happen in a new day. "It will be a lot of work."

"No one ever promised you it would be easy."

"No," he agreed, "but it would be *easier* to take the helm with help from family. You weren't planning on spending the rest of your life on that riverbank, were you?"

The witch narrowed her eyes at him. "What are you suggesting? That we both live here?"

"We don't have anywhere better to go," he pointed out. "We could rebuild this city from the bottom up. We could make it a center of trade and industry and learning. There is *some* good to what our family has done, creating a safe space for people who need it. What do you say?"

Huong looked at him, and for the first time, Bao could see himself in her face—in the tilt of her chin and the curve of her nose, and the way she carefully considered the question before answering. "It would be rather satisfying to order Vy's people around," she admitted, and that was how Bao knew that she was accepting his offer. He grinned at her, and she gave him his smile back with the same dimple.

"Did you really love my father?" he asked.

"More than anything. But there was nothing I could do to persuade him to love me."

"Not even magic?"

The woman laughed. "Magic has no effect upon the heart. It might temporarily control the mind, but it doesn't alter the core of a person's being or the deepest reaches of their soul. Love is a magic all its own," she said, placing her hand on Bao's shoulder, over his birthmark. "I've been alone all my life, even when I was here. I've learned to welcome solitude like an old friend, but perhaps it's time I changed that."

"We could build you a quiet, private sanctuary here," Bao suggested. "You could have a little house and a garden, like you had on the riverbank. But you'd have me nearby, too."

Huong patted his arm. "We have much planning to do, nephew. But for now, I think I'll go and get some rest. Your girl is awake, and I don't fancy being the third wheel."

Bao kissed her cheek, and she gave him another pat, groaning as her bones creaked when she stood up from the steps. He watched her stretch and walk back to the house, and then Lan was standing in front of him with her head tipped to one side, smiling. For a moment, he just sat there looking at her in silence, filling his soul with her lovely face.

"What are you thinking about?" she asked.

"How I was terrified, once, to look you in the eye," he said truthfully. "I didn't know how much I was missing."

Lan laughed. She took a seat two steps below his and leaned her head back against his chest. "How is Commander Wei doing? And Lady Yen?"

"The Commander is stable. The surgeon patched him up well, but it was more complicated than I thought," he said, wrapping his arms around her. "And Lady Yen is sleeping with a smile on her face." They sat in silence for a moment, gazing out at the sunrise. Somewhere beyond the wall that surrounded the city, Bao knew the grasslands were swaying in the gentle breeze, untouched by the violence and devastation.

"Did you ever think this would happen?" Lan asked dreamily. "When you first saw me at my father's house and loved me for all those years. Did you imagine that one day we would be sitting together in a burned garden, looking out at a wrecked city?"

Bao laughed. "No, I never imagined that. But I *did* imagine this," he said, tilting her head gently back so that he could kiss her the way he had always dreamed of doing. Her lips were like silk, soft and warm beneath his tongue. He knew in his bones that fifty years from now, his heart would still race at the sight of her. They had journeyed afar and broken a witch's spell together. They had gone from being two people with unrequited love, to two people broken apart, to two people come back together again: two halves of a whole, as they had always been meant to be.

Lan looked up at him, when they had pulled away at last, breathless from the kiss. "So how do I measure up to that imaginary version of myself?"

"You know, I was worried you wouldn't live up," he joked, and she hit his arm. "But it turns out the *real* you is so much better than the one I imagined."

She kissed his nose. "You made a great sacrifice tonight," she said softly. "I know it must have hurt to let your mother go. What do you think will happen to the city? Is it up to you?"

"That's what Auntie Huong and I were discussing just now," Bao said. "We'd like to stay and rebuild the city into something better than it was before. And I could truly picture myself living here and calling it home . . . once it's a different place, of course."

"And where does that leave me?"

"I think . . . I think that has to be your decision." He ran a hand over her petal-soft cheek, already hurting at the possibility of her living far away from him. The enchantment seemed to have had a lasting impact after all: it ensured that he would need her with him, always. "It's your choice, Lan. I'll understand if you choose your family."

"Don't you remember my promise? I told you I would help you and see you through to the end," Lan said. "I just didn't know, when I was making that promise, that *the end* would be the end of our lives together. You and me. A hundred years from now."

Perhaps that was another lasting effect of the spell: the almost unbearable lightness of his heart, as though it no longer wished to be tethered to earth. "We'll live that long?"

"Anything's possible," she said, smirking up at him.

"What about your parents? What will they think about you loving me?"

Lan raised her eyebrows. "You are the heir to the Gray City, and it needs a leader. It needs *you*. I don't think my father could refuse such a powerful son."

"A son?" Bao repeated.

She grinned up at him. "Will you marry me?"

The casual proposal nearly sent him flying backward. "I'm supposed to ask your parents first," he sputtered. "It's traditional and respectful. And they have to accept me, and then they need to speak to you, and . . . There's a proper way in which these things are done, Lan!"

Lan waved a dismissive hand. "I'm done with propriety and tradition. Bà nội never liked it much, either," she said, folding his arms back around her. "We survived a war together, Bao, and a witch's curse. I want you to marry me, and we will go home and tell my parents. *Tell*, not ask. I have a feeling Ba will be happy about the match, even if it takes Mama some time. That is, if you'll accept my proposal. Well?"

"Yes," Bao said without hesitation, his voice ragged. "I'll marry you, Vu Lan."

Their lips met once more, and Bao couldn't help smiling against her mouth.

"Will you play me the flute every night?" she asked playfully.

"Every night. Whenever you like," he vowed, and from his pocket he took out the bamboo flute that had started it all—none the worse for wear, despite all it had been through. It had been given to him with love, and now, he would give its music to the one he loved.

He might not know how the rest of his life would look, but he knew he would never be alone again. They would figure it out together.

ACKNOWLEDGMENTS

A few years ago, if you had told me that I'd be writing the acknowledgments for my third book in 2019, I would have laughed with disbelief. But here I am, writing the acknowledgments for my third book and laughing with sheer joy and gratitude toward everyone who has made this possible.

The first thanks goes to my loving and supportive family, both near and far. I'm so proud to have written a Vietnamese fantasy and I hope you think it does justice to our roots and beautiful culture. I am grateful to my mom, Mai, who helped me with the pronunciations, descriptions of the river market, and inspiration of the boatman story as the foundation for *Song of the Crimson Flower*.

Tamar Rydzinski, thank you for always having my back and believing in me. It is so comforting to know that you're always just a phone call away with excellent advice whenever I need it. Thank you to Laura Dail and everyone at LDLA for all that you have done for me these four years we've been together!

Thank you to Jill Santopolo, Talia Benamy, and everyone in the

Philomel phamily for everything you've done to help me bring these three books out into the world in tiptop shape! You are a group of wonderful, hardworking people, and I'm eternally grateful to you for giving my stories a home. Thank you to everyone at Penguin Young Readers, including my copyeditor Janet Pascal; my publicist Tessa Meischeid, and all of the sales and publicity team members; Felicity Vallence, Kara Brammer, Friya Bankwalla, and the all-star marketing team; and everyone involved with the art and design of my books, especially my cover designer Lindsey Andrews, for making *FOTL*, *Kingdom*, and *Song* look magnificent. Thank you also to the terrific teams at Listening Library and Penguin Random House audio and to Kim Mai Guest for creating such immersive audiobooks to accompany my stories.

Brian Geffen, you were one of the first to love Xifeng and her world, and you gave me the opportunity of a lifetime. There aren't enough dumplings to express my gratitude for your friendship. You're the best!

I am thankful for the following writers, all of whom I deeply admire, for their blurbs: Tochi Onyebuchi, loving brother and steadfast friend; E. K. Johnston, who taught me how skeletons *should* work; Margaret Rogerson, whose glorious writing inspires me; Beth Revis, one of the kindest authors I've met; and Emily X. R. Pan, who I forgive for writing a book that made me sob uncontrollably on a crowded plane.

Natalie Mae, you not only blurbed me, but you have also been my true friend and mentor for the past six years. We've come a long way since Pitch Wars 2013! Your editorial eye and sharp insight helped bring this book and its romance to the next level, and I am so grateful for you.

Thank you to my friends Marisa Hopkins and CB Lee for beta-reading and cheering me on. I always look forward to reading your comments and seeing the emojis you sprinkle throughout my manuscript!

A million thanks to the generous friends who joined me on my

Kingdom tour: Scott Reintgen, Patrice Caldwell, Tochi Onyebuchi, Emily X. R. Pan, Karen McManus, Rachel Strolle, CB Lee, Stacey Lee, and Stephanie Garber. It was an honor to do events with all of you!

I owe so much to the tireless, generous work of book bloggers, and I want to especially thank and acknowledge Erika (@TheNocturnalFey) and Rafael (@TheRoyalPolarBearReads) for heading the Philippines blog tour of *Kingdom* and for being such sweet, supportive readers. Huge thanks to Hailey LeBlanc and Monica Kim for leading a great Fall Into Fantasy Read-a-Thon for *FOTL* and *Kingdom*. And thank you to the lovely Mish (Chasing Faerytales) for hosting my #PhoenixFriday Twitter chat!

Thank you to Jon Cassir, Andrew Wang, Karen Frost, Johanna Lee, and David Henry Hwang for believing in my stories and asking brilliant questions that helped me further develop the world of Feng Lu.

I am forever indebted to the booksellers, educators, and librarians who have generously supported my work for the past two years. It was a privilege to meet some of you on my tour and thank you in person for embracing my stories and giving them to young readers hungry for a new fantasy world.

And, finally, to my readers: thank you for being the absolute best part of my dream come true. Thank you for reading, buying, and talking about my books; sending me lovely gifts, art, and messages; showing up to my events; and sharing your stories and dreams with me. If my life were an epic fantasy quest, you would all be the reward at the end. It is an honor to write for you.